Praise for the Violet Br

'An entertaining a

mystery set against a

Clare Chase

'A thoroughly enjoyable and suspenseful story'

Daily Mail

'A perfect cosy mystery with an engaging cast
of characters and a beautifully drawn setting'

Roz Watkins

'Violet Brewster is everything you could want in
an amateur sleuth; empathetic, determined,
and ruthless in her quest for truth . . . A must read!'

Charlotte Baker

'A book to put to the top of your "must read now" pile!'

C.L. Peache

'A murder mystery with a blossoming romance . . . what more
could one ask for? Delicious!'

Katie Gayle

JANE BETTANY is the author of the DI Isabel Blood crime series, set in the fictional Derbyshire town of Bainbridge, and the Violet Brewster cosy crime series, which is also set in Derbyshire.

Her debut novel – *In Cold Blood* – won the 2019 Gransnet and HQ writing competition, which was for women writers over the age of 40 who had written a novel with a protagonist in the same age range.

Before turning to novel writing, Jane had been writing short stories and non-fiction articles for over twenty years, many of which have appeared in women's magazines, literary magazines, newspapers and online.

Jane has an MA in Creative Writing and lives in Derby.

Also by Jane Bettany

The Violet Brewster Mystery Series
Murder in Merrywell

The Detective Isabel Blood Series
In Cold Blood
Without a Trace
Last Seen Alive

Murder at the Book Festival

JANE BETTANY

ONE PLACE. MANY STORIES

This novel is entirely a work of fiction. The names, characters and incidents portrayed in it are the work of the author's imagination. Any resemblance to actual persons, living or dead, events or localities is entirely coincidental.

HQ
An imprint of HarperCollins*Publishers* Ltd
1 London Bridge Street
London SE1 9GF

www.harpercollins.co.uk

HarperCollins*Publishers*
Macken House, 39/40 Mayor Street Upper,
Dublin 1 D01 C9W8

This paperback edition 2024

1
First published in Great Britain by
HQ, an imprint of HarperCollins*Publishers* Ltd 2024

A catalogue record for this book is available from the British Library.

ISBN 9780008589745

This book is produced from independently certified FSC™ paper to ensure responsible forest management.

For more information visit: www.harpercollins.co.uk/green

Printed and bound in the UK using 100% renewable electricity at CPI Group (UK) Ltd

In memory of
Alan Bettany
1935—2023

Prologue

I slip into the garden silently, grateful for the dim half-light that conceals my presence. Beneath my feet, a thick layer of ground frost sparkles like diamonds. The gloves I am wearing are ideal for the task ahead, but too thin to keep the early morning chill from nipping at my fingers. I shiver. Is it the cold making my hands tremble, or fear?

Rounding a group of fir trees, I enter the car park. The blue Audi stands alone at the far end, its distance from the other vehicles a distinct advantage. I can finish what I've come to do without fear of being observed or disturbed.

I approach stealthily, creeping through the shadows like a cat. The knife glints in my hand, its long, thin blade super-sharp and perfect for the job.

Something glistens as I draw near the car; something that isn't the frost or the knife.

A hat.

A ridiculous sequinned hat, sitting at a jaunty angle on a familiar blonde head.

The sight of it causes anger to surge through my veins. My breath quickens and a red mist descends, the colour of blood.

Gripping the knife, I lunge forward, through the darkness.

Chapter 1

Four weeks earlier

Violet Brewster was taking her lunch break in the reading nook at *Books, Bakes and Cakes*. She'd had a busy and slightly frenetic morning, and had chosen to unwind by browsing the pages of a beautifully illustrated guide to cottage gardening. On the coffee table in front of her was a cup of ginger-spiced hot chocolate, which she'd brought with her from the bakery next door.

The reading nook was a relaxing space, situated on the first-floor balcony of the bookshop. It consisted of four squishy armchairs, colourful cushions, a low coffee table, and a potted aspidistra. There was also a standard lamp in the corner, and a noticeboard on the wall advertising the regular activities taking place in Merrywell Shopping Village. Best of all, the nook was hidden away, tucked behind tall bookshelves, but still within eavesdropping distance of the conversations taking place at the ground-floor counter. Today it was presided over by the shop's proprietor, Eric Nash. He was currently being regaled by local council leader and village nitpicker Judith Talbot, who was castigating him about his choice of guest for the inaugural event at Merrywell's upcoming, and very first book festival.

'I can't believe you've invited *that* woman to open our festival,' Judith said, her waspish voice spiralling upwards to invade the quiet calm of the reading nook. 'What on earth were you thinking, Eric?'

The woman Judith was referring to was Leonie Stanwick, bestselling author of a series of raunchy romance novels. During her long writing career, Leonie's books had sold millions of copies, and in recent years, a few of them had even made it to the silver screen.

Violet heard Eric clear his throat. He was a shy man, and always polite, but she knew he wouldn't stand for any nonsense from Judith. Violet closed the gardening book, sat back, and listened to the unfolding conversation.

'Let me put you right on a few things,' she heard Eric say. 'First of all, Leonie Stanwick isn't *opening* the festival, although she is our first guest and the festival's big-name author. I thought long and hard about who that person should be, and I stand by my choice. Leonie has local connections, and her work is enormously popular. I sell more of her books in a week than almost any other author.'

'But this is supposed to be a literary festival,' Judith interjected. 'Leonie Stanwick's novels can hardly be classed as literature.'

'It's a *book* festival,' Eric said, his voice clear and unwavering. 'Which includes non-fiction authors and graphic novelists, as well as writers of genre and literary fiction.'

'Be that as it may, I do feel you could have been more selective in some of your choices. We want our festival to feature writers of a certain calibre, don't we?'

'If, by that, you mean authors of obscure or high-brow tomes, then no – that's not what I'm aiming for at all. And why are you calling it *our* festival? Because that's not strictly true, is it? When I asked the parish councillors for help with funding the event,

I was told there was no money available. In spite of that, I offered the council a place on the festival's organising committee, but that opportunity was also turned down.'

Judith began to bluster. 'There was no one available to attend,' she spluttered. 'We've been busy with other things.'

'So have I,' said Eric, his voice firm but courteous. 'And so have my wife and daughter – and yet, still we've found the time to knuckle down and organise everything. I'd say we've earned the right to choose which guest authors to invite.'

'I don't disagree, but surely the purpose of . . . *this* festival is to raise the profile of the village? Do you really think having Leonie Stanwick as a guest will achieve that?'

Eric gave a loud huff. 'I sincerely hope the book festival does . . . as you put it . . . *raise the profile of the village*, but that isn't the only reason we've set this whole thing up. The primary aim is to give readers a chance to meet or listen to their favourite authors, and discover new ones. The festival will also bring people into Merrywell Shopping Village at what is traditionally a very quiet time of year for the retailers. There's always a lull when the schools go back after the summer break, and before the Christmas rush begins. I'm hoping the events will bring an increase in footfall that will benefit everyone.'

A brief pause in the conversation caused Violet to sit up and tilt her head, wondering if she'd missed something. When Eric spoke again, he sounded slightly more conciliatory.

'Of course, an additional benefit of the festival is that people all over the world will get to hear about Merrywell,' he said. 'We'll be livestreaming four of the events – including the session with Leonie Stanwick. We've already sold over two hundred online tickets, and that revenue will go a long way towards recouping the financial investment I've made.'

Eric's lengthy explanation of the rationale behind the festival failed to pacify Judith's ill temper.

'If that's meant to be another dig about the lack of funding from the council, then please save your breath,' she said, sounding grumpier than ever. 'If you'd given us a little more notice, then perhaps we could have helped. The council's finances are planned well in advance, Eric. By the time you came to us, our budget for this year had already been allocated.'

'I understand that,' Eric replied. 'And I'm not having a dig, just stating the facts. The reality is, this is *my* festival, which means I get to decide who and what to include. I realise that Leonie Stanwick's novels aren't to everyone's taste, but no one's obliged to attend her event if they don't want to. There'll be plenty of other sessions on offer. We've put together a varied programme that has something for everyone.'

'Well, let's hope you've made the right decisions and the festival is a roaring success,' Judith said, her peevish tone contradicting her words. 'You see, the parish council is considering ring-fencing some funding from our next budget . . . assuming, of course, the book festival will run again next year. If this year proves to be an abject failure, I don't suppose the festival has much of a future. We'll have to wait and see, won't we?'

'Yes,' Eric said. 'I suppose we will.'

'As for choosing Leonie Stanwick as your star guest . . . trust me, that's a decision you'll come to regret. You mark my words, people like that are nothing but trouble.'

Judith had obviously delivered her parting shot, because Violet could hear her rubber-soled loafers squeaking a retreat across the wooden floor towards the exit. When the bell above the shop door had stopped jangling, Violet got up and peered over the balcony. Eric was leaning on the counter, running a hand through his brown, flyaway mop of hair.

She picked up the gardening book, and carried it down the staircase along with her empty cup.

'Are you OK, Eric?' she asked, when she reached the till.

'I am now,' he replied, exhaling sharply. 'I've just had a tongue-lashing from Judith Talbot but, thankfully, I appear to have come through it in once piece.'

Having incurred Judith's wrath herself in the past, Violet knew how he must be feeling, and she sympathised.

'From what I heard, you gave as good as you got . . . if not better. It's about time someone put Judith in her place.'

'You were listening to our conversation?'

'Yes. Sorry, I couldn't help overhearing. I've been up in the reading nook, browsing through this.' She held up the gardening book and placed it on the counter. 'I've decided to buy it.'

Distractedly, Eric scanned the barcode on the back cover of the book, and Violet presented her debit card to the contactless reader.

'You look worried,' she said. 'You mustn't let Judith unsettle you. The festival's going to be great. I can't think of anyone better suited to organising it than you.'

'Thanks, Violet,' he said. 'Between you and me, I've invested a lot of money in setting it all up. I can't afford for it to fail.'

'It won't. You know better than anyone what readers are interested in, and I'm sure the guests you've chosen will go down a treat with festivalgoers. As you say, Leonie Stanwick is hugely popular. People will be queuing round the block to see her.'

'Have you read any of her novels?' Eric said, as he handed over her book, along with a receipt.

Violet joggled her head. 'I can't say that I have. As you know, I'm more of a crime buff. I'm not really into romance . . . either in the fictional sense, or in real life.'

Eric laughed. 'That's not what I've heard. My missus tells me you've been seeing a lot of Matthew Collis recently.'

Eric's 'missus', Fiona, was Violet's friend and also the owner of the shopping village's bakery and café – both of which were housed under the same roof as the bookshop. Collectively the three businesses constituted *Books, Bakes and Cakes*, known locally as the BBC. Matthew Collis ran a furniture-making business, which was also based in the shopping village.

'Matthew and I have met up in the pub a few times,' Violet said. 'We're friends, that's all.'

'I believe you.' Eric grinned. 'Thousands wouldn't.'

Violet shot him a warning half-frown as she tucked the gardening book into her canvas shopping bag. She was fully aware that the locals enjoyed gossiping about her and Matthew – such rumour-mongering was one of the hazards of living in a small village. She usually chose to ignore the speculation – even though she found it annoying and (at times) intrusive.

'Actually . . .' Eric leaned on the counter and smiled ingratiatingly. 'I've been meaning to ask a favour. I've been thinking about who should interview Leonie Stanwick, and the conclusion I've come to is that I'm not the right person for the job. You, on the other hand, would be perfect. What do you say?'

'Me?'

'You interview people for a living, don't you? You're the obvious candidate. You did a brilliant job when you interviewed residents for the community film back in the spring. The locals know and trust you.'

'I'm not sure about that,' Violet said. 'I've lived in Merrywell for six months now, and I still feel like the village newbie.'

Eric smiled. 'Even Fiona and I feel like that sometimes, and we've lived here for over a decade. People like us . . . the ones who weren't born and bred in the village . . . we'll always be incomers, but that's not to say we're not made welcome. The locals have really taken to you, Violet. They like you.'

'Thanks,' she said, feeling an inner glow of satisfaction. 'That's nice to hear.'

'So, what you do say, then? Will you do the interview? I can pay you a small fee, and I'll also throw in a free festival pass, plus a copy of Leonie Stanwick's latest book.'

'Is that even out yet?' Violet said. 'I thought her appearance here in Merrywell was supposed to mark the official launch of her new novel.'

'Her publisher has sent me an advance reading copy.'

He reached under the counter and retrieved a hefty paperback.

'Voila!' he said, presenting it with a flourish. 'I give you *Hot Toddy* . . . featuring female protagonist Eliza Tiffen and her love interest Dominic Todd.'

Hesitantly, Violet accepted the book and examined its shadowy cover, which was dominated by the image of a ripped male torso – presumably meant to represent the novel's hero.

'Have you read it?' she asked.

'Bits of it,' Eric replied, smirking sheepishly. 'I kind of skipped to the juicy parts.'

'Eric!' Violet flashed him a look of mock horror. 'I thought your preferred reading matter was books on World War Two . . . or vintage buses. I didn't realise you had a penchant for racy romance novels.'

'That's just it,' he replied. 'I don't. I'll admit that Leonie Stanwick is one of my favourite authors . . . but only because I sell so many of her books here in the shop. Don't get me wrong . . . I have nothing against her novels per se. They're just not my cup of tea, which is why I'm not the best person to interview her at the festival.'

Violet had flipped the book over and was reading the blurb on the back cover.

When gallery owner Eliza Tiffen meets temperamental artist Dominic Todd, she finds him extremely attractive but intimidatingly intense. As they discuss an exhibition of his work, Eliza tries to understand what makes Dominic tick and what he's hiding.

As they embark on an unexpected and passionate love affair, Eliza finds herself falling in love with Dominic, but before she can give in to her emotions, she must uncover Dominic's deepest, darkest secret . . .

Although *Hot Toddy* wouldn't be Violet's usual reading choice, she found the prospect of interviewing its author surprisingly appealing.

She weighed up Eric's proposal and came to the conclusion that it was a no-brainer. Her fledgling business, *The Memory Box*, was becoming busier by the day, but interviewing Leonie Stanwick wouldn't take up much of her time – plus Eric was a friend, and she wanted to do whatever she could to support the festival.

'All right,' she said. 'You've got yourself a deal. I'll make a start on *Hot Toddy* just as soon as I've finished reading my current book. In the meantime, I'll do some research on Leonie Stanwick and put some questions together for the interview.'

'The festival isn't for another four weeks, so you've got plenty of time to prepare,' Eric said.

'Did I hear you tell Judith that Leonie has local connections?'

'Yes,' he replied. 'She was born here in Merrywell, although she hasn't been back much over the years. The book festival will be her first visit since her mother's funeral six months ago.'

'Does she have other family in the village?' Violet asked.

'There's a sister, but I don't think she and Leonie are close. You should talk to Fiona. She'll give you the low-down. She's read everything Leonie's ever written.'

'Really? I didn't know that.'

'Oh, yes,' said Eric. 'When it comes to Leonie Stanwick, my wife's quite a fan.'

Chapter 2

'Stanwick is Leonie's pen name,' said Fiona, later that evening. 'Her real name is Leonie Hammond.'

She and Violet were sitting in front of the log burner in Violet's living room at Greengage Cottage. They had gathered for a drink and a catch-up, and it hadn't taken long for the conversation to turn to the upcoming festival and its star guest.

'I had a quick look at Leonie's author website,' Violet said. 'It doesn't offer much in the way of personal information. It mentions that she was born in Derbyshire in 1970, and that she lived in the county until she was eighteen, but it's all very vague, and Merrywell isn't actually named.'

'Well, she definitely spent her childhood here in the village. A lot of local people remember her from back then,' Fiona said, as she sipped a glass of Zinfandel. 'Her first book came out in 2002 and it was an instant bestseller – quite a sensation at the time. Leonie's written a new book every year since. She has a huge fanbase.'

Violet nodded, impressed. 'What makes her books so popular, do you think?'

'They're very easy to read,' Fiona said, before pausing to ponder the question further. 'Raunchy and great fun . . . pure escapism . . .

but I suppose that's true of a lot of novels. The thing that makes Leonie's books stand out from the rest is her female protagonists. They're strong and sexy, and they live exciting, independent lives. Leonie has really nailed the art of creating characters that readers care about, and can relate to.'

'Or would like to be?'

Fiona laughed. 'Yes, maybe that's part of it. Whatever the reason, people can't get enough of her books.'

'Eric told me you've read every one of them. Maybe *you're* the best person to interview her.'

'No way!' Fiona pulled a shuddery face. 'If you put me in the spotlight, I'd get tongue-tied and muddled. I'm not cut out for all that stuff. You're so much better at it than I could ever hope to be. Besides, I'll be busy organising the catering for the event. I can't be in two places at once, can I?'

'OK, just so long as you're sure.'

'I am, providing you promise to introduce me to Leonie. I wouldn't want to miss the chance of meeting my favourite author. Eric told me he's already given you the advance copy of *Hot Toddy*. Bags I get to read it next.'

'Not a problem. I'll pass it over as soon as I've finished with it.'

'Cheers, Violet. Not that I'm going to have time to do any reading over the next few weeks. The run-up to the festival will be extremely hectic.' Fiona looked uncharacteristically anxious about what lay in store. 'On the festival weekend itself, we'll be keeping the café open late and offering a bistro menu on all three evenings.'

'Sounds like you'll be run off your feet.'

'It'll be hard work, that's for sure – but worth it, I hope. To be honest, any extra income is welcome at the moment. Things have been a bit slack in the café lately.'

'Why's that?' said Violet. 'Is it just a quiet time of year?'

Fiona shrugged. 'That's certainly a factor, plus a lot of people are tightening their belts at the moment. Fancy coffees and eating out are the first things to go when someone's on an economy drive. To make matters worse, Eric has pumped a fair chunk of his own money into setting up the book festival. It's a calculated risk . . . one that we're hoping will pay off . . . but quite frankly, we can't afford for it to fail. It *has* to be a success.'

'I'm sure it will be.' Violet squeezed her friend's arm. 'If anyone can pull it off, it's you and Eric.'

'Thanks, Violet. I appreciate the vote of confidence. Let's just hope everything goes to plan.'

'Why wouldn't it? You're two of the most organised people I know. What could possibly go wrong?'

Over a second glass of wine, they considered possible interview questions, and discussed Leonie's most memorable characters and some of the high-powered or exotic locations in which her novels had been set.

'She's never featured Merrywell in any of her books then?' Violet said. 'Or a village very much like it?'

'No,' Fiona replied. 'It's always London, or America, or somewhere hot and exotic. It's understandable, I suppose. Leonie's in her early fifties now: her days of living in Merrywell must be a distant memory. Besides, her readers have come to expect locations that are glamorous and chic – which rules Merrywell out.'

'Oooh, I wouldn't say that,' Violet said, struck by a fierce sense of loyalty to the place she now called home. 'Merrywell might not be glamorous, but it's got a lot going for it, and it has a charm all of its own.'

Fiona laughed. 'Perhaps when you interview her, you could suggest she uses the village as the setting for her next book . . . see what reaction you get.'

'I can just picture it,' Violet said, holding up her hands. 'A passionate love scene unfolding in the Merrywell Manor Hotel.'

Fiona gave a belly laugh. 'Or . . . even better . . . the village hall,' she said. 'I wonder what Judith Talbot would say about that?'

The idea of the village hall as a setting for a series of raunchy goings-on plunged them into a fit of giggles, and it took a few minutes for them to recover their composure.

'Tell me about Leonie's sister,' Violet said, as she wiped tears of laughter from her eyes. 'I'm assuming she still lives in the village?'

'She does, but I don't know much about her, other than her name's Angeline, and she's a district nurse . . . or possibly a health visitor. I'm never sure what the difference is.'

'Eric told me that she and Leonie aren't close,' Violet said. 'Which begs the question . . . do you think Angeline will come to see Leonie at the festival?'

'Now that *is* something I know about,' Fiona said. 'I checked the online sales before I came over here this evening, and I can confirm that Angeline Hammond has bought a ticket for Leonie's event. And interestingly, another name popped onto the list late this afternoon . . . a rather unlikely one.'

'Who?'

'Judith Talbot. She's booked a ticket for the livestream.'

Violet's eyebrows disappeared into her fringe. 'What? After everything she said to Eric?'

'Yep. Judith might not approve of Leonie Stanwick, but she obviously intends to watch the interview from home.'

'She's got a nerve, I'll give her that,' said Violet, with a shake of her head.

'Who knows . . .' Fiona grinned. 'Perhaps she's a secret fan.'

Chapter 3

The following day was Saturday, and Violet had arranged to meet Matthew for lunch in the local pub. She arrived first, and chose a table close to the roaring log fire. Sipping half a pint of the White Hart's finest draught bitter, she began to read the first chapter of *Hot Toddy*.

'Sorry I'm late,' Matthew said, when he took a seat at the table a few minutes later. 'Not that you appear to have missed me. You look engrossed. What are you reading?'

Smiling, Violet placed a marker between the pages and held up the book for Matthew's inspection.

'Blimey.' His eyes widened as he took in the front cover image. 'Doesn't look like your usual fare. *That* guy looks a lot more lively than the bodies you normally read about. I take it this isn't a crime novel?'

'No.' Violet laughed. '*This* is homework. It's the new one by Leonie Stanwick. Eric's asked me to interview her at the book festival.'

'Has he now? That's good. Are you pleased?'

'I am, although I'm at something of a disadvantage, having never read any of her books.'

'You've got a few weeks to put that right,' Matthew said. 'And

I'm sure you'll do a great job regardless. You always seem to know what to say to people.'

'Do I?'

Matthew nodded. 'You have a knack for making people feel comfortable, and getting them to confide in you. I look forward to seeing you in action with Leonie Stanwick.'

'Oh! Are you coming to the event then?' Violet said. 'I didn't think it'd be your scene.'

'It wouldn't be, ordinarily, but now that I know you're doing the interview, I'll make a point of being there. I've already bought myself a festival pass, so I can go to as many of the sessions as I like. And I must confess, I am slightly intrigued about Leonie. I went to school with her, so I'm interested to hear how her life has panned out.'

'You were at school together?' Violet narrowed her eyes. 'You've kept that quiet. Were you in the same class?'

Matthew took a swig of beer and wiped his mouth before replying. 'She was in the year above me, but I used to see her around . . . and on the school bus. To be honest, you couldn't really miss her. Leonie was one of those people who attracted a lot of attention, although I'm pretty sure she didn't know I existed back then. I was a scrawny little squirt . . . easily overlooked.'

Violet stared at Matthew's impressive, six-foot-two, broad-shouldered frame and smiled. 'I find that hard to believe. I can only think you must have had a late growth spurt.'

'I did, but not until after Leonie Hammond had left the sixth form.'

'Was she nice?' Violet asked. 'Did you like her?'

'She was very popular. Clever, without being too swotty, if you know what I mean. To a naïve young lad like me, she was sophistication and glamour personified.'

'I see.' Violet sipped her beer. 'Sounds to me like you had a thing for her.'

He laughed. 'I think almost every lad in the school was smitten with Leonie. She was quite a looker.'

'Ah . . . right,' Violet said, smiling to herself as she pictured a besotted young Matthew in school uniform. 'Now we're getting down to the real reason you've decided to go to her event. Admit it. You want to sit and admire your schoolboy crush.'

'Who knows, perhaps she'll notice me this time,' Matthew said, staring deep into Violet's eyes. 'It's about time I had some luck in love.'

Chapter 4

Over the course of the next four weeks, various items of equipment arrived at Merrywell Shopping Village, transforming it piece by piece into a festival venue. Banners went up; a small, elevated stage was erected in the bookshop, where the majority of the author events would take place; and a supply of hired foldable chairs arrived, ready to seat the audience.

The day before the festival, two street food vendors set up in the shopping village's courtyard area, and a collection of sturdy outdoor tables were positioned on its cobbles.

'What's with the mobile eateries?' Violet asked Fiona, when she went into the BBC. 'I thought you and Sophie were doing the catering for the festival.'

Fiona's daughter, Sophie, managed the café and occasionally helped out in the bakery.

'We are,' Fiona replied. 'But there's limited space in the café, and the number of festival tickets we've sold well exceeds our catering capacity. We thought it would be a good idea to bring in a few extra food vendors for outdoor dining. Who knows, if it goes down well, it could become a regular thing.'

'What about the bistro evenings in the café?'

'Fully booked every night,' Fiona said, smiling from ear to ear.

'And festival sales have really taken off over the last couple of weeks. Several of the author events have sold out, and most of the workshop places have been filled. We've posted everything on social media and we're getting a huge number of shares. The support's been amazing.'

'Eric must be feeling relieved.'

'He is,' Fiona said. 'All we need to do now is deliver on our promises. It's going to be a busy few days, but I'm looking forward to it.'

'Good,' Violet said. 'That's the spirit.'

'What about you? Are you all set? Have you finalised your questions for the interview with Leonie?'

'Yes, I sent them over to her publicist yesterday,' Violet said. 'I'm slightly disappointed they've asked to see the questions in advance. I'm worried it'll make things too staid. I was hoping for spontaneity, rather than Leonie trotting out a set of preprepared and well-rehearsed answers.'

'Perhaps it's standard practice,' Fiona said. 'Anyway, there's always the questions from the audience. That's something the publicist won't be able to vet. I take it you're going to leave time at the end for a Q and A?'

'I am, plus I'll be keeping a couple of extra questions of my own in reserve, should I need them.'

Digging around in her shoulder bag, Violet pulled out the now slightly dog-eared copy of *Hot Toddy*.

'Here,' she said, handing the book to Fiona. 'I've finished my final read-through. Sorry it's taken me so long. I know you've been dying to get your hands on it.'

'I have.' Fiona grabbed the book and clutched it to her chest. 'I'm planning to buy a signed copy at tomorrow's event, but I'll make do with this for now. I'll start it tonight. What did you think?'

'I enjoyed it,' Violet said. 'I'm still not a total convert to the genre, but it is an exceptionally well-written novel; fast-paced and utterly gripping. I'll admit to getting a lump in my throat at one point. There's this bit where—'

'Stop!' Fiona held up a hand. 'Don't tell me *anything*. No spoilers, please. I want to read it for myself.'

As she crossed the courtyard on her way back to her desk at *The Memory Box*, Violet spotted Joyce Collis, Matthew's mother, emerging from *The Epicurious* – the shopping village's deli, famous for its range of locally produced cheeses, preserves and pickles.

'Hello,' Violet said. 'Have you been treating yourself to something nice?'

'Just this.' Joyce held up a pot of gooseberry jam. 'It's absolutely divine, and delicious on scones.'

They were standing in the centre of the courtyard, surrounded by the picnic tables that were dotted around the cobbles.

'I assume you're coming to the book festival tomorrow?' Violet asked.

'I wouldn't miss it for the world,' Joyce replied, glancing approvingly at the outdoor furniture. 'Everything's shaping up nicely, isn't it?'

'Yep. Merrywell's buzzing. Most of the traders are staying open late to make the most of the increased footfall. Hopefully, the festival will be extremely good for business.'

'It's a real cultural boost too,' Joyce said. 'A book festival is exactly what the village needs. I can't wait.'

'Which sessions are you going to?'

'As many as I can,' said Joyce. 'I've bought a full three-day pass, and I intend to get my money's worth.'

'So, you'll be at the opening event tomorrow? With Leonie Stanwick?'

'I most certainly will. I've also signed up for her novel-writing masterclass on Saturday morning. I've had to pay extra for that, of course, but I'm sure it'll be worth it.'

'I didn't know you were a writer.'

'I'm not.' Joyce smiled bashfully. 'At least, not yet, but I'm hoping Leonie's workshop will inspire me. Mind you, at my age I've probably left it too late.'

Violet smiled encouragingly. 'I don't think it's ever too late . . . not if you're determined enough.'

Joyce gave an uncertain shrug. 'We'll see,' she said. 'If I'm no good at it, or writing turns out to be too much like hard work, I'll probably just stick with my crafting.'

Violet knew that Joyce had a penchant for knitting and crochet. She was a regular customer in the shopping village's yarn and fabric shop, *Sew-in' to Knitting*.

'Do you still go to the crafting club here at the shopping village?' Violet asked.

'I do,' said Joyce. 'We took a break for the summer, but we're getting back into it again now. Did you know that Leonie Stanwick's mother, Elizabeth, used to be a member? She attended right up until the week before she died.'

'No, I didn't know that. I didn't realise you were friends with Leonie's mum.'

'We weren't big buddies or anything,' Joyce said, with a brief shake of her head. 'Elizabeth was very quiet and reserved, but we'd chat occasionally. She lived on the outskirts of Merrywell . . . a mile or so along Stanton Lane. For that reason, she and her family weren't big mixers. They always stayed on the periphery, if you know what I mean?'

'You mean socially?'

'Yes, the Hammonds were a self-contained bunch. They rarely came along to village events.'

'I didn't think that was allowed here in Merrywell.' Violet grinned. 'Isn't being involved in village life obligatory?'

'As a general rule, yes, but somehow, the Hammonds managed to buck the trend. They avoided getting dragged into things by developing a sort of collective aloofness. It could be quite off-putting, even for the most determined of Merrywell's organising do-gooders.'

Violet made a mental note to resort to the same approach herself, should the pressure to get involved in the community ever become too intense.

'I only got to know Elizabeth properly after her husband had passed away,' Joyce said. 'That's when she joined the craft group and started to join in a bit more.'

'She must have been proud of Leonie,' said Violet. 'Did she talk about her much?'

'To be honest, it was her younger daughter, Angeline, that she was always going on about. If someone happened to mention Leonie, or talk about her books, Elizabeth would respond politely enough, but I got the impression she and Leonie didn't exactly see eye to eye.'

'I wonder why?'

'Elizabeth was a bit of a prude, so maybe she didn't approve of Leonie's books. She told me once that she hadn't read any of them. Can you believe that? She also said that Leonie was hopeless at keeping in touch. Apparently, after she went off to uni, Leonie hardly ever came back to Merrywell. By then Angeline had been born, so I think Elizabeth and her husband lavished all their attention on her instead.'

Violet frowned. 'During the interview, I was planning to ask Leonie about her memories of growing up in Merrywell – but maybe that's not a good idea. If there was a family feud, the question might get vetoed by the publicist.'

'I wouldn't go as far as to say there was a feud,' Joyce said. 'Leonie was obviously still in touch because she came back for Elizabeth's funeral earlier this year.'

'Did you go? To the funeral?'

Joyce nodded. 'I did. I was hoping I'd get the chance to speak to Leonie, actually . . . to offer my condolences . . . but she only came to the church service and the crematorium. She didn't come back for the wake.'

'That's odd,' Violet said. 'You'd think she would have made the effort, if only to support her sister.'

‘I agree,’ Joyce said. ‘Although I don’t think anyone need worry about young Angeline. She’s got her head screwed on . . . knows how to look after herself does that one. She’s very self-reliant.’

Violet smiled. ‘An independent spirit, is she?’

‘Very much so, but nice with it. Angeline’s quiet-natured, like her mother. She lives here in Merrywell . . . stayed on in the family home after Elizabeth died. The way I heard it, Angeline inherited everything. Leonie didn’t get a bean – although it’s not as if Leonie needs the money. Rumour has it she lives in a fancy house in some posh north London suburb – whereas Angeline lived with her mum right up to the end. I suppose it’s only right she got the house.’

‘Do you think Angeline will stay in Merrywell long term?’ Violet asked. ‘Now that her mum’s no longer around?’

‘I’d say so. For a while, I did wonder if she might sell up and move somewhere new, but she seems settled where she is. Every time I’ve driven by the house recently, there’s been work going on . . . new windows, repairs to the roof. There was even a kitchen fitter’s van parked outside a few weeks ago. It looks to me like Angeline intends to stay.’

‘Either that, or she’s doing the place up, getting it ready to put on the market.’

Joyce shook her head. ‘I doubt it. Unlike her sister, Angeline has a strong connection to Merrywell. She works in the area, and she has friends in the village.’

‘But she’s not close to Leonie?’

Joyce seesawed her head. ‘No, but that’s understandable. Leonie left home before her sister was even born. Elizabeth was getting on in years when she had Angeline. Just when she thought her baby-making days were behind her . . . boom! She discovered Angeline was on the way. There were complications with the pregnancy, so she didn’t have an easy time of it. She must have been relieved when it was all over and Angeline was safe in her arms.’

Violet smiled. ‘I bet she didn’t relish going through the whole sleepless nights routine again. Being plunged back into the days of nappy changing and two-in-the-morning feeds must have been a real shock to the system.'

'It would have been for most people . . . but for Elizabeth, I think it offered a second chance. She told me once she was very young and naïve when Leonie was born, and totally unprepared for motherhood. She admitted she'd made mistakes the first time around. Having Angeline gave her an opportunity to do it all over again . . . and get it right.'

Violet wondered what Elizabeth's mistakes had been. The dynamics within a family were always a rich source of intrigue and dissatisfaction.

'Do you think Leonie's agreed to appear at the festival so that she can spend time with her sister?' Violet asked. 'Perhaps the siblings will grow closer, now that it's just the two of them.'

'I hope they do,' Joyce said. 'Family is the most important thing there is, and Leonie and Angeline would do well to remember that.'

'Perhaps Leonie's visit to Merrywell will strengthen the bonds of sisterhood.'

'I'd like to think so,' said Joyce. 'Although it's not something *we* can influence. At the end of the day, it'll be up to Leonie and Angeline to sort things out between themselves.'

'Absolutely,' Violet agreed. 'What will be, will be. My job tomorrow is to make sure the interview with Leonie goes well. Eric's put an enormous amount of effort into the festival. I don't want to let him down.'

'You'll do a grand job,' Joyce said, giving Violet a reassuring smile. 'You have a way about you . . . a natural warmth. You make people feel comfortable by always saying the right thing.'

Violet smiled bashfully. 'It's kind of you to say so. I only hope you're right. I guess we'll find out soon enough.'

Chapter 5

Eric had hired three of the studio rooms at the shopping village for the duration of the festival. Two were set up for events that were due to take place on each of the three days of the festival, and the third and smallest room was being used as a 'green room' for guest authors. Flasks of hot water and teabags were laid out on a side table, along with a filter coffee-maker, jugs of cold orange juice, mugs, plates and glasses, and a selection of muffins, cookies and fresh fruit.

It was the first day of the festival, and Violet was sitting in an easy chair in the corner of the green room, checking her notes as she awaited the arrival of Leonie Stanwick. Over by the door, Eric was prowling, arms folded, glancing down at his watch every few seconds. The atmosphere was growing increasingly tense. The festival's opening event was due to start at noon, and it was already five minutes to. Leonie was late. Uncomfortably so.

'I specifically asked her to be here no later than eleven-forty-five,' Eric said. 'I need to go through the running order with her . . . plus we have to fit the lapel mics.'

'Is she still not answering her phone?'

He shook his head. 'It's going straight to voicemail.'

'Perhaps she's been held up in traffic,' Violet said, in a feeble attempt to calm Eric down.

'That's extremely unlikely,' he replied. 'She travelled up yesterday evening and stayed overnight at the Merrywell Manor Hotel – so, it's not as though she has far to travel.'

A soft knock brought a relieved expression to his face, but when he opened the door, his beaming smile faded. Instead of welcoming Leonie Stanwick, he found himself staring into the pale face of a woman wearing a black leather coat and a purple bobble hat.

'Hello,' she said. 'Is this the green room? Would it be possible to have a quick word with Leonie, please?'

She peered suspiciously over Eric's shoulder, eyeing the magnolia-emulsioned walls with scepticism, perhaps puzzled as to why they weren't painted a calming shade of green.

'Leonie hasn't arrived yet,' Eric said. 'And when she does, we're going to be very short on time. Can I suggest you talk to her after the event? She'll be signing copies of her latest novel in the bookshop, so you can speak to her then.'

'I was rather hoping to have a word with her in private,' the woman said, her face a picture of disappointment. 'My name's Karen Avery. Leonie and I were at school together. She was my best friend, actually. I was hoping to invite her over for dinner on Sunday. I'd love to catch up with her while she's in Merrywell.'

'I'm not sure how long she intends to stay in the village,' Eric said. 'She's running a workshop in the morning, but after that . . . who knows?'

Karen Avery tucked an escaped curl back inside her hat. 'Could you at least let her know I was here?' she said, appealing to Eric with sad, grey eyes. 'Tell her I'll try and catch up with her later.'

'Yes, yes, I'll do that . . . of course,' Eric said, sounding uncharacteristically impatient. 'For now, the best thing you can do is head over to the bookshop and take your seat. We'll be there shortly.'

Closing the door on Karen Avery's retreating figure, Eric leaned against it and ran his hands up and down his face.

'Where the hell is she?' he said, sounding exasperated. 'Unless she turns up within the next minute, we'll have no choice but to make a late start.'

'Shall I ring the hotel?' Violet said. 'See what time she left?'

'Would you? Thanks, Violet.' He pushed himself away from the door and began to pace. 'We really are cutting things fine. Darren's on standby to start the livestream . . . and the audience is waiting. What will I do if she doesn't turn up?'

'She'll be here,' Violet said, in the cheeriest voice she could muster.

As she searched on her phone for the telephone number of the Merrywell Manor Hotel, the sound of female voices drifted in from the courtyard.

'That sounds like it could be them,' she said.

Eric yanked open the door and gave an audible sigh of relief as Leonie Stanwick and another woman were directed into the green room by his son, Tom.

Leonie looked exactly like the publicity photo on her website: tall, with a rangy figure, and long, wavy blonde hair. She was wearing tight black jeans, high-heeled ankle boots, a flowing saffron-coloured blouse, and a black-sequinned fiddler cap. Violet, who was wearing a plain navy-blue dress, felt dull and dowdy in comparison. The woman at Leonie's side – presumably the publicist – was small and mouselike, a look accentuated by her rodent-grey trouser suit.

'Welcome, welcome,' Eric said effusively. 'It's wonderful to meet you, Leonie. Thank you so much for agreeing to appear at Merrywell Book Festival.'

The author offered a jewelled hand for him to shake.

'This is Yvette Finch, my publicist,' she said, indicating the woman at her side.

Yvette held out limp fingers, which Eric shook rather too vigorously.

'This is Violet Brewster,' he said, turning in Violet's direction. 'As you know, she'll be doing the interview with you this evening.'

Violet stood up and exchanged brief greetings with the two women, fully aware that time was running short.

'Thanks for sending over your plan for the interview, Violet,' Leonie said. 'I appreciate it.'

'Not a problem,' she replied, pleased that Leonie hadn't voiced any objections to the proposed questions.

Her sense of relief was short-lived.

'I've taken the liberty of making a few notes,' Yvette Finch said, pulling a wad of folded papers from her shoulder bag and handing them to Violet. 'There you go. There are a couple of questions that Leonie doesn't want to answer, and I've put a slightly different spin on some of the others.'

Violet seethed inwardly as she looked down at the printed questions. Some had a thick black line drawn through them – presumably the ones that were off the table – and others had copious alterations.

'I wish you'd emailed this to me earlier,' she said. 'I would have liked an opportunity to read through the changes. As it is, we're running short on time. We need to get mic'ed up and start the interview.'

'I'm aware of that.' Yvette bunched her lips into a pout and glowered at her boss. 'Unfortunately, Leonie has only just finished reading through the questions . . . last minute as always, I'm afraid.'

Leonie curled her lip and gave a disdainful and unapologetic shrug.

'I'm sorry I couldn't let you know about the changes any sooner,' Yvette added. 'Given the short notice, and if you feel unable to incorporate the revisions, I suppose it would be all right to go with your original wording. But please, don't ask the questions that I've crossed out. If you do, Leonie will simply refuse to answer.'

At that moment, Tom's partner, Darren, materialised and began to attach wireless mics, and explain the setup for the livestream.

'Someone dropped in to see you a few moments ago, Leonie,' Eric said, as the author wriggled her mic into place. 'She said her name was Karen Avery and that she'll catch up with you later.'

'Not if I can help it,' Leonie muttered, as she flicked open a compact mirror to check her appearance.

'She said you were friends at school,' Violet said. 'Best friends.'

Leonie snapped the mirror shut and sprayed perfume behind her ears and onto her wrists, filling the green room with a heady rose-scented aroma. 'Karen and I *were* at school together, but that's about as far as it goes. I haven't seen or spoken to the woman for well over thirty years. If we'd been best friends, I think I would have made the effort to keep in touch, don't you?'

Violet wasn't sure how or whether to respond – but thankfully, Eric chose that moment to herd everyone out of the door, across the courtyard and into the bookshop.

Leonie's appearance was met with tumultuous applause from the audience, and as Violet led the author onto the stage, it became clear that this was one of the festival's sell-out events. The bookshop was packed. Every seat was taken, and there were more people upstairs, leaning over the balcony.

Eric's voice quavered with nervous excitement as he thanked everyone for coming and declared the Merrywell Book Festival officially open. After he'd encouraged everyone to attend as many of the festival events as possible, he formally welcomed Leonie Stanwick and handed over to Violet.

As she introduced Leonie, Violet noticed that mother and daughter duo Cathy and Molly Gee were sitting on the front row, directly in front of the stage. Cathy and her husband, Billy, ran the local pub, the White Hart, and their grown-up daughter Molly was a familiar and friendly presence in the village.

Violet's attention was drawn to the woman sitting on Molly's right. She was in her thirties, with flowing blonde hair and an open, naturally pretty face. Her arms were folded across her body, and her long legs were stretched out in front of her, crossed at the ankles. The likeness to Leonie was uncanny. She had the same flashing eyes . . . even the same tilt of the head. It was like looking at a youthful version of Leonie. Her double.

This then, must be Angeline Hammond. Leonie's younger sister.

On Violet's left, Leonie was gazing out at the audience, smiling – looking in every direction except that of her younger sister.

In stark contrast, Angeline was staring directly at Leonie, her eyes boring into her. But unlike her sister, Angeline wasn't smiling.

Chapter 6

Violet had planned to open the interview by asking about Leonie's childhood memories of Merrywell, but that was one of the questions that had been crossed out by the publicist. So instead, she began by asking Leonie why she had chosen to become an author.

'I was working on a cruise ship when I first started writing,' she replied. 'It was a busy job, with long hours, and when I did get any free time, I liked to spend it alone, in my cabin, curled up with a good book. One day I realised I'd worked my way through virtually all of the fiction in the ship's library, and I was desperate for something new to read. The trouble was, we were at sea, forty-eight hours from the next port, so there was no chance of getting my hands on a new book. That's when I decided to have a go at writing one of my own. I suppose it was a bit of fun to begin with. A lark.'

'Your novels are set in some very interesting and exotic locations,' Violet said. 'Are those the places you visited when you worked on the cruise ships?'

'Some of them,' Leonie replied. 'Others are countries I've travelled to in more recent years. I've been on some fascinating journeys, and rather than letting those experiences go to waste, I use them in my stories. Authors are always being told to *write about what you know* . . . and as my first book was called *The Love Cruise*, I think we can safely say I took that advice to heart.'

A murmur of laughter rippled through the audience.

'Overall then, would you say that working on a cruise ship was a good career move for you as a writer?' Violet said. 'It seems to have provided you with motivation and inspiration, as well as plenty of background material for your novels.'

'Yes, from that point of view, it was the perfect job. Prior to that, I'd been a bit lost . . . career wise. When I was in my early twenties, I was restless. I moved around a lot, taking whatever work I could get. I've waited tables in a restaurant, been a holiday rep, and I've lost count of how many sales jobs I've had. I even worked in a dog grooming parlour once . . . but that only lasted a few weeks.' She pulled a face. 'Dogs can be unpredictable little so-and-sos. It's the tiny, cute ones with the sweet faces that you have to look out for.'

Another rumble of laughter from the audience.

'You've clearly had a varied but . . . shall we say . . . unconventional work history,' said Violet, taking a risk and going off script with the question. 'Weren't you tempted to settle for a steady job after you graduated from university? Didn't you want to start a career and climb the promotional ladder?'

Leonie gave a half-hearted laugh. 'There was a time when that's *exactly* what I wanted to do,' she said. 'I couldn't wait to go to university to study law, and I had every intention of becoming a barrister, but by the end of the first semester . . . things had changed. I realised my life was destined to go in a different direction. I dropped out of uni and went off-piste. For a while, things were pretty wild. Some people thought I'd lost my way, but I prefer to think of that period as a time of freeing myself from expectations.'

'So, if you'd stayed at university, you'd be lawyer now, rather than a novelist?'

'Without a doubt,' Leonie agreed. 'My novels would still be buried deep in my imagination, having never seen the light of day – a scenario I'm sure my fiercest critics would have wholeheartedly preferred.'

Violet nodded towards the people in the audience, who were listening intently. 'Whereas, I'm sure your readers are all exceedingly grateful that you abandoned your plan to become a barrister.'

Violet moved the conversation on, asking questions designed to elicit Leonie's views on why romantic novels were so popular with female readers, and how the genre had evolved over recent decades. The answers Leonie gave were intelligently thought out, eloquent, and delivered with genuine passion.

During the interview, Violet sneaked several glances at the rapt faces of the audience, the majority of which were female. In fact, other than Eric and Matthew, there were only two other men in the crowd.

On the front row, Angeline Hammond sat motionless as a statue, her face devoid of emotion, as though she was keeping herself in check. Why had she come to the event? Her refusal to smile suggested it wasn't to offer moral support to her sister. So what were Angeline's reasons for being here? Curiosity? A show of unity? Or a genuine interest in Leonie's books?

It took a while to spot Karen Avery among the sea of faces. After her last-minute visit to the green room, she'd obviously had no choice but to take one of the last remaining seats on the back row. She was leaning forward, soaking up every one of Leonie's words. The expression on her face was curiously indecipherable: a combination perhaps of awe and astonishment. Violet found herself wondering whether Karen Avery had really been Leonie's friend, or whether she was simply an ardent and possibly overwrought admirer.

'Let's talk now about your latest book, *Hot Toddy*,' Violet said, as the interview progressed. 'It's out today and is being officially launched here at Merrywell Book Festival. Without giving too much away, can you tell us what the book is about and what inspired you to write it? And then, maybe you'd like to read a short extract for us.'

Leonie picked up the hot-off-the-press copy of her new book from the coffee table in front of her. Running a manicured finger-nail across its cover, she gave a succinct overview of the story's premise.

'There was no one particular moment that triggered the idea for the novel,' she said. 'When I write, it's the characters that come first. They sort of . . . appear, fully formed. This will sound weird – but what I do then is *interview* them, question them about their lives. And as each character responds, I ask myself: *what is this person hiding*? Because we all have secrets, don't we?'

Instead of looking at Violet, Leonie had turned to stare at the audience, her voice tinged with a sense of urgency.

'Every one of us has something to hide, even from those closest to us,' she said. 'And it's the secrets we keep that shape who we are. They alter our behaviour: change the way we speak, the things we say, the decisions we make. It's that intrigue that I look for in my characters. Secrets are pure gold to a writer. They are the basis of all the best stories.'

Without further ado, she opened up *Hot Toddy* and began to read from a chapter halfway through the book.

Violet was surprised, having assumed that Leonie would read from chapter one. To save everyone's blushes, she hoped the section Leonie had selected wasn't one of the love scenes.

As she tuned in to the reading, Violet realised that the extract was in fact the highly charged, emotional scene that had brought a lump to her own throat when she'd read the book.

She leaned back, listening to the melodious sound of Leonie's voice.

The reading began with Eliza Tiffen interrogating Dominic Todd about his past, furious that he was refusing to open up to her. The scene ended with Dominic explaining the reasons for his reticence. It was a narrative that had resonated with Violet.

'There are certain things that are just too hard to talk about,' Dominic said. 'Sometimes in life, something happens . . . something so catastrophic . . . so hurtful that you have no alternative but to bury the memory, deep inside your soul. You carry on and try to forget about it, but it's always there, burning away at your consciousness. If I could open up to you about what happened, I would, but I find it impossible.'

'If you truly loved me, you'd be able to tell me anything,' Eliza said.

He placed his hands on his head. 'I do *love you, but I'm sorry . . . it's still too raw, too painful. Do you understand what I'm saying?'*

Eliza lifted her chin defiantly. 'No, Dominic. I'm not sure that I do.'

'In that case,' he replied, 'consider yourself lucky. You've obviously not experienced the worst of life's cruelties – at least not yet. Let's hope it stays that way.'

As Leonie finished her reading and closed the book, the audience gave an enthusiastic round of applause.

'Thank you,' she said, smiling gratefully. 'I really appreciate you coming here today for the launch of *Hot Toddy*. There's nothing I like more than celebrating publication day with my readers.'

'And can I remind you that the book will be available to buy at the end of the session,' Violet added, getting in one final plug to help Eric sell as many copies as possible. 'In a short while, Leonie will move to the book-signing table and she'll be there for at least half an hour – but before then, we have a few minutes remaining to take your questions. Does anyone have anything they'd like to ask?'

Half a dozen hands shot up. Violet pointed to Molly Gee on the front row, indicating that she should go ahead and ask her question.

Molly grinned broadly, obviously happy to be chosen. 'You mentioned that you try and write about what you know,' she said. 'Does that apply when you're writing the love scenes?'

The audience laughed.

'Remembering that discretion is the better part of valour,' Leonie said, smiling enigmatically and refusing to be drawn, 'I'll let my readers work that one out for themselves.'

Violet pointed to a woman on the balcony, who was waving her arm, desperate to ask a question. 'Up there . . . the lady in the green dress.'

'I'd like to ask Leonie's advice on the writing process,' she said. 'What's the most important quality an aspiring writer needs in order to succeed?'

'That's easy,' Leonie said, in a beat. 'Persistence.'

Somewhere in the audience, someone reacted with a loud, disbelieving huff. It was a disrespectful and insolent sound, and Violet felt embarrassed. She tried to work out where the noise had come from, but it was impossible to tell.

Thankfully, Leonie didn't seem to have noticed. She carried on, blissfully unaware that someone in the audience disagreed with her. 'Being an author has its fun moments,' she said, 'but you have to remember that it's also hard work. There will be times when you won't feel like writing, when you'll look for an excuse to do something else . . . *anything* else. Those are the days when it's most important to write. You *have* to keep going. Be persistent. Every writer has periods when they feel disinclined to work. It's the people who keep going, despite their reluctance, who go on to succeed.'

It was almost one o'clock, and the session was drawing to an end. There was time for one more question, two at the most. Violet scanned the raised hands and pointed to the long arm of a man sitting in the second row.

The sound of his voice brought a warm smile to Leonie's face – so warm, in fact, that it made all her previous smiles seem inconsequential in comparison.

'Why romance?' the man said, his expression intense. 'Why not crime, or science fiction, or horror? Why do you choose to write about love?'

'Because,' Leonie said, her voice quivering with emotion, 'love is the most important thing there is. Once experienced, it can never be forgotten. Not all relationships last, but love . . . *true* love . . . goes on forever.'

Violet thought fleetingly of her own failed marriage. The demise of her relationship with her ex had been a gradual thing . . . a slow, sad fizzling out . . . but they had loved each other once. They must have done, otherwise their divorce wouldn't have felt so painful.

The man smiled back at Leonie. 'It seems to me your female protagonists are strong and independent, more than capable of managing on their own,' he said. 'But there's also a sense that they're looking for *the one*. Is that the case for you? Who is the love of your life?'

'That's a very personal question,' Violet said, deciding to intervene to save Leonie's blushes. 'And not something we can expect Leonie to answer. Has anyone else got a question?'

Several more hands shot up, but Leonie was intent on continuing her conversation with the man.

'Before we move on,' she said. 'I *am* willing to respond to the question, although you're right, Violet, I'm not going to reveal who the great love of my life is, or was. What I will say is this: I found my one true love many years ago, but sadly it was a relationship that wasn't destined to last. But I've never forgotten that person.' She tapped a hand against her chest. 'They will always be here . . . in my heart.'

Violet cleared her throat. The interview was taking an unexpectedly serious turn, and she was determined to lighten the mood and get the conversation back on track.

'There you go, ladies and gentlemen,' she said, laughing nervously at the audience. 'You've heard it from the queen of romance herself . . . *true love never dies*. And if you want to find out if Eliza Tiffen and Dominic Todd find happiness together, you'll have to buy the book. Now . . . we have time for one more quick question . . .'

Joyce Collis put up her hand.

'Can you tell us what you're working on at the moment?' she asked.

Before responding, Leonie glanced over at her publicist, who was sitting in a reserved seat at the end of the front row. Was it Violet's imagination, or did Yvette Finch give an almost imperceptible shake of her head? Was there something she didn't want Leonie to share with her readers?

Smirking, Leonie turned and addressed Joyce directly.

'My publicist will kill me for saying this . . . but what the heck. The book I'm working on right now isn't a novel. It's a tell-all memoir that will cover all aspects of my life, including my journey as an author. In order to complete it, I'm having to take some time out from my normal publication schedule, which my publisher has agreed to, albeit reluctantly. The imprint I write for doesn't publish autobiographies, so my agent is negotiating a separate contract for the memoir. Whether or not it will be with the same publishing house remains to be seen.'

Yvette Finch was scowling furiously. Clearly, Leonie had revealed something she shouldn't.

'The autobiography is a project I've been considering for a while,' Leonie added. 'It does mean that fans of my romances will have to wait a little longer for my next novel to be published – but for now, at least, you have *Hot Toddy* to look forward to. I hope you enjoy it.'

It was a suitable note on which to end the interview.

'Thank you for sharing that with us, Leonie,' Violet said. 'I'm sure your autobiography will be absolutely fascinating, and something your readers will relish.'

Leonie smiled cryptically. 'Perhaps not all of them,' she said. 'However, it's something I feel I must do. It's time.'

Violet wondered whether the death of Elizabeth Hammond had freed Leonie up, removed any constraints that would have prevented her from writing candidly about her early family life, as well as her adult years.

'And talking of time . . .' Violet said, keen to wrap things up. 'Sadly, it's something we've run out of – but if you do still have a question, you can chat to Leonie during the book signing, here in the shop. In the morning, she'll be delivering a masterclass for budding novel writers – although I'm reliably informed that tickets for that workshop are now sold out.'

Violet smiled.

'All that remains is for me to thank Leonie for being Merrywell Book Festival's very first guest. I'm sure you'll agree it's been fascinating to get her take on writing romantic fiction, and listening to her read from her latest book. Ladies and gentlemen, please put your hands together for Leonie Stanwick.'

Chapter 7

As a vigorous round of applause echoed around the bookshop, Leonie stood up, stepped off the stage and allowed Eric to lead her to the signing table. It was positioned at the rear of the shop, next to a towering pile of her novels.

As Violet descended from the stage, the audience shuffled to its feet and people began to form an orderly queue to buy books. With the interview over, Violet's job was done. She stood aside, listening in to people's conversations and observing their body language to gauge their reaction to the event.

The first person to get in line to buy a book was the man who'd quizzed Leonie about love. When he reached the signing table, paperback in hand, Leonie gave him a dazzling smile. Bending their heads together, the pair began to chat and laugh flirtatiously.

Surprisingly, Angeline Hammond showed no inclination to stick around. As soon as the interview was over, she put on her coat and headed straight out through the main door, into the courtyard.

What was even more astonishing was that Karen Avery, Leonie's erstwhile *bezzie mate*, was close on Angeline's heels. Violet would have put money on Karen hanging around in the hope of getting reacquainted with her 'friend'. Instead, Karen had pulled on her hat and headed outside. Perhaps she intended to waylay Leonie later, over a drink in the café or courtyard.

The bookshop was packed, and not just with people queuing to buy copies of *Hot Toddy*. Now that the event was over, customers were pouring back into the shop, milling around and browsing shelves in almost every aisle, as well as on the balcony. Eric's endeavours to boost business seemed to be paying off big time – and it wasn't just the bookshop that was benefiting. A sizeable crowd was also wandering around in the courtyard, with people going in and out of the antiques emporium, the yarn and fabric shop, and the deli.

As Violet watched their movements through the shop window, someone came and stood at her elbow. Turning, she saw that it was Matthew.

'That's the first event over and done with, then,' he said.

She smiled warmly, glad of his company. 'Was Leonie how you remembered her?'

'Pretty much,' he said, making a sound that wasn't quite a laugh. 'Older, of course – but aren't we all?'

Violet nodded sagely.

'I thought she was very relaxed and chatty,' Matthew added. 'But she didn't really *say* very much, did she?'

Violet faltered, wondering whether his observation was a criticism of her interviewing style.

'She was very forthcoming about her writing,' she said.

'True, but rather more cagey about the more personal aspects of her life.'

'I'd say she was vague rather than cagey,' Violet said. 'The publicist did warn me that might be the case. As an author, Leonie's obliged to discuss her books and her writing process, but it's up to her to decide whether to divulge anything more personal.'

'Fair point. I must confess, I found the question about *her one true lurve* a tad intrusive and cringeworthy.' He pulled a face. 'What was that all about, do you suppose?'

'Search me.' Violet shrugged. 'The question threw me a little, particularly as the publicist had told me not to ask about Leonie's early years in Merrywell. I took that to mean I was to steer clear of anything *too* personal . . . so I was gobsmacked that she was so keen to answer that bloke's question. Who was he, I wonder?'

'That,' Matthew said, 'was Rupert Dalloway. He was at the same secondary school as me, but a couple of years older. He was in the sixth form with Leonie. For a while, they were rumoured to be an item. Not sure if that was true or not. If it was, it was certainly never official.'

'Does he live in the village? I haven't seen him around.'

'He lives up near Hassop, in a massive house. He and his family are absolutely loaded. I remember his parents came to the school once. They wandered around with their noses in the air, looking as if they'd trodden in something unspeakable.'

'If they were that rich and stuck-up, I'm surprised they didn't send their son to a private college, or boarding school.'

'They did, but Rupert was expelled when he was seventeen . . . and before you ask . . .' Matthew held up his hands '. . . I've no idea why. All I know is, he ended up doing his last year in sixth form at my school in Bakewell.'

'Sounds like he was a rebel,' Violet said, her curiosity piqued. 'Do you suppose Rupert Dalloway could be Leonie's *one true love*?'

Matthew grinned. 'I haven't a clue,' he said. 'Who cares? Leonie will be gone tomorrow and, by next week, everyone will have forgotten about her again. It'll be years before she comes back to Merrywell, if she bothers to come back at all.'

'Don't you think she'll visit her sister?'

'I doubt it. Angeline was there today, sitting right on the front row, but she took off as soon as the interview was over. It doesn't look like their mother's death has brought them any closer.'

'That's a shame,' Violet said, standing aside as a group of excited women pushed past, clutching autographed copies of *Hot Toddy*.

Over at the signing desk, Leonie was embracing a woman with dark hair styled in a short pixie cut.

'Who's that with Leonie?' she said. 'They look very chummy.'

'It's Zoe Corndale,' Matthew said. 'She and Leonie used to hang out together, back in the day.'

'Leonie looks pleased to see her,' Violet said. 'I didn't have her down as the huggy-kissy type, but Zoe Corndale's certainly getting a warm reception.'

Another group of people pushed past, smiles on their faces and books in their hands.

'Looks like the festival's off to a flying start,' Matthew said, watching as a group of customers exited the bookshop via the side entrance, into the bakery. 'I've never seen this many people here before.'

'Is someone looking after your shop while you attend the festival?' Violet asked. 'I hope you're not missing out on potential customers.'

'Rhys has stepped in this afternoon, and he's working tomorrow and Sunday too,' Matthew said.

'Do you need to get back and help him out?'

He shook his head. 'My son's more than capable of holding the fort on his own. Besides, he owes me a favour and I fancy trying the street food on offer out in the courtyard. Care to join me?'

'I'd love to,' Violet replied, feeling disproportionately thrilled at the prospect of a simple lunchtime snack. 'But can you give me about twenty minutes? I want to make sure Fiona gets a chance to meet Leonie Stanwick. My life won't be worth living if I let the star author slip away before Fiona's had a chance to get her book signed.'

'That's fine, I don't mind waiting,' Matthew said. 'Are you planning to open up *The Memory Box* this afternoon? I know it's not a shop, but the festival is a brilliant opportunity to promote your services.'

'Maybe later,' Violet said. 'Although I'm not sure how much

extra work I can take on at the moment. Things have been really busy the last few months. I've even been toying with the idea of getting an assistant.'

Matthew gave a cautionary frown. 'Taking on an employee is a big undertaking.'

'I know,' Violet said. 'Which is why I'm not going to make any rash decisions. And if I do take someone on, it'll only be for a few hours a week to do the admin tasks that have been falling by the wayside.'

'Have you thought about asking Molly Gee?' Matthew said. 'As you know, she takes the minutes at the parish council meetings . . . and she's very efficient. I know she'd like to take on more work, but it'd have to be flexible hours, so that she can work around childcare availability.'

'That's an excellent idea,' Violet said. 'I like Molly, and I'd be more than happy for her to vary her days, as long as she gets the work done. I'll give it some thought, and sound her out sometime – but not today. I happen to know that she and her mum are spending the rest of the day at the festival.'

'I'll probably do the same,' Matthew said. 'The next event starts in just over an hour, so I'll need to grab some lunch before then.'

'Go without me, if you're in a hurry.'

'No.' He smiled at her and winked. 'It's all right. You're worth waiting for. Shall I meet you in the courtyard in twenty minutes?'

'Yes, OK,' she said, unable to stop a smile from spreading across her face. 'Where will you be if I manage to get away earlier?'

'In the shop. I'll go and check on Rhys . . . take him a cappuccino.'

As Matthew wandered towards the bakery to buy a takeaway coffee for his son, Fiona came from the opposite direction, looking hot and flustered.

'Are you all right, Fi?' Violet asked. 'You look stressed.'

'That's because I am,' Fiona replied. 'Some of the temporary staff we've brought in to help out are useless, and Sophie's got a strop on.'

'Why? What's up with her?'

'She was planning to go to one of the events this evening, and I've told her she can't. She's supposed to be running the café, not swanning around like a festivalgoer. We're absolutely run off our feet.'

'That's good news, isn't it?' Violet said, as she peered through to the packed bakery and the noisy, bustling café beyond. 'Having said that, it does look rather hectic in there.'

'We've had a rush on the "hot toddies". They're on offer today only, to celebrate the launch of Leonie's book. They're going down a storm.'

'What a brilliant idea,' Violet said, making a mental note to try one herself.

'You'd think so, wouldn't you? But it's caused controversy in some quarters. The café doesn't have a licence to sell alcohol, so I had to submit a temporary event notice. I've done everything properly, but a couple of minutes ago, one of the ladies from the WI strolled in and started complaining about us selling alcoholic drinks in the café.'

'If you've got a temporary licence, what's the problem?'

'There isn't a problem, not as far as most people are concerned, but this woman's a teetotaller – that's why she's unhappy. She told me in no uncertain terms that I should be offering an alcohol-free version as well.'

'A hot toddy without the alcohol?' Violet pulled a face. 'That would be a glass of hot water, lemon and honey, wouldn't it?'

'Exactly,' Fiona said. 'It sounds more like a cold remedy to me.'

Violet laughed. 'Come on, Fi, don't let her get to you. As Abraham Lincoln once said, you can't please all of the people all of the time. Forget your catering responsibilities for a few minutes and come with me. I'll introduce you to Leonie Stanwick.'

'Let me go and buy a copy of *Hot Toddy* first,' Fiona said. 'Can you believe Eric is making me pay full price for it? You'd think being married to a bookseller would have its advantages, wouldn't you?'

Ten minutes later, leaving Fiona with Leonie at the book-signing table, Violet crossed the crowded courtyard. When she entered *Collis Fine Furniture*, she found Matthew engaged in conversation with a young couple who were admiring a small table in the shop window.

While she waited, Violet picked up a wooden fruit bowl. It was smooth and sinuous, and would look great on her kitchen table. As she checked the price tag, Rhys Collis emerged from the workshop area carrying a beautifully carved blanket box.

'Hey, Violet,' he said, sounding very chipper. 'How's it going?'

'Good thanks, Rhys. Are you having a busy afternoon?'

'We are,' he said, as he placed the box next to a tall oak dresser. 'Eric's idea for bringing in the crowds is genius. So far today, I've sold two cabinets and a set of dining chairs.'

Violet grinned. 'You'll have to ask your dad for a bonus. Erm . . . actually, I've come to drag him away for a while. I hope you don't mind?'

Rhys smiled enigmatically. 'Not at all. If he sticks around, he'll only mosey in on my sales pitch. Feel free to take him away.'

'I heard that.'

The young couple had left, and Matthew was walking back across the shop, his hands in his pockets.

'Did they put in an order?' Rhys asked, nodding towards the retreating couple.

'They're thinking about it,' said Matthew.

'You should have left them to me, Dad. I'd have got the order written up. No problem.'

Matthew shot his son an old-fashioned look. 'I hope you're not giving people the hard sell,' he said. 'That's not how I like to do business.'

'You're too soft, Dad.' Rhys shook his head and laughed. 'You need to learn how to close the deal.'

'I was running this shop when you were in nappies, Rhys. I may be a humble furniture maker, rather than a smarmy salesman – but I think I know how to run my own business.'

Rhys squared his shoulders. 'I hope you're not calling *me* smarmy. I'm as charming as they come, me. Violet reckons you should give me a bonus.'

She cast an apologetic smile in Matthew's direction. 'Sorry,' she said. 'I didn't mean to interfere.'

'Don't worry about it.' Matthew grinned. 'As a matter of fact, I was thinking the same thing. Me laddo here may be a bit cocky, but he is in charge of the shop for the whole weekend of the book festival . . . and, if he continues selling at the same rate as today, he'll definitely have earned himself a bonus. He can put it towards his trip.'

'Trip?' Violet said. 'Where are you going, Rhys?'

'Haven't decided yet,' Rhys replied. 'Canada, maybe. Or Australia and New Zealand. I'm taking three months out . . . going travelling.'

'When's this?'

'In the new year,' he replied. 'January, February maybe . . . or possibly the spring, depending on where I decide to go to.'

'Sounds like fun,' said Violet. 'I wish I'd done that when I was your age. Wherever you end up, I'm sure you'll have an amazing time.'

It was Violet's turn to buy lunch. They chose pitta wraps from the Greek food stand, served with halloumi fries.

As they carried their food to one of the picnic tables in the courtyard, Violet asked the question that had been on her mind since they'd left the shop.

'If Rhys is going travelling for three months, who'll look after the shop on Saturdays?'

'I guess that'll be me,' Matthew said. 'I'll just have to work six days a week, instead of five.'

'Bad luck,' Violet said, wrinkling her nose. 'Just be grateful it's only for a few months.'

Matthew rocked his head from side to side. 'I'm not sure that it will be,' he said. 'If Rhys gets a taste for travelling, he might decide to extend his visit.'

'Do you think that's likely?'

'I'd say it's a definite possibility. Anyway, even if he does come back after three months, I think it's time I made some changes. I can't expect him to keep working every Saturday at the shop. Not indefinitely. He's got his own career to think about.'

Rhys was a freelance illustrator, who did most of his work from home.

'He doesn't seem to mind working in the shop,' Violet said. 'In fact, I'd go as far as to say he enjoys it, and he's a great salesman. Better than you.'

Matthew laughed. 'I agree, and I know he appreciates the chance to earn some extra money, but when he gets back from his travels, I'd like him to focus on his career. He's considering giving up the freelance work and getting a job in a design agency . . . as a proper employee . . . and not necessarily in Derbyshire.'

'You'll miss him if he moves away.'

'I know. More than I care to admit,' Matthew replied. 'But I can't expect him to stick around in Merrywell just to keep me company. Rhys has his whole life ahead of him, and he needs to do whatever it takes to follow his dreams. It won't be easy managing without him, but I'll have to find a way . . . maybe I can take on an apprentice. Someone I can train up to help run things.'

'And make furniture?'

'Yes, that as well, if they're interested in learning.'

'I thought you said taking on an employee was a big undertaking,' Violet said, as she bit into a halloumi fry. 'A decision that shouldn't be taken lightly.'

Matthew gave a self-deprecating laugh. 'Yeah . . . I did say that, didn't I. Maybe I need to start listening to my own advice.'

Chapter 8

The following morning Violet stayed in bed until after eight. Snuggling beneath the warmth of her quilt, she stared at her vaulted bedroom ceiling and reflected on the events of the previous day.

After lunch, she'd ended up staying on at the festival, accompanying Matthew to the next session – which was a talk by the author of a book on the history of British workhouses, which she had found surprisingly fascinating.

After that, she'd lingered in the shopping village, ostensibly to get some work done at *The Memory Box* – but on her way there, she'd dropped into the café for a swift cappuccino and ended up staying until early evening, chatting to the locals and drinking several cups of coffee and a couple of the hot toddies. At six-thirty, she'd attended the festival's third author event: an interview with a writer of psychological thrillers. Inevitably, she had found herself unable to resist buying a signed copy of the author's book. It was now on the towering 'to be read' pile, next to her bed.

As she was about to turn over and go back to sleep, Violet heard the faint sound of feline feet on the stairs. Seconds later, her tortoiseshell cat, Rusty, leapt onto the bed and came to sit on Violet's chest.

'What can I do for you, Rusty-roo?' she said.

The cat stared at her with pale green eyes and meowed loudly.

'Are you hungry?' She stroked the cat's ear. 'I suppose you want me to get up and feed you, do you?'

With a trilling meow, the cat jumped off the bed and looked back at Violet, as if to say: *Yes. Come on then! What are you waiting for?*

With a sigh, Violet pulled back the warm quilt and obeyed.

She didn't usually work at weekends, but today Violet had resolved to spend some time in *The Memory Box*, catching up on all the pesky paperwork she'd neglected to do yesterday. The truth was, she was still coming to terms with being self-employed. As a 'one-man-band' business with no one to delegate to, she was responsible for every single task, including accounting – and there were several invoices that needed to be sent out urgently if she wanted to get paid for the work she'd done. Her days of regular employment and an automatic monthly salary were well and truly over.

She zipped herself into a long, quilted coat with a fur-lined hood, and left Greengage Cottage at nine-twenty. There was a residual nip in the air from an overnight frost, which had coated the ground with sparkling particles of ice. In the heart of the village, the ancient and beautifully majestic trees were shedding their leaves, gilding the pavements with dazzling hues of yellow and gold. As she strolled along, Violet sighed contentedly. She loved these tranquil autumn mornings, when the world seemed to stand still, holding its breath, as if readying itself for the arrival of winter.

It was nine-twenty-five when she approached her tiny business premises in Merrywell Shopping Village. *The Memory Box* was nestled in the corner of the courtyard, next to a shop selling arts and craft supplies and jigsaw puzzles. Along the adjacent side of the courtyard, next door to *The Epicurious* deli, was the suite of studios available for hire – three of which were booked for the weekend's festival activities. This morning, in the largest of the rooms, Leonie Stanwick would be delivering her masterclass in novel writing. Violet had been tempted to book a place on the workshop herself, but, ultimately, had decided against it. Right now, she had enough on her plate running *The Memory Box* and ensuring her relatively new business ran smoothly. Writing a book would require commitment and effort – and Violet lacked the time needed for such a project.

As she approached the door of her business unit, Eric Nash emerged from the bookshop and dashed towards the studio area. He was holding a bakery box, and looked deep in thought. His shoulders were stooped, as if they were supporting the worries of the world.

'Good morning, Eric!' Violet hollered to get his attention. 'Looks like you'll be in for another busy day.'

The sound of her voice stopped him mid-stride.

'It may be morning,' he said, turning in Violet's direction, 'but it isn't a good one . . . at least, not so far.'

'Oh, dear.' She walked across the courtyard and met him in the middle. 'Problems? Anything I can help with?'

'It's Leonie Stanwick. She's late. *Again*. The woman is turning out to be a complete nightmare. Her shoddy time-keeping is stressing me out . . . I tell you, this festival will be the death of me.' He pointed to a first-floor window in the studio. 'I've got a roomful of eager beavers in there who've paid good money for a masterclass in novel writing, and Leonie hasn't even turned up yet. If you ask me, Ms Stanwick would benefit from attending a masterclass herself . . . on the importance of punctuality.'

'I take it she's not answering her phone?'

'It's going to voicemail again,' Eric said. 'I've left a message, and so has Yvette Finch, her publicist, but we've not heard back from her.'

'Have you spoken to anyone at the hotel? I assume Leonie stayed there again last night?'

He nodded. 'Yvette's there as well. She went up to Leonie's room a little while ago and knocked on the door, but there was no answer. The hotel staff say she hasn't been down for breakfast either.'

'Maybe she stayed at her sister's house last night,' Violet suggested. 'Or somewhere else . . . *with* someone else.'

'Regardless of where she spent the night, she knows the workshop's due to start at nine-thirty.' Eric scratched his head. 'What is she playing at? I'd never have invited her to the festival if I'd known she was going to be a liability.'

He was obviously stricken with worry: his cheeks were flushed and his hair was standing up in wispy strands.

'I must say, it's extremely inconsiderate of her to be late,' Violet said. 'I hate tardiness.'

'Me too,' said Eric. 'I've got enough to think about today without having to run around after people who're incapable of arriving on time. I'm going to have to tell everyone that the workshop will now start at ten o'clock . . . assuming Leonie will have arrived by then. In the meantime, I'm hoping to keep the attendees sweet by providing some complimentary Danish pastries from the bakery.'

He held up the box, looking less than confident about the persuasive powers of its contents.

'Would you like me to drive over to the hotel to see if I can find out what's happening?' Violet offered, aware that Eric couldn't abandon the festival to go and hunt for Leonie himself. 'I walked here this morning, but I can go home and get my car and be at the hotel within minutes.'

'Would you?' He smiled gratefully. 'Thank you, Violet. You're a true friend, although presumably you're here on a Saturday because you have something important to do? I don't want to drag you away unnecessarily.'

'I'm only here to get my accounts up to date,' Violet said. 'Trust me, any distraction is welcome. I'd consider it a favour if you gave me something to do other than boring old paperwork.'

* * *

Five minutes later, Violet was driving down the tree-lined driveway of the Merrywell Manor Hotel. The imposing building was a Grade 2 listed former manor house, which had been built in 1794 by a local landowner. In the 1990s, after years of neglect, the property had been converted into a boutique hotel. At the same time, its outlying stable block, barn and other outbuildings were developed into the retail units that now formed Merrywell Shopping Village.

The front of the hotel was covered in Virginia creeper which, at this time of year, was a vibrant crimson colour. The stunning display of red leaves softened the appearance of the otherwise dour-looking façade. Violet steered to the right, and then turned into the car park next to the hotel.

Leaving her vehicle in the nearest available parking space, she walked back to the main entrance and entered the lobby through a pair of huge double doors. A curving staircase swept upwards from a sprawling reception area, and from behind a wood-panelled desk, a haughty-looking man lifted his chin and stared at Violet through narrowed eyes.

'Can I help you?'

'I'm hoping you can point me in the direction of Leonie Stanwick,' she said. 'I'm here to take her over to the book festival.'

It was a white lie. She was there in no formal capacity, as a driver or anything else, and the guy at the reception desk seemed to sense this.

'I have no idea where she is,' he said, making zero effort to be helpful. 'And you're not the only one looking for her either. Another one of our guests . . . a Ms Finch . . . has been enquiring about Ms Stanwick.'

'Maybe I should liaise with her then . . . Yvette Finch . . . if you can tell me where she is.'

'I believe you'll find her in the breakfast room.'

With a thin smile, he indicated a door to the left, off the main reception hall. Nodding her thanks, Violet walked towards it.

Apart from the gentle chinking of china and crockery, the breakfast room was a quiet, relaxed space. There were around twenty tables, only half a dozen of which were occupied, mostly by silent couples sipping orange juice, tucking into bacon and eggs, or munching on breakfast cereals. Yvette Finch was at a table by the window, nursing a teacup and looking out over the hotel's formal gardens. Her serene expression and surprisingly calm demeanour were not what Violet had been expecting.

As Leonie's publicist, shouldn't she be doing everything possible to track her down? Wasn't she concerned? What on earth did she expect to achieve by guzzling tea and staring out of the window? Violet wondered if she was expecting Leonie to materialise miraculously in the hotel grounds, wandering back from wherever it was she had been.

'Yvette?'

The publicist placed her cup in its saucer and looked up.

'Hello.' She frowned slightly. 'It's Violet, isn't it?'

'Yes, I was hoping Leonie Stanwick would be with you. I'm here as a favour to Eric Nash. He's desperate to find out where she is. Leonie's supposed to be running a novel-writing masterclass, but she hasn't turned up.'

'Yes, I know,' Yvette replied, her tone dismissive. 'Eric rang me earlier and asked me to check Leonie's room. There was no answer when I knocked, and I'm told she hasn't been down for breakfast. I'm sorry, but I don't know where she is.'

'Aren't you worried about her?' Violet said, irked by the publicist's offhand manner.

Yvette lifted a bony shoulder half-heartedly. 'Not really. When you've worked with Leonie for as long as I have, you get used to this sort of thing. She does it all the time. She's unpredictable, and punctuality definitely isn't her strong suit.'

'But isn't that why *you're* here?' Violet said, failing to disguise her irritation. 'To make sure Leonie gets to her engagements on time? Isn't that part of your job?'

'It was my responsibility yesterday,' Yvette said, reaching for the teapot and pouring herself another cupful. 'Which is why Leonie arrived on time for her interview at the festival.'

'Only just,' said Violet. 'She made it by the skin of her teeth.'

'I can assure you, that wasn't down to me,' Yvette said, as she dropped two lumps of sugar into her tea and stirred it vigorously. 'As I said, Leonie is unpredictable . . . a law unto herself. It makes life extremely difficult for those of us tasked with managing her appearances – but, thankfully, that's not something I have to concern myself with now. I told Leonie last night that I don't want to work for her anymore.'

Violet was nonplussed. Pulling out a chair, she flopped onto it. 'Can you do that?' she asked, placing her hands on the table. 'Aren't you employed by Leonie's publisher?'

'No. Leonie hires my services in addition to the work done by her publisher's publicity team. They organise loads of promotional opportunities, but it's never enough for Leonie – which is why she brought me in. I've always liaised with the publishing house, but worked independently of them to arrange complementary activities.'

'So why don't you want to work for her anymore?' said Violet. 'Isn't Leonie one of your most important clients?'

'She likes to think so.' Yvette laughed bitterly. 'But the truth is, I've had enough. My contract is up for renewal and I've decided I don't want to continue with it. Quite honestly, it's a relief to bring the arrangement to an end. It's liberating to think I'll no longer have to run Leonie's errands, or put up with her foibles. This morning, I've been able to relax and have a leisurely breakfast. And now . . . I'm going to finish my tea, check out of the hotel, and catch the train back to London.'

'Before you do,' Violet said. 'Would you be willing to give Leonie another call? Please? I need to get her over to the book festival, pronto. As we speak, there's an eager bunch of budding novelists desperate to learn how to write a bestseller. They'll be gutted if Leonie doesn't show up for the workshop.'

Yvette pursed her lips. 'That definitely wouldn't be good PR,' she said. 'But thankfully, it's no longer my problem.'

'I realise that, but Eric Nash is my friend, and he's put an enormous amount of effort into organising this book festival. If Leonie is a no-show, it'll create a lot of negative publicity.'

Yvette surrendered with a resigned sigh. 'OK. I will ring her again, but only to help you out. There's not much chance I'll get hold of her though. Her phone was going straight to voicemail when I tried earlier. It's possible she's switched it off, or she's not taking my calls because she's still angry with me.'

Violet's ears pricked up. There had obviously been a falling-out, and she yearned to know the cause of it, but time was running short. If Yvette could locate Leonie *now*, there was still a slim chance Violet would be able to pick her up and drive her back to the book festival in time for the workshop's revised start time.

Yvette grabbed her phone from the table and called Leonie's number. As she listened and waited, she took dainty sips from her teacup.

'Sorry,' she said, shaking her head. 'It's still going to voicemail.'

A heavy feeling settled in Violet's stomach. Had something happened? Even if Leonie *was* notoriously unpredictable, she surely wouldn't be this unprofessional. Would she?

'Why would Leonie commit to running the workshop and then not turn up for it?' Violet said. 'Has she done this sort of thing before? Or do you think she could be ill?'

'Leonie's never ill,' Yvette replied. 'Unless you consider unreliability an ailment.'

Violet stood up. 'We should check her room, just in case.'

'I told you, I've already been up there. There was no answer when I knocked.'

'What if she's incapacitated?' Violet said. 'She could be lying there, passed out or unconscious. We need to double-check.'

'I doubt the hotel staff will let you into her room. You're not even a guest here.'

'No, but you are – and you checked in at the same time as Leonie. They know you're acquainted, so they might let *you* take a look. Will you come with me and talk to the receptionist?'

Yvette rolled her eyes, making clear her reluctance to get involved. Pinkie finger raised, she drained her teacup and then, begrudgingly, got to her feet.

Violet walked behind her into the lobby, where they explained their concerns to the man on duty. After a brief discussion, he arranged for a member of the housekeeping team to take them up to Leonie's room.

Chapter 9

Leonie was staying in room 22, which was on the first floor, at the rear of the hotel. The young female member of staff who was escorting them drummed her knuckles on the door and waited. When there was no reply, she knocked again. Harder. Still, the knock went unanswered.

'Can we go into the room?' Violet said. 'Just to make sure Leonie isn't inside?'

Pulling an electronic key card from her pocket – presumably a master key – the housekeeper opened the door.

The room was elegantly and luxuriously furnished, with gold brocade curtains and a matching bedspread. The wall behind the bed was decorated with exquisite green wallpaper, patterned with tree silhouettes. Over by the window, draped over the back of a winged armchair, was the saffron-coloured blouse Leonie had worn for the interview the previous day – but that was the only visible clue that the room was occupied. There was no other sign of Leonie, and the neatly made bed clearly hadn't been slept in.

Looking perplexed, Yvette ran a hand over the unrumpled bedcover. 'She must have spent the night somewhere else,' she said.

Violet turned to the housekeeper. 'Has the room been cleaned this morning?' she asked. 'Is it possible someone's already been in and made the bed?'

'No one's been in yet,' the housekeeper replied. 'Ms Stanwick is due to leave today, but she prearranged a late checkout time . . . two o'clock. The cleaners always wait until guests have checked out before they prepare the room for the next guest.'

The writing masterclass had originally been due to finish at twelve-thirty. Even if it ended later, at one o'clock, that would still give Leonie plenty of time to get back to the hotel and check out by the two o'clock deadline.

Violet wandered over to the wardrobe and pulled open the door. There were several items of clothing on hangers, as well as two folded pairs of jeans and a sweater on the built-in shelves.

'Most of her clothes seem to be here,' she said, somewhat unnecessarily.

Yvette was poking her head around the door to the adjoining bathroom. 'Her toothbrush and toiletries are still in the en suite. Her handbag isn't here though, and there's no sign of her phone.'

'It might be in a drawer somewhere,' Violet said. 'Can you call her number again? See if we can hear it ringing?'

Yvette did as Violet asked, but there was no ringtone anywhere within earshot.

'It's still going to voicemail,' Yvette said, as she ended the call and wandered over to the tall sash window. 'If the phone's switched off, we wouldn't hear it ringing anyway.'

Feeling frustrated, Violet cast one final look around the room. Yvette's lack of enthusiasm for the search was plain to see. She was gazing out of the window, her hand gripping one of the brocade curtains, unashamedly indifferent to Leonie's whereabouts.

'Come on,' Violet said. 'She's obviously not here. We may as well go.'

Yvette didn't need telling twice. Letting go of the curtain, she turned away from the window and followed Violet out of the door, back down the stairs to the reception area.

'It's fairly obvious to me that Leonie has gone AWOL,' Yvette announced. 'It's unfortunate, but it's not the first time this has happened, and I'm sure it won't be the last. I'm afraid I can't stick around to help find her, because I have a train to catch . . . I need to pack my bag and check out.'

Violet fished around in her handbag for a business card.

'If you do hear from Leonie in the next hour or so, could you let me know, or ask her to call me on this number?'

She handed the card to Yvette, who slipped it into her pocket.

'I can't imagine she'll have any reason to call *me*, but if she does, I'll pass on your message. I think you should ring the book festival guy . . . Eric? Tell him the bad news.'

Violet nodded. It was a call she was dreading. Eric would be gutted.

'How are you getting to the railway station?' Violet asked.

'I'll get a taxi. I came up with Leonie, in her car, but I don't want to have to travel back with her. Not with the way things are between us . . . I don't think either of us would be comfortable with that.'

Unable to keep a lid on her curiosity, Violet gave an enquiring smile. 'You didn't say exactly why you and Leonie are parting company.'

'No. I didn't,' said Yvette, her voice razor-sharp. 'Because it's no one else's business.'

'I'm sorry.' Violet grimaced awkwardly. 'It's wrong of me to pry. I'll get going and let you do your packing.'

With a nod, the publicist spun away.

'Actually . . .' Violet was struck by an idea. 'Before you go, can you tell me what kind of car Leonie drives?'

Yvette turned back. 'It's a blue Audi coupé. Why?'

'Do you know if it's still in the car park?'

'I've no idea. I didn't think to check.'

'Perhaps I should go and have a look before I ring Eric.'

Yvette shrugged. 'Please yourself, although I'm not sure how it will help. It's Leonie you need to find, not her car. Anyway, if you'll excuse me . . . I really must get going. Good luck. I hope you find her.'

Using her key card to enter the corridor leading off to the ground-floor bedrooms, Yvette gave a brief wave before disappearing through the opened door.

In the corner of the reception area, a grandfather clock was ticking loudly. According to the clock's ornate face, it was five to ten . . . five minutes until the workshop's revised start time.

Violet gave a frustrated sigh. The chances of the writing class going ahead were becoming more unlikely with every second that slipped by.

Chapter 10

Leaving the hotel by the front entrance, Violet retraced her steps to the car park, all the while trying to recall if she'd seen a blue Audi when she'd parked her own Toyota there.

When she reached her car, she leaned against it and scanned the rest of the vehicles. There was no sign of an Audi.

Knowing she couldn't put off the call to Eric any longer, she pulled out her phone and scrolled her contacts to find his number. As she started to make the call, she noticed that the car park curved left at the far end, around a jutting copse of firs. Pushing her phone back into her pocket, she walked as far as the trees and looked beyond them. The car park continued for another couple of hundred feet or so.

Parked nose-first at the end, away from the other vehicles, was a blue Audi.

Wherever it was Leonie had gone to, she obviously hadn't taken her car. Had she travelled somewhere on foot, or taken a taxi? Or had someone picked her up?

Violet wasn't sure why, but she felt compelled to go over and inspect the Audi. Perhaps she could check to see if the engine was warm, to determine whether it had been driven recently.

The end section of the car park was overshadowed by the

towering fir trees, which were blocking out the hazy morning sunshine. It was cold here, and very quiet. As she approached Leonie's car, Violet shivered.

A thin film of frost covered the roof, suggesting it had been there all night. Violet stood for a moment at the back of the car. Did Audis have a rear engine? She touched the metal, but it was cold beneath her fingertips, so she stepped to the side of the car, intending to check at the front.

What she saw when she rounded the vehicle froze the air in her lungs. Consumed by a chilling sense of dread, she edged closer.

Protruding from beyond the front of the Audi were a pair of booted female feet, lying prostrate on the tarmacked surface of the car park. Violet moved closer, her heart thumping furiously in her chest.

The boots were attached to a pair of long, jean-clad legs, which in turn were attached to the slim torso of a woman. Long, blonde hair flowed in waves from beneath a black-sequinned fiddler cap.

She was lying face down, and there was a knife in the centre of her back.

Chapter 11

Violet stared down at Leonie's body, pressing a hand over her mouth to hold in the scream that was erupting deep inside her chest. Shock and fear were clutching at her heart and slowly squeezing the air from her lungs, making it increasingly difficult for her to breathe.

What she longed to do was run towards the hotel, screeching like a banshee – but that was impossible because her legs had turned to jelly. Besides, this wasn't the time for histrionics. She needed to hold herself together, stand still, remain calm and observe Leonie's body to establish whether or not she was breathing.

Violet stared hard at the prone form in front of her, hoping to see the gentle expansion of still-functioning lungs, willing them to be working – but the lifeless body lay motionless.

Staggering backwards, Violet pulled out her phone and, with trembling fingers, dialled 999. She felt nauseous and light-headed. Worried she might throw up or pass out, she stumbled to the rear of the vehicle and stepped away from it. Having spent twenty years of her life married to a police detective, she knew how important it was not to touch the body or contaminate what was clearly a crime scene.

'Emergency. Which service do you require?'

'Police,' Violet said, her voice a stuttering wail. 'Ambulance . . . I'm not sure. Someone's been stabbed . . . I think she's dead.'

'Are you with the person now?'

'Yes,' Violet replied.

'Is the person breathing?'

'No.'

'OK, stay calm and tell me where you are.'

'At the Merrywell Manor Hotel, in the car park. She's lying on the ground. There's a knife in her back, and she isn't breathing. Definitely not breathing.'

Violet realised that *she* didn't seem capable of breathing either. Her chest felt cold and rigid, frozen solid by fear.

'All right, the police are on their way,' the call handler said. 'Please don't touch anything. Remain where you are and tell me what happened. Were you with her when she was stabbed?'

Violet sucked air into her uncooperative lungs. 'No,' she said. 'I walked over to her car and saw her lying on the ground . . . I don't know how long she's been here.'

'Was anyone else in the vicinity when you approached the vehicle?'

'I didn't see anyone. There was no one here . . . just me.'

'Do you know the victim?'

'Yes. It's Leonie Stanwick. The author. She's been staying here at the hotel. I interviewed her at the book festival yesterday. She was supposed to be there today as well, but she didn't turn up. That's why I came here. Looking for her.'

Violet was aware that she was firing out words, staccato fashion. She needed to slow down, speak clearly, and try to make sense of all this.

Had Leonie been lying here all night? Who had done this to her? And why?

And how the hell was she going to break the news to Eric that the star guest at his book festival had been murdered?

Chapter 12

The emergency call handler stayed on the line, calming Violet down and asking more questions. After what seemed like an age, but was probably less than ten minutes, a police car pulled into the hotel car park and two uniformed officers got out.

Violet almost fainted with relief – such was her eagerness for the authorities to take charge of the situation.

Breathing shakily, she pointed to where the body was, watching as one of the officers bent down, presumably checking for a pulse. He obviously didn't find one, because he stood up quickly, stepped back and spoke into his radio, while the other officer began to cordon off the area with police tape.

The finality of his actions left a cold, hard ache in the pit of Violet's stomach. As she waited to give a statement, an ambulance arrived.

'You've had a wasted journey, mate,' she heard one of the officers say. 'The body's still warm, but there's no sign of life.'

Violet shuddered. *I hope she hasn't been lying here for ages*, she thought. *Waiting in vain for help to arrive.*

When the taller of the two police officers came over to ask Violet a series of questions, she answered as accurately but concisely as possible. She was keen to get her statement over with, so that she could get away from here, out of the cold.

'Can I go home now?' she asked, when the officer had finished questioning her. 'I feel weird . . . and a bit faint.'

'You're probably in shock,' he said. 'But I'm sorry, you're going to have to stick around for a while longer. There's a detective on his way. He'll want to talk to you.'

'But I've already told you everything I know. Can't the detective read my statement? The truth is, I need to sit down, otherwise I think I'll pass out.'

'I'll take you into the hotel reception area. You can sit there until the detective arrives,' the officer said. 'I need to speak to the hotel staff anyway . . . let them know what's happened.'

Violet waited in the hotel lobby on a long, teal blue, velvet couch. She felt better, now that she'd taken the weight off her feet and had pulled in a few calming breaths to clear her head.

On the low, glass-topped table in front of her was a vase of scented freesias, and a collection of upmarket magazines. Violet picked up a copy of *The Lady*, staring in a daze at its front cover as she listened to the conversation that was unfolding at the reception desk.

The hotel manager had been summoned. He was young and hipsterish, dressed in a slim-cut suit – not at all the kind of person Violet had imagined would run the hotel. His skinny body was youthful, but fragile-looking, and his face twitched with shock and alarm as the police officer informed him that the hotel car park was now a crime scene.

'We'll need to look at the hotel's security footage,' Violet heard the officer say.

'We only have a couple of CCTV cameras,' the manager told him. 'One by the main gate at the end of the driveway, and one at the hotel's front entrance.'

'You don't have cameras covering the car park?' the officer said, sounding both incredulous and annoyed.

'No. Sorry.'

'What about inside the hotel?'

'Nope,' the manager said, folding his wiry arms and glaring defiantly. 'I realise that's not what you want to hear, Officer, but I'm not going to apologise. We're an upmarket boutique hotel and our guests pay a lot of money to stay here. They come to us expecting privacy and discretion. The last thing they want is for their every move to be monitored by a security camera.'

'In my experience, people are reassured by CCTV cameras, not unsettled by them,' the officer said. 'But I suppose I'll just have to be grateful for whatever footage you do have. I take it there's only one way in and out of the car park?'

'For vehicles, yes, but it can be accessed on foot from several points within the hotel grounds. The car park also borders a spinney and a stretch of open fields, so it's open to almost anyone.'

The police officer puffed up his cheeks. 'Based on what you've told me, I can't say I'm impressed with the hotel's security arrangements,' he said. 'For the benefit and wellbeing of your guests, I'd recommend you install a more robust system.'

'Why?' said the hotel manager. 'A dearth of CCTV isn't the reason this crime has been committed, surely?'

The police officer held up his hands to defuse what was rapidly becoming a confrontation. 'I didn't say it was,' he said. 'You're absolutely right, a slicker security system wouldn't have prevented this from happening, but extra CCTV footage might have helped us track down the perpetrator.'

'I'm sorry we aren't able to make your job easier,' the manager replied, his sarcastic tone contradicting the sentiment of his words. 'As for reviewing our security arrangements . . . wouldn't that be like shutting the stable door after the horse has bolted?'

Violet smiled to herself. The hotel manager might be young, but beneath his fragile exterior was a steely frame.

Dragging her attention away from the frosty exchange at the desk, she threw the magazine back onto the coffee table, pulled out her phone and called Eric's number. It was important she let him know what had happened. As soon as the media got wind of the story, they would be all over it. She wanted to give him a heads-up, so that he could prepare himself for an onslaught of journalists. The incident would create a lot of publicity for Merrywell Book Festival, just not the kind Eric had been hoping for.

His phone rang several times before going to voicemail. Unwilling to break such tragic news in a voice message, Violet spoke only briefly.

'Eric, it's me,' she said. 'Call me as soon as you get this. It's important. I need to tell you something and, unfortunately, it's not good news – so brace yourself.'

As she slipped her phone back into her pocket, the hotel door swung open and a tall figure walked into view on her left. The man's loping gait, scraggy hairstyle and scruffy coat were uncomfortably familiar.

Violet slunk back into the couch. When the police officer had told her a detective was on his way, she'd hoped it would be anyone other than DS Charlie Winterton. And yet, here he was, large as life: the lead detective in the murder investigation Violet had become embroiled in earlier in the year. She was certain he wouldn't be pleased to see her again.

DS Winterton headed straight to the reception desk, striding across the lobby. Violet sat back, unnoticed, watching as he fired questions at the uniformed officer. It wasn't long before the officer turned and nodded in Violet's direction. DS Winterton spun around, raising his eyebrows as he and Violet made eye contact. Thirty seconds later, he marched across and loomed over her, shaking his head.

'You again?' he said. 'Is this a hobby of yours, then? Getting yourself involved in murder investigations?'

Violet looked up and gave him her sweetest smile. 'Hello to you too, DS Winterton. Are you going to sit down, or are you hoping to gain some sort of psychological advantage by towering over me?'

He harrumphed and lowered himself onto the couch. 'Argumentative as ever, I see.'

'Not at all,' Violet replied. 'And I can assure you the last thing I want is to become entangled in another murder investigation. It's hardly my fault I found the body.'

'Just stumble across it, did you? Or were you in the car park for a reason?'

'As I'm sure your officer has already told you, I came here looking for Leonie Stanwick. She failed to turn up for an event at Merrywell Book Festival this morning and – as there was no sign of her inside the hotel – I went to check whether her car was in the car park. And that's when . . . when I found her.'

'And are you and the victim acquainted?'

'Not exactly,' Violet replied. 'I met her for the first and only time yesterday. I interviewed her for the festival's opening event.'

'OK, and are you aware of anything that might account for what's happened this morning?'

Violet rubbed the tips of her fingers across her forehead. 'No, unfortunately not,' she said. 'But you do know that Leonie was originally from Merrywell? She grew up here, so she knows people locally, and she has a sister in the village . . . Angeline Hammond.'

DS Winterton nodded. 'We'll get in touch with her . . . let her know what's happened. Do you know if the victim has been in touch with anyone else while she's been in Merrywell?'

'One of her old school friends was trying to make contact,' Violet said. 'But I'm not sure if they actually met up or not.'

'Who was that?'

'Someone called Karen Avery. I'm told she lives in Merrywell.'

DS Winterton made a note of the name. 'Can you think of anything else that might be relevant?' he said. 'For instance, was there anyone who was unhappy about Leonie Stanwick being back in the village?'

Violet wavered, thinking back to the heated debate she'd overheard between Judith Talbot and Eric Nash. Should she tell DS Winterton about it? It didn't seem fair to peg Judith as a suspect just because she'd objected to Leonie appearing at the book festival. The council leader was many things: a snob and a bossy-boots, an all-round termagant – but a murderer?

DS Winterton had spotted her hesitation. 'Come on,' he said. 'Out with it. If there's someone I should know about, you need to tell me.'

Violet bit down on her bottom lip. 'There is someone who didn't want Leonie Stanwick at the festival, but I put that down to sheer bloody-mindedness.'

'I'll be the judge of that,' DS Winterton said. 'Who are you referring to.'

'Judith Talbot . . . but there's no way she could be involved. She's the leader of the parish council, one of Merrywell's most upstanding citizens. She may be guilty of snobbery, but there's no way she's a killer.'

'I'll need to have a chat with her nonetheless . . . find out what her issue is with Leonie Stanwick. Is there anyone else I should know about?'

'Not that I'm aware of, but Leonie had a publicist with her at yesterday's event, so perhaps you should speak to her. She'll know who Leonie has been in touch with over the last few days.'

'Does this publicist have a name?'

'Yvette Finch. Although, technically, as of this morning, she and Leonie are no longer working together. Yvette ended their contract yesterday.'

'Did she now.' DS Winterton frowned. 'Do you happen to know where she is?'

'As far as I know, she's still here . . . at the hotel,' Violet replied. 'My guess is, you'll find her in her room, packing. She's due to check out soon, so if you want to talk to her, you'll have to be quick.'

'I'll speak to her as soon as I can. But don't you worry . . . until then, she won't be going anywhere.'

'But she has a train to catch . . . back to London.'

'She can always catch a later one, if necessary.'

Violet wondered if such unconcealed contrariness was the detective's way of reminding her who was in charge. As he opened his mouth to ask another question, Violet's phone began to vibrate in her pocket. She pulled it out and glanced at the screen. It was Eric.

'Can I take this?' she said, feeling obliged to ask the detective's permission. 'It's Eric Nash, the chap who's organised the book festival. I need to let him know what's happening. Am I allowed to do that?'

'Yes, but keep it brief.' DS Winterton nodded. 'Tell him only the bare facts . . . and let him know I'll be speaking to him later, as part of the investigation.'

With trembling fingers, Violet accepted the call.

'Eric,' she said. 'Thanks for calling back. Where are you?'

'In the bookshop, setting up for the next event. Why?'

'Are you sitting down?'

Eric groaned. 'Oh, no. What's happened?' he said. 'Please tell me it's nothing to do with the festival.'

Violet closed her eyes before replying. 'It's Leonie,' she said. 'There's no easy way to say this . . .'

'Just tell me, Violet.'

'You asked me to find her, and I have,' she said. 'I'm sorry, Eric, but Leonie's dead.'

He laughed: a low, raucous cackle. Violet held the phone away from her ear, appalled at his crass reaction. She could only assume he was in shock, or denial.

'What are you talking about?' Eric said.

'Leonie's dead,' she repeated. 'I was the one who found her body.'

He laughed again, an irritated snicker this time. 'This is a wind-up, yeah?'

'Of course it isn't,' she said, trying not to snap. 'I wouldn't joke about something as horrific as this.'

'Nice try, Violet, but you can't kid a kidder. I know Leonie isn't dead . . . because she's here, at the shopping village. She finally turned up half an hour ago to deliver her writing class.'

Chapter 13

DS Winterton was sitting on the edge of the velvet couch, leaning forward and tapping his knees.

'So,' he said. 'Let me get this straight . . . the woman you told me was lying dead in the car park is, in fact, alive and well?'

Violet squirmed. She was relieved that Leonie was OK, but she felt utterly mortified and embarrassed about her error. What must DS Winterton think of her?

'So it would seem,' she said. 'Eric says she turned up half an hour ago.'

'Did he not think to let you know?'

'He must have forgotten. He's been busy.'

The detective smiled cheerlessly, obviously taking great pleasure from Violet's discomfiture.

'And is he absolutely certain?' DS Winterton said, curling his finger to beckon the police officer over. 'He's seen Leonie Stanwick with his own eyes, has he?'

'Yes,' said Violet. 'She's delivering a workshop as we speak.'

DS Winterton breathed heavily through his nose. 'Which begs the question . . . who's the woman in the car park?'

Violet edged forward, rocking slightly as she considered her answer.

'I think . . .' she said. 'Maybe . . . it could be her sister. Angeline Hammond.'

The more Violet thought about that possibility, the more likely it seemed.

'Let me explain why I thought it was Leonie,' she said, determined to defend her error. 'The body was lying face down, so I didn't get a proper look. It was the long blonde hair that convinced me, and the sequined hat Leonie wore yesterday. It *looked* like Leonie, and Leonie was missing, so I assumed it was her.'

'You do know that when you assume, you make an ass out of you and me?' DS Winterton said.

Violet scowled. 'Yes, thank you. I am familiar with that old adage. I'm sorry if you think I've made a fool of you, or myself – but I'm sure, in the circumstances, most people would have come to the same conclusion. I didn't touch the body or get close to it . . . mainly because I found the whole situation horrifying, and also because I didn't want to contaminate the crime scene. I thought I was doing the right thing by standing back and observing from a distance. I took in what I *thought* I saw . . . *expected* to see. But I was wrong. I'm sorry. I made a mistake.'

'One case of mistaken identity is unfortunate,' DS Winterton said. 'But two would look like carelessness. So, think long and hard before you answer my next question . . . How sure are you that the victim in the car park is Leonie Stanwick's sister?'

Violet wondered how many more clichéd maxims Charlie Winterton would use over the course of the investigation. She recalled he had a habit of trotting them out whenever he was under pressure.

'I'm not a hundred per cent sure,' she replied. 'And I wouldn't want to incur your wrath by making any more assumptions.'

'Never mind that,' he said. 'Tell me what you're thinking. If you're not hundred per cent certain, how sure are you? Fifty per cent? Ninety?'

'Stop!' Violet held up a hand. 'Please don't trivialise this.'

'I can assure you there's nothing trivial about murder, Ms Brewster.'

'No, there isn't,' Violet said. 'So, why are you turning this into a game of "Guess Who?"'

He let out a sigh. 'All I want to do is establish the identity of the victim.'

'My gut feeling is that it *is* Angeline Hammond, Leonie's sister,' Violet said. 'I saw the two women in close proximity at yesterday's event, and it struck me how alike they were. Leonie's older, but she has a similar build and they both have the same coloured hair. But what I don't understand is why Angeline would be wearing Leonie's fiddler cap. How and when did it come to be in her possession?'

DS Winterton tapped the side of his nose. 'That's for me to work out. It's something I'll talk to Leonie Stanwick about when I ask her to confirm whether the victim is indeed Angeline Hammond. If it is, Ms Stanwick might be able to shed some light on why her sister was in the car park.'

He turned to the uniformed officer who was hovering nearby, and told him to collect Leonie Stanwick from the shopping village and bring her back to the hotel.

'Would you like me to stay?' Violet said. 'From what I've heard, Leonie and Angeline weren't close, but they *were* sisters. Leonie is bound to be upset and she might appreciate some emotional support. She knows me a little . . . I'd be happy to stick around if you think it would help.'

DS Winterton raised an eyebrow. 'So you can eavesdrop on the investigation, you mean?'

'No! That's not what I meant at all,' Violet said, miffed by his deliberate misinterpretation of what had been a genuine offer of help.

He smirked benignly. 'In that case, I apologise. Nevertheless, I think we're done for now. Thank you for your time, Ms Brewster, but your presence is no longer required. I'll be in touch if I have any more questions.'

* * *

Violet headed straight to the bookshop to talk to Eric. He was standing behind the counter, looking pale and shaken. Fiona stood on his left, pressing a comforting hand on his shoulder.

'The police have taken Leonie away,' Eric said, when he saw Violet approaching. 'They've asked her to identify the body. They think it could be her sister.'

'Yes,' Violet said. 'I know.'

'I'm glad you're here,' Fiona said. 'Perhaps you could have a word with this one?' She pointed to Eric. 'See if you can talk some sense into him. He might listen to you.'

'About what?'

Fiona took a step back and folded her arms. 'He's talking about cancelling the rest of the book festival.'

'Why would you want to do that?' Violet said, addressing Eric directly.

'As a mark of respect to Angeline Hammond,' he said, placing his left hand across his eyes and shaking his head. 'In the circumstances, it seems like the right and proper thing to do.'

'But we don't even know for certain that it's Angeline who's died,' said Violet. 'And trust me, DS Winterton won't be happy if you start making assumptions.'

'The police officer who came here said they thought the victim was Angeline. He wouldn't have told us that unless they were pretty sure.'

'Even so, you shouldn't jump the gun,' Violet said. 'You need to wait until the body has been formally identified. For heaven's sake, don't cancel the festival as a mark of respect to Angeline before the police have even named the victim. For now, the best thing you can do is carry on as planned.'

'I don't know about that,' Eric said, rubbing a hand across his chin. 'It doesn't seem right, carrying on as though nothing's happened.'

'I can understand where you're coming from,' Violet said, reaching across and squeezing Eric's forearm. 'And I totally get why you're thinking of cancelling.'

Fiona put her hands on her hips. 'Thanks a bunch, Violet,' she said. 'I was hoping you'd back me up, not go along with this madness.'

'It is Eric's festival,' Violet reminded her. 'We have to support whatever decision he makes. Anyway, you know better than anyone how stubborn he can be. If his mind's made up about cancelling, there's nothing you or I can say to dissuade him.'

'I wish the two of you wouldn't talk about me as if I wasn't here,' Eric said, twisting his neck to glare at them. 'Anyone would think I'm incapable of thinking or speaking for myself.'

'Sorry,' Violet said. 'Like I say, you have my full support, whatever you decide.'

Fiona obviously didn't agree. 'That's all well and good, but this afternoon's events are fully booked,' she said, sounding panic-stricken. 'Most of the tickets for tomorrow have been sold as well, and some of the guest authors have already arrived. They've travelled long distances to come here, as have some of the festivalgoers. In my opinion, cancelling would be foolish. A complete disaster.'

'What you really mean is a *financial* disaster,' Eric said, giving his wife a sideways look. 'And, of course, you're right. If I *do* cancel, Merrywell Book Festival will go from being a successful, break-even venture to a complete financial catastrophe. But, be that as it may, I don't see that I have a choice. If we plough on regardless, it'll be disrespectful to Angeline, or whoever it is that died this morning.'

Violet thought for a moment. 'There is another option,' she said. 'Once the police have confirmed the identity of the victim, you could announce that the festival *will* continue as planned, and that the remaining events will be dedicated to the memory of Angeline . . . or whoever the victim turns out to be.'

Nodding vigorously, Fiona smiled. 'I like the sound of that. It's the perfect solution to the problem. What do you think, Eric?'

He gave a single, sharp nod, but remained silent.

Fiona touched his elbow. 'Come on, love. Say something.'

'I'll think about it,' he said, begrudgingly. 'The next session is due to start in two hours. If the police have confirmed the woman's identity by then, I'll do as Violet has suggested. If not, I'll have no option but to cancel the remaining events.'

Chapter 14

Within an hour, the police had issued a statement and named the victim as Angeline Hammond.

Violet was sitting at a table in the corner of the café when Fiona dashed over to tell her the news.

'At least we know for definite who it is now,' Fiona said, looking upset and also a little relieved. 'Eric's taken your advice. The remaining events will be dedicated to Angeline's memory. It's the right thing to do if he wants to save the festival, although I don't think he's entirely comfortable with carrying on. He's torn between being respectful and doing what's best for everyone involved.'

'It's a good compromise,' said Violet. 'A way for Merrywell to pay its respects to Angeline without putting the future of the book festival in jeopardy.'

'I agree,' said Fiona. 'But you know Eric. He's one of life's worriers. He cares what people think, and he sets great store by doing the honourable thing.'

'That's one of the reasons he's so well liked around here,' Violet said, as she sipped her coffee. 'And I can't imagine for one minute anyone will criticise him for doing what he thinks is best. Has he let Leonie know what he's planning?'

'Yes, he rang her a few minutes ago to offer his condolences and explain what he intends to do. She was fine with it . . . said she was glad the festival was continuing.'

'How has she taken the news of Angeline's death?' Violet asked.

'Eric didn't say. He only spoke to her briefly, so I don't suppose he could tell. But *I* thought something seemed off earlier . . . a bit strange.'

'Strange how?'

'When the police officer arrived this morning, it was me who went to get Leonie out of the class she was teaching. I took her to the green room, so that she could talk to the policeman in private. I waited in the corridor while they had the conversation, so obviously I couldn't hear what was said . . . but the door was open, and I could see Leonie's face. When the officer spoke to her, her expression *froze*. She completely shut down. It seemed odd to me, certainly not the reaction I was expecting.'

'I'm not sure I know what you mean.'

'Perhaps I'm not explaining myself very well,' Fiona said. 'I just thought it was weird, that's all. Try to imagine how you'd feel in those circumstances. If a police officer told you that a body had been found and they thought it was your sister, what would you do?'

'I'm not the best person to answer that question,' Violet said. 'I'm an only child.'

'Well, I have two sisters,' Fiona said, tapping the tabletop with her index finger to drive home her point. 'And I'm telling you, I'd have shown a hell of a lot more emotion than Leonie did. If I'd been in her shoes, I'd have broken down, or cried out, or at least shown some outward sign of distress.'

'And Leonie didn't do any of those things?'

'Not one.' Fiona shook her head, slowly. 'Instead, she stood still as a statue, staring down at the floor. It was as though she was holding everything in, like she didn't want to show her true feelings.'

'Everyone has their own way of dealing with stress and grief,'

Violet said. 'The way you or I would cope in that situation isn't necessarily how everyone else would handle it. And we have to remember that Leonie and Angeline weren't close.'

'Maybe not, but they were sisters. Close or not, that's got to mean something.'

'Perhaps she was controlling her emotions until she knew for certain whether Angeline was the victim.'

'I hadn't thought of that,' Fiona said, looking a little shamefaced. 'You're right. Maybe I'm being unfair. It's not for me to judge others or measure them against how I'd behave in similar circumstances. Perhaps what I witnessed wasn't so much Leonie holding on to her emotions, but rather her clinging on to hope . . . hope that the victim would turn out to be someone other than Angeline.'

After Fiona had returned to the bakery, Violet sat and finished her coffee. As she was putting on her coat, ready to leave, her phone rang.

'Hello?' she said.

There was no caller ID, so she was half-expecting an unctuous sales spiel, preceded by the usual *how are you today?* question.

Instead, an angry female voice boomed in her ear.

'What have you been saying to DS Winterton?'

'I beg your pardon,' Violet replied. 'Who is this?'

'Yvette Finch,' came the reply. 'I want to know what you've said to the police.'

Violet bristled. 'I didn't *say* very much,' she replied. 'Not about you at any rate. I assume the police told you that a body's been found?'

'Yes, of course they did.'

'Well, I was the one who found it. Initially, I thought it was Leonie, and when the police talked to me, I told them you'd been working for her in a PR capacity.'

'You must have said more than that, otherwise they wouldn't have been so keen to talk to me.'

'I mentioned that you'd recently ended your working relationship. Nothing else.'

'Well, thank you *very* much,' Yvette said, her voice soaked in sarcasm. 'As a direct result of your meddling, the police have told me to stay in the area. It's outrageous, especially as I've now been told Leonie is fine.'

'She is, but it turns out the victim is her sister,' Violet said. 'This is a murder investigation. The police will be talking to a lot of people. I'm sure you have nothing to worry about.'

'I'm not worried, just annoyed. It's inconvenient. I have to get back to London. There are things I need to do.'

'Maybe you'll be able to change your rail ticket and catch a later train.'

'I'm not going to be able to leave today,' Yvette said. 'DS Winterton has told me to stick around for at least another twenty-four hours. I have no idea where I'll stay. I certainly can't afford another night at the Merrywell Manor Hotel – not now that Leonie isn't picking up the tab.'

'You could try the White Hart,' Violet said. 'It's the pub in the village. They've recently started letting out a room to bed and breakfast guests. I'm not sure if it'll be available though, what with the festival and everything – but it's worth a try. Failing that, you might have to go further afield. Bakewell or Matlock.'

Yvette sighed. 'I've a good mind to send the bill to the local constabulary.'

'You can try,' Violet said. 'But I'd imagine you'd get short shrift. You're better off viewing this as a brief, enforced holiday. You have to admit, there are worse places to be holed up than the Peak District.'

'I suppose so,' Yvette said, sounding slightly less hostile. 'And thanks . . . for recommending the White Hart.'

'You're welcome. Let's hope they can accommodate you.'

* * *

Violet went to *The Memory Box*, hoping that work would take her mind off the morning's tragic events. She'd taken on a project with a nearby retirement village, filming interviews with its residents to capture their recollections of life in the 1950s and 60s. The interviews had been completed – all Violet had to do now was edit the best bits and arrange them into the most suitable order for a fifteen-minute film.

As she worked on the edits, niggling questions about Angeline Hammond's murder swam around in her head, swirling back and forth until she began to feel dizzy. She rubbed her temples and swallowed a paracetamol, quelling any temptation to try and solve this latest mystery. The last murder that had taken place in Merrywell had landed her in big trouble, and this time, Violet was determined not to let curiosity get the better of her.

She sat back and watched one of the interviews she was working on, aiming to focus on her job, rather than random theories about Angeline's death. Ten minutes later, a text arrived from Matthew.

I heard what happened to Angeline Hammond. Are you OK? I gather you were the one who found her body.

So much for trying to forget about things.

Violet tapped out a reply.

I'm still quite shaken TBH. I don't understand why someone would do that to her. It doesn't make sense. I'm working this afternoon, to divert my thoughts away from what's happened, but I'll admit I'm finding it hard to concentrate!

Matthew responded almost immediately.

If you're looking for something to take your mind off things, why don't you come with me to the White Hart tonight? They're running a special literary-themed quiz to celebrate the book festival. It'd be great if you could join team Collis for the evening ☺

Violet wasn't really in the mood for socialising, but taking part in a quiz had to be better than staying at home, alone, brooding on the events of the day. And time spent with Matthew was always a pleasure.

OK. Sounds like fun 😉

Matthew's reply pinged back a minute later.

Excellent. Come and join us in the pub just before 8 p.m.

After sending a quick 'thumbs-up', Violet placed her phone face down on the desk and went back to her editing. Within minutes, she was completely absorbed in the task.

Half an hour later, her concentration was broken by the sound of the door opening. Violet dragged her eyes from the screen and looked up.

Leonie Stanwick was walking into *The Memory Box*.

Chapter 15

'Leonie!'

Unsure what else to say or do, but knowing she had to say something, Violet pushed her chair back and stood up. 'I'm so sorry about your sister.'

The words seemed feeble and inadequate, but Leonie must have appreciated the sentiment, because she managed a grateful smile.

'Thank you. Is it OK if I sit down?'

'Yes . . . yes, of course. Can I get you a cup of tea? Coffee?'

'No.' Leonie waved away the offer. 'It's kind of you, but in the last couple of hours, I've been handed more cups of tea and coffee than I've known what to do with. I've reached the point of being waterlogged.'

Violet offered a sympathetic smile. 'It's what we Brits do at times like this, isn't it? When words fail us . . . when we're unsure how to comfort someone, we resort to copious pots of tea.'

'Yes, I suppose it's the good old standby . . . the panacea for all ills,' Leonie said, as she lowered herself onto one of the visitors' chairs.

'I can't begin to imagine how you must be feeling,' said Violet.

Leonie trailed a finger across her left eyebrow. 'I'm not sure that I know myself,' she said. 'I'm numb. I don't think it's quite sunk in.'

'It's not an easy thing to come to terms with . . . losing someone close to you so suddenly.'

'That's the thing . . .' Leonie smiled regretfully. 'Angeline and I weren't close. Not at all. The truth is, we hardly knew each other, but she *was* my flesh and blood. Some bonds can't be broken, no matter how much you pull them apart. I've been hoping our relationship might change for the better, but that's never going to happen now, is it?'

'No.' Violet sat down. 'It's always hard, thinking about *what might have been*.'

'It feels as though someone's stolen something precious from me,' Leonie said, biting her lip and battling with tears. 'Something I didn't even know I had.'

Swiping her knuckles across her eyes, she distracted herself by picking up one of Violet's business cards from the stack on her desk.

'What is it that you do in here?' she asked, glancing around the cramped workspace.

Violet smiled. 'When I'm at my computer, I'm usually editing or doing administration of some kind.'

'Editing what?' Leonie looked down at the business card, turning it over in her hand. 'What sort of business is it that you run?'

It was a question Violet was asked regularly, but not one she found easy to answer succinctly. On numerous occasions she'd tried and failed to come up with a strapline or mission statement for her quirky business, something that precisely and concisely described the services she offered.

'In a nutshell, I record people's memories,' she said. 'Either in writing, on audio, or on film. I've worked with clients to record family histories, business histories, community memories. I'll tackle almost anything . . . whatever it is people want to talk about, or document for posterity.'

Leonie looked sceptical. 'I'm astonished anyone would want to go on record with those kind of things,' she said. 'I'm firmly of the opinion that most memories are best forgotten . . . but I'm sure that makes me the exception, rather than the rule.'

'Yes, I think it does,' Violet said. 'And thank goodness for that, otherwise I wouldn't have a viable business.'

Another moment of silence descended, and Violet floundered for something else to say.

'That's another reason people offer tea,' she said, smiling apologetically. 'It gives them something to do with their hands when the conversation runs dry. I'm sorry. It's hard to know how to behave in these circumstances. I'd like to offer some words of comfort, but I'm not sure what to say.'

Leonie clasped her hands together. 'Don't worry, I didn't come here looking for comfort. The reason for my visit is to seek information . . . about what you saw. The police told me that you were the one who found Angeline's body.'

Violet felt a stab of anguish as she recalled that awful moment of discovery. Pressing her lips together, she breathed through her nose and suppressed a sudden urge to weep.

'What is it that you want to know?' she said, once she was back in control of her emotions.

'Whether Angeline looked peaceful when you found her,' Leonie said. 'I realise it sounds silly, but I can't bear to think of her life ending in fear. I suppose what I'm looking for is reassurance.'

'She was lying face down, so I couldn't see her expression,' Violet said. 'As I'm sure you're aware, Angeline was attacked from behind. It's possible she didn't even see her assailant.'

'Do you think she died instantly? She wouldn't have suffered, would she?'

Violet shifted uncomfortably. If the knife that killed Angeline had pierced her heart, death would have been instantaneous. She wanted to be honest, but sometimes the truth wasn't what people needed to hear.

'I really don't know,' she said. 'The only thing I can tell you for certain is that there was no sign she'd tried to escape, or crawl away. I'm sorry I can't be more helpful than that. The fact is, I didn't look too closely. When I saw that she wasn't breathing, I stepped back. I didn't want to contaminate what was evidently a crime scene.'

Violet paused to let her words sink in.

'I don't know if the police told you this,' she continued, 'but initially, I thought it was *you* lying there.'

'Me?' Leonie pulled her shoulders back and stared into Violet's eyes. 'Why would you think that?'

'Because you hadn't turned up for the workshop. Eric Nash sent me off to look for you. You weren't at the hotel, and you weren't answering your phone. Nobody knew where you were. In the end, I went to check whether your car was in the car park, and that's when I saw your sister . . . lying there, next to *your* Audi. Perhaps now you can understand why I assumed it was you.'

Leonie buried her face in her hands.

'Before I went into the car park, Yvette and I went up to your room with a member of the hotel staff,' Violet explained. 'We thought you might be ill, so we went inside, but it was obvious you hadn't spent the night there.'

'I stayed with a friend,' Leonie said. 'The reason I wasn't answering my phone was because I'd switched it off. I didn't want anyone pestering me.'

Violet wondered about the identity of the 'friend'. Was it a man? Rupert Dalloway, for instance? Or a female friend? Zoe Corndale, Karen Avery, or someone else? Another childhood buddy?

As Leonie seemed in the mood to talk, Violet risked another question, one that had been baffling her ever since she'd discovered the body.

'Why was Angeline wearing your fiddler cap?' she said. 'I recognised it immediately. It was the sequinned one you wore when I interviewed you. That's the thing that convinced me it was you in the car park.'

Leonie swiped at her cheeks, which were wet with tears. 'Angeline admired the hat,' she said. 'So I gave it to her.'

'When?' said Violet.

'After the book festival event, later in the afternoon. I was wearing it when I went to see her. It was around teatime. I had one of those hot toddies at the festival, and another drink when I got back to the hotel, so I went to Angeline's on foot . . . across the fields. It was the first time I'd been home in years.'

'Was she pleased to see you?'

Leonie lowered her eyes. 'Not at first, but she let me in and we talked. There was stuff I wanted to say to her, things I needed to explain.'

'What kind of things?' said Violet.

Leonie lifted her head and shook it dismissively. 'Nothing you need concern yourself with. The things we discussed were private family matters. It's not important now.'

'Are you sure about that?' Violet said. 'The fact is, someone killed your sister today. I can understand your reluctance to tell *me* what was discussed – but, please, don't hold anything back from the police. Tell them everything, regardless of how irrelevant you think it might be.'

'I'm sure that scruffy-looking detective will find a way to wheedle everything out of me,' Leonie said, smiling crookedly. 'He wanted to talk to me earlier, but I told him I wasn't up to it. I feel slightly better now, more composed, so I suppose I should go back and have a chat with him . . . get it over with. I get the impression he won't rest until he's squeezed every bit of information he can from me.'

'In fairness, he is only doing his job.'

'Maybe,' said Leonie. 'Although it wouldn't surprise me to learn that I'm his prime suspect.'

'Why would he think that?'

'Isn't that what they always think? Even I know that most murders are committed by someone connected to the victim.'

Violet nodded. 'That's true, but regardless of what DS Winterton might think, once the time of death has been established, you'll be able to prove you were with your friend when Angeline was killed,' Violet said. 'You'll have a watertight alibi.'

'Something tells me that won't be nearly enough to satisfy the police,' Leonie said. 'Think about it . . . I come home for the first time in years, and hours later, Angeline turns up dead. Everyone in Merrywell knows I was estranged from my family. It's only a matter of time before the village gossips start whispering in DS Winterton's ear, if they haven't done so already.'

'If you don't mind me asking, why *were* you and your family estranged?' Violet said.

'That's none of your business.'

Violet flinched: at both Leonie's bluntness and the inappropriateness of her own question.

'I'm sorry,' said Leonie. 'That was harsh. I didn't mean to be rude . . . but my relationship with my family is not a subject I care to talk about right now. Since my mother died, I've tried to put the rift behind me. It's water under the bridge, as far as I'm concerned.'

'Is that how your sister saw it?'

'I think she was coming round to that way of thinking, yes. But like I said, it's not something I want to discuss today. The reason I came here was to establish that Angeline hadn't suffered.'

Violet reached across the desk and squeezed Leonie's fingers, trying desperately to muster some words of comfort.

'Based on what I saw, I don't believe she did.'

'Thank you, Violet. You've put my mind at rest.'

'The thing I don't understand,' Violet said, 'is why Angeline was in the hotel car park in the first place.'

'She must have gone to fetch the car,' Leonie said.

'You asked her to get it for you?'

'No, I meant she'd gone to collect it for herself. As well as giving Angeline my hat, I also gave her my Audi.'

'*Really?*' Violet coughed in an attempt to hide her astonishment.

'Angeline's job required her to do a lot of mileage,' Leonie explained. 'When I turned up to see her, I discovered she was driving around in a clapped-out Fiesta. It was parked at the house, and I could see the damned thing wasn't safe, so I told her she could have my car.'

Violet didn't think an Audi coupé was necessarily the best choice of vehicle for a district nurse, but she kept the thought to herself.

'That was a very generous gift,' she said, instead. 'Angeline must have been delighted.'

'She was, although I got the impression she intended to trade it in for something more sensible, with better fuel consumption. Unlike me, Angeline wasn't overly impressed by flashy cars. She was blessed with a lot more common sense.'

'How were you planning to get back to London without your car?'

Leonie shrugged. 'By train, I suppose. I didn't really give it much thought. I have this terrible habit of acting impulsively, you see – and gifting my car to Angeline was definitely a spur-of-the-moment thing. I'm not going to lie though, I do have a new BMW on order. It's being delivered next week. That was at the back of my mind when I gave Angeline the Audi . . . letting her have my old car struck me as the logical and kind thing to do. I handed her the keys and told her I'd transfer the logbook over as soon as I got back to London. She said she'd go and collect the car early this morning.'

'So that's why she was at the hotel,' Violet said.

'It must have been.'

'Why was the car parked on its own?' Violet asked. 'It was right at the far end of the car park.'

'Trust me, it was surrounded by cars when I left it there. When I got back to the hotel on Friday, after the festival, there was a huge party taking place in the hotel's main function room.

The car park was full, and the only space I could find was right at the end.'

'So when the party guests drove away, your car was left out on a limb.' Violet nodded. 'That explains it.'

'It did occur to me that someone might have been hanging around the car park . . . eyeing up the Audi when Angeline got there.'

'A car thief, you mean?'

'Why not? They steal to order these days, don't they? Maybe Angeline disturbed someone, or caught them in the act.'

'It's possible.' Violet nodded. 'But why would a car thief be carrying a knife?'

Leonie let out a puff of air. 'I don't know. For the purposes of protection or intimidation? I really have no idea how these gangs operate.'

'There is another possibility,' Violet said, furrowing her brow and wondering how best to phrase what she was about to say. 'I don't wish to alarm you, Leonie, but *I* thought Angeline was you . . . What if her killer did as well? What if the person who murdered Angeline thought they were killing you?'

'No.' Leonie held up a hand to ward off Violet's theorising. 'Please don't say that. It would make Angeline's death even more futile.'

'I'm sorry. I'm not saying this to upset you, but I do think it's something you should consider.'

'But who would want to kill *me*?' Leonie asked.

'I have no idea. But as a successful, well-known author, I'd say you're a far more likely target than your sister.'

'I honestly can't think of anyone who would wish me harm,' Leonie said, sounding supremely confident about her own safety. 'Maybe Angeline was targeted by someone who held a grudge. One of her patients, maybe?'

'You could be right, and I'm sure the police will investigate every possible angle,' Violet said. 'Even so, you should talk to

DS Winterton. It must have crossed *his* mind that you were the intended victim. Why don't you flag it up with him, see what he has to say?'

Leonie stood up and smoothed down her dress. 'Forgive me, but it's not a scenario I care to think about. I'll speak to the police and answer their questions, but I'd prefer to leave it to them to work out what happened.'

'But what if I'm right?' Violet said. 'If you were the killer's real target, they may try again. If you stay here in Merrywell, you could be putting yourself in danger.'

Leonie moved towards the door.

'Thank you for your concern, Violet, but I think you're worrying unnecessarily. Angeline's killer was most likely a car thief who panicked when she showed up unexpectedly. Her death is a tragic case of being in the wrong place at the wrong time.'

Clearly, Leonie was staking her hopes on the most palatable explanation for Angeline's death. Violet thought that was a mistake.

'You need to be careful, Leonie. Keep your wits about you.'

Leonie acknowledged the warning with a nod. 'I always do,' she said, as she opened the door. 'Goodbye, Violet.'

After she'd gone, Violet placed her elbows on the desk and rested her head in her hands. There was no doubt about it: the Hammonds were an enigma. There was something about the family that puzzled her. Violet was convinced the undercurrents in their relationship were a lot more complicated than Leonie was letting on.

As she rubbed goosebumps from her arms, she recalled what Leonie had said during her interview.

Every one of us has something to hide . . . secrets alter our behaviour: change the way we speak, the things we say, the decisions we make.

What was Leonie hiding? Were her secrets the reason Angeline had been killed?

Chapter 16

When she got home, Violet ate a light dinner and then went upstairs to shower and get ready for her evening in the pub.

As venues went, the White Hart was unfussy and casual; definitely not the sort of place to dress up for. With that in mind, she slipped on a pair of black jeans and a bright red sweater, and spritzed her neck with her favourite perfume. As she checked her appearance in the mirror above the dressing table, she heard a knock on the front door. After giving her reflection one last look, she bounded down the stairs, hoping whoever it was wouldn't delay her too long.

She entered the hallway, pulled open the door and stared open-mouthed at the man standing on the threshold. He was probably the last person on earth she'd expected to see.

'Hello, Vi,' he said. 'You look nice.'

She blinked twice, wondering if she was hallucinating.

It was Paul. Her ex-husband.

The shock of his unexpected appearance had made her throat constrict. She swallowed hard, and looked at him with wide eyes.

'What are you doing here?' she said, aiming to sound casual, despite the knot of anxiety that was building in her chest.

'I've come for the book festival,' he replied. 'Aren't you going to invite me in?'

Feeling confused, she tightened her grip on the door handle and thought about her best course of action. Paul's unexpected arrival was an unwelcome curveball. Obviously, she couldn't leave him standing on the doorstep – but neither was she keen to invite him in.

She stood her ground as she gathered her thoughts, torn between feelings of obligation and resentment. Glancing at her watch, she noted that it was seven-thirty. The White Hart was only a couple of minutes' walk away, so she supposed she could spare Paul twenty minutes. Twenty-five tops.

Plastering a smile onto her face, she stood back and opened the door wide. 'By all means come in,' she said. 'But I am going out shortly. You should have messaged me to let me know you were coming.'

She stiffened as Paul stepped into the hallway and moved in for a hug. What was he doing? They'd rarely hugged, even before their divorce. Why start now?

'You smell nice,' he said. 'Still wearing the same perfume, then?'

Ignoring the comment, she closed the front door and led him into the living room.

Paul looked around, nodding approvingly. 'Nice cottage,' he said.

'There are other adjectives, you know . . . other than "nice",' Violet said, irritation breaking through the veneer of politeness she was struggling to maintain.

Paul stuck out his bottom lip. 'What?'

'You've told me I *look* nice, I *smell* nice, and I have a *nice* cottage. Since when did your vocabulary become so limited?'

'Bloody hell, Violet.' He laughed. 'You could have given it a few minutes before you started taking pot shots.'

Violet pinched the back of her hand, hoping this was all a bad dream. Sadly, the sharp nip of fingers on skin confirmed she was wide awake. Paul's presence in her living room was all too real.

She watched him peel off his coat, seething inwardly as he threw it onto the back of the sofa and sat down.

Make yourself at home, why don't you?

'Have I come at a bad time?' he said.

'It's not ideal. Like I said, I'm going out.'

Paul's eyebrows rose momentarily. 'Are you off to one of the book festival events? If so, I'll come with you.'

Talk about presumptuous.

'As a matter of fact, I'm going to the pub,' she replied. 'To a quiz night.'

He leaned his head against the back of the sofa and smirked. 'That's something I never thought I'd hear you say. Not the bit about going to the pub, obviously . . . but a *quiz* night? Is that what passes for entertainment round here then?'

Violet narrowed her eyes, fighting an overwhelming urge to grab him by the collar and throw him back out through the front door.

'Why do you always have to mock?' she said.

'I'm not mocking,' he replied. 'But since when have quiz nights been your thing?'

'Since not long after I moved here. I go more for the social side than the quiz.'

Why am I explaining myself? she wondered. *What I do with my life is none of Paul's business. Not anymore.*

'I suppose when you live in a village, you have to take whatever's on offer,' he said. 'But rather you than me.'

'Correct me if I'm wrong, but haven't you just travelled all the way from London to attend our book festival? I don't think Merrywell is quite the cultural void you're making it out to be, is it?'

Paul winked, cocking a finger in her direction. 'You got me there. And, from what I've seen of it so far, Merrywell seems like a—'

Violet held up a hand to cut him off. 'Please don't say *nice*.'

He smiled. 'Like an *interesting* place to live. I like the Peak

District – you know I do. You and I used to come walking here all the time when we were students.'

'So why do you find it necessary to be so scathing?'

'I'm not being scathing. I've got nothing against village life per se . . . but I've always been a city boy at heart – you know that.'

'How could I not? It's something you've made crystal clear over the years. As I recall, you wouldn't even consider a move to the countryside to try and save our marriage.'

'Yeah . . . well.' He fidgeted uncomfortably. 'Maybe that was a mistake. Perhaps I should have listened to you.'

Violet cringed inwardly. There was a time when she might have welcomed those words, but not anymore. 'We can't backtrack now,' she said. 'That boat sailed a long time ago. And admit it, you'd have been miserable if you'd been forced to leave London.'

When he wobbled his head, looking uncharacteristically uncertain, Violet decided to change the subject.

'Does Amelia know you're here?' she said, making a mental note to call her daughter at the earliest opportunity.

'She was the one who told me about the festival. I'm here primarily for the Clive Kitchner event.'

Clive Kitchner was a writer of popular thrillers, but Violet wasn't aware that Paul had read any of his books.

'I didn't realise you were a fan,' she said.

He nodded. 'Over the last six months or so, I've read pretty much every novel he's ever written. He's my new favourite author.'

'I thought Clive Kitchner was appearing in the morning,' she said.

'He is. I thought it'd be easier to drive up this evening.'

Violet lowered herself into the armchair by the window.

'Are you staying at the Merrywell Manor Hotel?'

'You're joking, aren't you?' Paul said. 'According to their website, they charge nearly six hundred quid a night.'

Violet was aware that the hotel was exclusive and a tad snooty, but she hadn't realised the room rates were quite so exorbitant. The hotel was obviously an important contributor to the local business economy, and she hoped the police investigation wouldn't cause too many problems or put people off staying there.

'Normally, I'd suggest you stay at the White Hart, but I suspect their one and only room is already taken,' she said. 'There are some great B&Bs in Bakewell though. Or there's a Premier Inn in Matlock if you're on a really tight budget.'

'Actually . . .' He gave her a doe-eyed look. 'I was hoping you'd put me up.'

'*What*?' Hit by a wave of panic, Violet sat up straight and stared at him.

He couldn't possibly be serious. After the pettiness and acrimony of their divorce, how could he expect her to comply with such an outrageous request? This was a wind-up, right?

'Are you having a laugh?' she said. 'You can't just turn up unannounced and expect me to give you a bed for the night.'

'A couple of nights, actually . . . if that's all right,' Paul said. 'I thought I'd stick around for another one of the events tomorrow night. I'm planning to drive home on Monday morning.'

Violet struggled to her feet, determined not to get snared in a trap of Paul's making.

'Didn't you hear what I said?' She scrunched up her nose and fought off the urge to squeal with frustration. 'This isn't on, Paul. And don't try looking all big-eyed and innocent. You've always been a cheeky sod, but even *you* must know this isn't acceptable. People don't behave like this in polite society.'

'Hey, this is me you're dealing with.' He winked again and gave an irritating click of his tongue. 'You know I play by my own rules. Anyway, we're family, and you always used to say that family were welcome any time.'

Violet folded her arms. 'We're divorced, Paul. We're not family anymore.'

'Yes, we are. We're Amelia's parents.'

'That means we have family in common. It doesn't mean I'm obliged to give you free accommodation at the drop of a hat.'

Paul wriggled uncomfortably. At least he had the good grace to look guilty.

'I suppose I should be grateful you've not brought Janis with you,' Violet said, arching an eyebrow.

Janis was Paul's new partner. Welcoming her to Greengage Cottage would have been a bridge too far.

Paul shrugged nonchalantly. 'Janis and I broke up,' he said. 'It was nice while it lasted.'

There it was again: that word. Violet cast her eyes upwards.

'Don't pull a face,' Paul said. 'We weren't suited. End of.'

'It was your use of the word *nice* that made me roll my eyes,' she explained. 'Your love life is nothing to do with me, although I'll admit I'm surprised the two of you have split up. Amelia told me that Janis was lovely.'

'Yeah, well . . . Amelia's not the one going out with her, is she? Janis *is* lovely. We're just not compatible.'

'If you say so.' Violet pulled back her sleeve and glanced at her watch. Seven-forty-five.

'Anyway,' she said. 'Much as I'd love to sit and chat, I'd better get a shift on. Like I said, I'm going out. As for you staying here tonight? I'm sorry, but that's not an option. The bed in the spare room isn't even made up.'

'You're kidding me.' Paul looked at her aghast. 'You're not going to throw me out at this time of night, are you?'

'Paul, it's quarter to eight, not the middle of the night.'

'Yeah, but it's a bit late in the day to be finding a hotel.' His voice had begun to wheedle. 'Come on, Vi. Please. If you point me in the direction of the airing cupboard, I'll make the bed up myself. I promise I won't be any trouble, and if you don't want to leave me here on my own, I'll even make the ultimate sacrifice and come to the quiz night with you.'

Violet scowled as she weighed up her options. What she *should* do was harden her heart and turf Paul out into the night – but that wouldn't be very friendly, and she wanted to keep things amicable between them, for Amelia's sake.

Another option was to let Paul stay, and give him free rein of Greengage Cottage while she went to the White Hart. That was slightly preferable to the alternative – which was to take him with her to the pub (definitely a non-starter). The thought of Paul encroaching on her new life in Merrywell was excruciating.

She wanted to growl with anger, furious that he was putting her in such an impossible position.

In the end, she took a deep breath and, against her better judgement, decided to put him up in the spare room, forego the quiz and stay at home. Of all the options, it was the one that called for the biggest sacrifice on her part, but at least it would mean she could keep an eye on what Paul was up to while he was in Merrywell.

'Cheers, Vi, I appreciate it,' he said, when she told him her decision. 'Don't feel you have to stay in though. If you want to go out, I'll be fine on my own. Don't miss the quiz on my account.'

'Will you please shut up about the quiz,' she said. 'My decision's made. I'm not going. There's nothing more to be said.'

'In that case, do you want me to send out for a takeaway? We could make an evening of it. You can *get* takeaways delivered here, yeah?'

She shot him a look. 'Yes, Paul. We can. Merrywell isn't completely cut off from civilisation. If you want a takeaway, that's fine, but count me out. I've already eaten.'

'Lucky you. I've not had anything since lunchtime. I'm starving.'

'No change there, then. You're always hungry,' Violet said. 'I'll happily make you an omelette or a sandwich, or you can send out for something. It's up to you.'

When she'd woken up that morning, the last thing Violet could have predicted was that she'd be spending the evening with her ex-husband. Then again, finding Angeline's body hadn't exactly been on her agenda either.

Maybe she could take advantage of Paul's presence by getting his views on the murder. As a chief superintendent with the Met, he was sure to have an opinion.

Chapter 17

After thirty seconds of dithering, Paul opted for a tuna mayo sandwich, which Violet prepared while he was upstairs, making up the bed in the spare room.

Once the sandwich was made, she pulled out her phone and composed a message to Matthew.

> Sorry for the short notice, but I can't make it to the pub tonight. An unexpected visitor has arrived. Good luck with the quiz.

Violet's chest tightened as she pressed send. Not only did she feel guilty about letting him down, she was also disappointed about missing out – not on the quiz (that she could take or leave), but on being with Matthew. He was interesting and easy-going, and he always knew how to make her laugh. She'd been looking forward to spending time with him. Trust Paul to turn up and put a spanner in the works.

Violet stared anxiously at her phone, fervently hoping that Matthew would read the text message and not ask any awkward questions. He replied almost immediately.

Bring your visitor along . . . the more the merrier. Team Collis needs all the help it can get.

She squirmed. Why couldn't he have sent her a thumbs-up and left it at that? The idea of drafting Paul onto the quiz team was unthinkable. Violet would much rather his presence at Greengage Cottage go unnoticed.

She composed a reply; something suitably vague and ambiguous.

Better not. It's complicated. I'm coming to some of the festival events tomorrow, so hopefully we can catch up then.

This time, Matthew did send her a thumbs-up. It arrived as Paul's heavy footsteps thundered down the stairs. Violet was filling the kettle when he strolled into the kitchen.

'That's all done,' he said, sounding as if he'd single-handedly built a new bed, rather than put on fresh sheets and a duvet cover. 'It's a cosy little room, certainly comfortable enough for a couple of nights.'

Talk about damning with faint praise, Violet thought. He was right, the spare bedroom was small, but this was an eighteenth-century cottage. What did he expect?

'I've made you a sandwich,' she said, pointing towards the plate on the kitchen table. 'You said you were hungry, so I've done a couple of rounds. There's some leftover quiche in the fridge as well, if you want it.'

'Ooh, yes please,' he said, rubbing his hands together.

She retrieved the half-quiche and placed it on the table.

'Am I eating in here?' he said. 'At the table?'

'I usually do,' she replied.

'You never used to. We always used to have dinner on trays, in front of the TV.'

'The operative words in that sentence are *used* and *to*,' said

Violet. 'I do things differently now, now that I only have myself to please.'

Looking suitably chastened, Paul pulled out a chair and sat down at the kitchen table.

'Would you like tea, or coffee?' Violet asked, as he bit into one of the sandwiches.

'I don't suppose you've got anything stronger, have you?' he said, speaking with his mouth full. 'A nice glass of wine would go down a treat.'

'I thought you were supposed to be cutting down on the drinking,' she said, looking at him out of the side of her eyes.

'I have cut down,' he said, as he sliced into the quiche. 'But I'm on my holidays.'

Holidays? What did he think this was? His own personal B&B with a free dinner thrown in for good measure?

'There's a bottle of white wine in the fridge,' she said, knowing that he preferred red. 'You're welcome to a glass of that.'

There were a couple of bottles of Châteauneuf-du-Pape stashed in the cupboard under the stairs, but she had no intention of letting Paul get his hands on the good stuff.

'If it's that or nothing,' he said, 'then I won't say no.'

As Violet poured the wine, she noticed him staring at the food bowls on the floor, and the cat flap she'd had installed in the back door.

'Have you got a cat?'

She nodded. 'Her name's Rusty. She spends most of the day outside, but she usually comes home round about now. I'll introduce you as soon as she arrives.'

He wrinkled his nose. 'You're OK. Cats don't tend to like me. I'll keep my distance.'

'That might not be possible,' Violet said. 'She likes sitting on people's knees. She also likes tuna, so I shouldn't hang about . . . eat your sandwiches before she comes in.'

Paul questioned her with a look, obviously unsure whether

she was kidding or not.

'Are you not having a glass of wine?' he said, after he'd taken another bite of his sandwich.

Violet smiled. 'You know what?' she said. 'I think I will have one. I reckon I deserve it.'

She removed another glass from the cupboard and carried it to the table.

'I found a body this morning,' she said, making the bombshell announcement as she filled the glass.

Paul almost choked on the quiche he was eating.

'What?' He screwed up his face.

'You heard me. I found a body . . . a woman's body. She'd been stabbed.'

'Bloody hell!' He put his shoulders back and stared at her. 'Where was this?'

'In the car park at the Merrywell Manor Hotel.'

Paul stared at her. 'You're pulling my leg.'

Violet shook her head and sat down. 'I only wish I was.'

'Strewth!' He slapped the edge of the table with his fingers. 'It's not many months since you were involved in that other murder. What sort of place is this? When you said you were moving to Merrywell, I didn't realise it was the Derbyshire equivalent of Midsomer.'

Violet clenched her jaw. 'Do you want me to tell you about it, or not?'

'I do,' Paul said. 'Believe me, I'm all ears.'

As he continued to eat, she explained what had happened. Paul listened intently, saying nothing, even when Violet expounded her theory that Angeline may not have been the intended victim.

'Leonie Stanwick thinks her sister might have disturbed a car thief,' she said, eager to hear his opinion. 'What do you think to that idea?'

Paul bunched up his lips and pushed them to the left-hand side of his mouth.

'It doesn't really matter what I think,' he said. 'It's not my case, is it?'

'Come on, you can do better than that.' Violet pointed to the empty plate. 'You need to start singing for your supper.'

'All right,' he said, folding his arms and blowing air through his nose. 'It's not a bad theory, but criminals who steal high-value vehicles tend to target specific models and steal to order. They might nick a car from someone's driveway, or off the street, or even from a public car park if there isn't much in the way of security, but how could they have known that Leonie Stanwick's Audi was going to be there?'

'It was all over social media that Leonie was appearing at the festival, so it's not much of a leap to assume she'd be staying at the Merrywell Manor. But even if they *didn't* know, you said yourself it's an upmarket hotel. It stands to reason that anyone who can afford to stay there is likely to be driving an expensive vehicle. Maybe the thieves turned up on spec, or were casing the joint.'

'That's a valid point, and you make it well,' Paul said. 'But realistically, what are the chances of a criminal gang coming to Merrywell to steal a motor?'

'You're the detective; you tell me.'

'I work for the Met,' he said. 'I'm no expert on rural crime.'

'Don't give me that. I've watched enough episodes of *Police Interceptors* to know that county forces work together, and that the police track and chase stolen vehicles over long distances. Merrywell's as likely a place as any for thieves to target, especially as the car park doesn't have CCTV cameras. If someone got wind of that, it would make easy pickings of any vehicle left there.'

'I'm not so sure . . . I'm more inclined towards your theory that the dead woman was a victim of mistaken identity.'

Violet straightened her back. 'Really? Do you think that's something the investigating team will consider?'

'If they're worth their salt, they will,' Paul said. 'Relax, Vi. I'm sure they've got everything in hand. They certainly won't need your help, so don't even think about interfering.'

'Hey!' she snapped. 'I have no intention of *interfering*, as you put it.'

'All right, don't take umbrage. I'm just saying . . . you need to keep your nose out.'

Violet squeezed the stem of her wine glass. 'Are you suggesting I'm nosy?'

'It's not a suggestion, it's a fact.'

'Paul!'

'What?' He laughed. 'It's true. You *are* nosy.'

'I am not.' She scowled at him. 'I'll admit I have a strong sense of curiosity, but there's a difference between that and being a busybody.'

Paul chuckled as he drained his wine glass.

'Stop trying to wind me up,' she said. 'And stop laughing. I'm not a meddler . . . I don't go around sticking my nose into things that are nothing to do with me. But I was the one who found Angeline's body, remember? It's only natural for me to be curious about the investigation.'

Paul straightened his face, perhaps remembering where it was he was sleeping that night.

'A little curiosity is fine,' he said. 'Just make sure you don't step on the toes of the investigation team. The last thing they need is civilian interference.'

After Paul had finished eating, they took the bottle of wine into the living room and poured themselves a second glass. Thankfully, the conversation moved away from the murder. They talked about Amelia, the holiday to Italy Paul was planning, and how things were progressing at *The Memory Box*.

With the log burner glowing and the cat curled up on her knee, Violet leaned back and relaxed. The sound of Paul's laughter in her ear was familiar and reassuring, but she reminded herself that these weren't 'old times'. This was *new* territory; both of them behaving far more politely than they would ever have done prior to their divorce. Even so, it felt (to use Paul's favourite word) *nice* to enjoy each other's company again, albeit temporarily.

Violet knew this easy companionship was only possible because they were no longer beholden to each other. After years of unhappiness, she was glad they'd had the good sense to untangle their relationship and establish separate lives.

At ten o'clock, she stretched her arms and yawned.

'I'm going up,' she said, as Paul tore open the bag of peanuts Violet had supplied from the pantry. 'I know it's early, but it's been a long and eventful day, and I've got a lot planned for tomorrow.'

She went out into the kitchen to lock up at the back, and then into the hallway to lock the front door.

'Night, Paul,' she said, pausing at the bottom of the stairs. 'Feel free to stay up as long as you want. There's Sky and Netflix if you want to watch TV. I've locked up, so all you need to do is switch off the lights when you come up.'

'Cheers, Vi,' he said, as he tipped a handful of peanuts into his mouth. 'And thanks for letting me stay. I appreciate it.'

Chapter 18

Violet woke the next morning at eight o'clock. Downstairs, Paul was clattering around in the kitchen. The sound was accompanied by the distant rumble of a boiling kettle, and the faint sizzle of a frying pan. He was obviously hungry again.

The cat had slept on Violet's bed overnight, but as the smell of bacon began to drift up the stairs, Rusty was unable to resist temptation. Jumping off the bed with a thud, she pawed at the narrow gap in the partly opened door and scurried downstairs, where she would no doubt pester Paul vociferously, until he gave in to her demands.

Violet sat up, pushed a pillow behind her back, and checked her phone. No missed calls. No messages. Nothing to keep her in bed a moment longer. It was time to get up, take a shower and start the day.

'You found the bacon then?' she said, when she entered the kitchen half an hour later.

'You don't mind, do you?' Paul said. 'I like a decent breakfast on Sundays.'

'I know you do – and no, I don't mind. Just so long as you do the washing up.'

She nodded to the kitchen sink, where the frying pan and a plate had been wedged into the plastic washing-up bowl.

'No problem. I'll sort everything out just as soon as I've finished my tea. There's more in the pot, if you want one?'

'I prefer coffee in the mornings these days,' she told him, as she tipped muesli into a bowl. 'What's your plan for today?'

'The Clive Kitchner thing starts at eleven-fifteen,' he said. 'I thought I'd leave here around ten . . . have a wander around the village and then head up and spend some time in the bookshop before the event kicks off.'

'Make sure you leave time to explore the rest of the shopping village,' said Violet. 'There are a couple of shops you'll definitely want to check out, and there are places to eat there too, so you won't go hungry.'

Paul laughed. 'Is that your less-than-subtle way of asking me to stay out for the whole day? I take it you don't want me coming back here, eating you out of house and home?'

'You're welcome to come back if you need to . . . I'll give you a spare key,' she said. 'You did come to Merrywell for the festival though, so you may as well make the most of it. There are loads of things happening throughout the day.'

'Will I see you at any of the events?'

'We'll probably run into each other at some point,' Violet said. 'I have a festival pass, but I'm undecided about which sessions to go to.'

'Aren't you going to the Clive Kitchner event?'

'Probably not. It clashes with a reading by a local poet. I might go to that instead.'

True to his word, Paul left Greengage Cottage at ten o'clock. Violet had drawn him a rough map, showing a route that would take him on a circular tour of Merrywell, ending up at the shopping village.

As soon as he'd disappeared along the lane, she picked up her phone and called her daughter.

Amelia answered after the fourth ring, sounding groggy and half asleep.

'Mum? Why are you calling so early?'

'It's ten o'clock,' Violet said. 'You're not still in bed, are you?'

'Of course I am. It's Sunday. I always have a lie-in on Sundays.'

'Honestly.' Violet tutted. 'It's a lovely sunny morning, Amelia. You should be up and about and making the most of the day.'

'Give me a break, Mum. It's not a work day. I'll get up when I feel like it. Anyway, it's not sunny here in London. I can hear rain pattering against the window.'

'It makes a change for London to be getting the worst of the weather,' Violet said. 'It's good news for us, though . . . with it being the book festival this weekend.'

'Oh, yes,' said Amelia. 'Is it going well?'

'Yes and no.'

Violet took a deep breath and filled her in on the murder.

'Bloomin' heck, Mum. So much for a quiet life in the countryside. I didn't realise you'd moved to the murder capital of the Peak District.'

'Funny you should say that . . . Your dad made a similar quip when I told him.'

'Dad? You've spoken to him?'

'I've spoken to him *and* seen him. He's here for the book festival. I got the impression you knew he was coming.'

'No . . .' Amelia sounded hesitant. 'I told him Clive Kitchner was appearing, because I knew he'd been reading a lot of his stuff lately – but I didn't think he'd actually want to *go*, otherwise I'd have given you a heads-up. I take it you ran into him at one of the events? That must have been a surprise.'

'I didn't run into him. He came knocking on my door, last night – and it was more of a shock than a surprise, especially when he asked if he could stay here for a couple of nights.'

'At Greengage Cottage?' Amelia gasped. 'You're having me on. What did you say?'

'A few choice things.' Violet laughed. 'Then, eventually, I gave in. He stayed last night and he's staying tonight as well.'

'Ewwkk. That must be awkward.'

'It's not as bad as I was expecting. He's on his best behaviour.'

'Did he tell you that Janis has given him the elbow?' Amelia said.

Violet frowned. 'He told me they'd split up, but he made it sound like it was a joint decision.'

'Nah. She kicked him into touch . . . told him he was selfish, and too wrapped up in his job.'

'Oh dear.'

'Unless he takes early retirement, I think he'll keep getting the same complaint, no matter who he goes out with,' Amelia said. 'Don't go saying anything though. If he's making out the break-up was a mutual decision, it's best you play along.'

'No worries,' Violet said. 'If his pride's hurt, the last thing I'd want to do is rub his nose in it. What I don't fully understand is why he's come to the festival. It's a long way to drive for an hour-long event.'

'Maybe it's an excuse to see you,' Amelia said.

'I doubt it. Why would he want to see me?'

'I don't know, Mum. Could it be he's missing you?'

The phone call with Amelia left Violet feeling unsettled and confused. The thought of there being a hidden agenda behind Paul's visit was disconcerting.

She retrieved the festival programme from the noticeboard in the kitchen and cast her eyes down the list of the final day's events. The poetry reading started at the same time as the Clive Kitchner session: eleven-fifteen. Violet would time her arrival at the shopping village with only minutes to spare. It would reduce the chances of running into Paul.

After switching on the radio, she began to put away the pots, pans and cutlery Paul had washed and dried and left on the worktop. At ten-thirty, when the local station ran a short news summary, Violet turned up the volume, waiting to see if Angeline Hammond's murder would be mentioned. Sure enough, it was the lead item.

'Police have confirmed this morning that a man has been taken in for questioning in connection with the suspicious death of a woman in Merrywell. The thirty-three-year-old victim has been named as Angeline Hammond. Her body was discovered in the car park of the Merrywell Manor Hotel at 10 a.m. yesterday. Anyone who was in the area between 6 a.m. and 10 a.m. is asked to get in touch with the police by calling 101.'

Violet sat at the kitchen table and stared down at the flagstone floor, replaying the news segment in her head.

A man has been taken in for questioning.

She was both stunned and impressed that the police had managed to home in on a suspect so quickly. But who on earth was this mystery man?

She picked up her phone and composed a text.

I've just heard on the news that the police are questioning a man in connection with Angeline Hammond's death. Any idea who?

Ordinarily, she would have sent the text to Fiona, who always had an ear to the ground when it came to local gossip. Today though, Fiona would be busy with the festival, and wouldn't be paying attention to the Merrywell rumour mill. Nor would she have time to reply to non-essential texts.

So, instead, Violet sent the message to Matthew, whose opinion she valued even more than Fiona's. He responded instantly.

It's the first I've heard of it. Has this man been arrested?

Violet rattled off a reply.

The word 'arrest' wasn't mentioned.

Matthew's next text arrived a minute later.

Hats off to the coppers involved. They're obviously not hanging around. Let's hope someone is arrested and charged soon. I'm heading over to the festival in a minute. I'm going to the Clive Kitchner event. Should be good.

Violet crossed her fingers, hoping he wouldn't end up sitting next to Paul. The thought of the two men striking up a conversation made her shudder. Paul was bound to mention her name . . . what if Matthew put two and two together and came up with the wrong answer? The situation was a potential car crash waiting to happen.

I'm going to give that one a miss. Might go to the poetry session instead.

Another message alert sounded as she went upstairs to put on her shoes and grab her bag.

My mum's going to that one. Enjoy! Might see you later 👍

Violet glanced at her watch. Ten-fifty-eight.

She hurried back downstairs, tipped some cat crunchies into Rusty's bowl, and locked the back door.

As she walked through the living room towards the front hallway, her phone began to ring.

'Hello?' Violet said, perching on the armchair by the window to take the call.

'Ms Brewster. It's DS Winterton.'

‘Detective Winterton. I was just thinking about you.’

‘Were you?’

‘I heard on the radio that you’re questioning someone. Has this man been arrested?’

‘No, he’s being interviewed under caution,’ DS Winterton replied. ‘Not that it’s any business of yours.’

‘So why are you calling me?’ she said. ‘Why aren’t you in the interview room, interrogating your suspect?’

‘We have specially trained officers to conduct interviews.’

‘Then shouldn’t you be observing through a one-way mirror or something?’

DS Winterton laughed. ‘I may have said this to you before, but it’s worth repeating. You read too many crime novels, Violet.’

‘That’s how I prefer to experience murder,’ she said. ‘As fiction. The real thing is a lot less palatable. So, come on then . . . is there something you want to ask, or are you calling just to make fun of me?’

‘I want to talk to you about the interview you did with Leonie Stanwick.’

‘It was livestreamed,’ Violet told him. ‘If you speak to Eric Nash, he might be able to provide you with a recording. That way, you can listen to it yourself and find out what was said, verbatim.’

‘I’ve already done that. The interview *was* recorded and I’ve watched it a couple of times. For obvious reasons, the camera was focused on you and Leonie Stanwick, but it’s the people in the audience I’m interested in. From your position on the stage, you must have had a good view of those watching . . . Did you happen to notice whether there was a young male in the audience? Average height, longish brown hair, thirtyish? I appreciate it’s a long shot. I know the event was a sell-out and there were a lot of people there.’

‘It *was* a sell-out and the room was packed, but Leonie Stanwick is a romantic novelist,’ Violet said. ‘Consequently, the audience was predominantly female. From what I saw, there were only four men present, including Eric Nash.’

'Do you know the names of the other three?'

'Matthew Collis was there,' she replied. 'And someone called Rupert Dalloway. I don't know the name of the fourth man, but he was older. He certainly didn't fit the description you've just given me.'

'Is it possible the man I described *was* there, but you didn't notice him?'

Violet thought for a moment. 'He definitely wasn't in the downstairs seating area,' she said. 'But there were people on the balcony, and I didn't have a clear view of everyone up there.'

'So, he could have been on the balcony?'

'Yes . . .' Violet felt she was being pressured into saying something she wasn't entirely comfortable with. 'He *could* have been there, but then so could George Clooney, for all I know. You can't expect me to confirm the presence of someone I didn't see, or who might not have been there in the first place.'

'I'm not asking for a definitive answer, I just want your observations,' DS Winterton said. 'You're saying there was definitely no one of that description sitting downstairs, but you had a restricted view of the people up on the balcony?'

'I didn't say restricted view, I said I didn't have a *clear* view . . . not of everyone . . . although most of the people upstairs were in plain sight. They were there to see Leonie . . . so, naturally, they were leaning over the balustrade, looking down. I can't imagine why anyone would have wanted to hide away at the back.'

'The person I'm asking about may have had other reasons for being there,' DS Winterton said.

'You think he was there to see Angeline? Is the man you're asking about the guy you're questioning?'

'I can't tell you that.'

Violet huffed. 'Just as I can't tell you, categorically, whether the man you described was on the balcony,' she said. 'You do know that tickets for the festival have all been sold online? The best way to check who was at the event is to ask Fiona or Eric Nash for a list of attendees.'

'That's something else I've already done,' the detective said. 'But there's nothing to stop someone booking a ticket under a false name, using an unidentifiable email address. Which is why I'm talking to possible eyewitnesses.'

'I'm sorry I've not been able to help.'

Violet glanced at her watch. Five past eleven.

'You mentioned yesterday that you saw Angeline Hammond at the event,' DS Winterton continued.

'That's right.'

'What about afterwards? Did you see her once the interview was over?'

'I saw her leave,' Violet said. 'She made a real point of not hanging around at the end. She stood up, pulled on her coat and headed straight out of the bookshop.'

'Did you notice if anyone followed her?'

'There was someone close on her heels, but it wasn't a man. It was Leonie's old schoolfriend, Karen Avery.'

'Do you think this Karen Avery might have been following Angeline?'

'I didn't get that impression, no.'

'And you didn't see anything else? Anything unusual?'

'Not really,' Violet said. 'I stood for a while and watched people queuing to get their books signed. I was right opposite the staircase . . . and, for what it's worth, I don't recall seeing a long-haired thirty-something man come down from the balcony.'

'OK, well thanks anyway,' DS Winterton said. 'I appreciate you talking to me. I'll let you get on. You have a nice day now.'

It was ten past eleven when Violet ended the call. She needed to get her skates on.

Chapter 19

The poetry reading was being held in one of the studio rooms at the shopping village. Violet slipped into a seat at the back with less than a minute to spare. When she looked up, she realised Matthew's mother was sitting directly in front of her. Joyce turned around and smiled when Violet tapped her on the shoulder.

'You're cutting it fine,' she said, keeping her voice low.

'I know,' Violet replied. 'I wasn't sure I was going to make it. How are you? Are you enjoying the festival?'

'I am. Obviously I'm shocked and saddened about Angeline . . . but I'm glad the festival's gone ahead, regardless.'

A door opened behind them, and Eric led the guest speaker down the centre aisle, towards the podium at the front.

'Do you fancy getting a quick coffee after this?' Joyce whispered. 'It'd be good to have a proper chat.'

'Sure,' Violet replied. 'I'd like that.'

After dedicating the event to the memory of Angeline Hammond, Eric introduced the tall and rather serious-looking poet. Opening up a slim volume, she launched into her reading with aplomb. She began with a haiku about autumn, and ended on a high thirty minutes later with a haunting poem about a nearby drowned village.

'Are you staying to buy a copy of the book?' Violet asked, when the reading had concluded.

Joyce shook her head. 'I don't think so. I enjoyed listening, but some of it was a bit over my head. Let's go and get that coffee, shall we?'

They crossed the crowded courtyard and joined the queue in the café. The place was packed and noisy, but as they paid for their drinks, they spotted two stools being vacated at the long bar along the rear wall.

'I've never been very good at getting onto these things,' Joyce said, as she clambered inelegantly onto one of the tall stools.

'There's definitely a knack,' Violet said, hoicking herself upwards. 'But, like you, it's not one I've mastered.'

'Tell me how you're feeling,' Joyce said, once she'd settled comfortably. 'After your awful discovery yesterday.'

Violet stirred her coffee. 'Sad and shaken up, but slightly more optimistic – now that I know the police are questioning a suspect.'

'I heard about that,' Joyce said, leaning in to close the gap between them. 'And I happen to know who it is.'

'Really?' Violet said, feeling in awe of Merrywell's bush telegraph.

'It's someone Angeline used to work with,' Joyce said, speaking in a hushed tone. 'He had a thing for her, apparently . . . made quite a nuisance of himself at one time.'

'Are you sure about this, Joyce?'

'One hundred per cent,' she replied. 'My friend's sister-in-law worked with Angeline at the health centre. This bloke . . . his name's Harry something-or-other . . . he really fancied Angeline . . . asked her out loads of times, but she wasn't interested. He obviously didn't take the hint, because supposedly he kept turning up wherever she was, sort of accidentally on purpose going into the same pub or café.'

'You mean like a stalker?'

'Erm . . . I don't think it was *quite* that bad, but enough to make her feel uncomfortable.'

'Did she report it to the police?'

'I don't think so,' Joyce replied. 'But yesterday, when her colleagues heard what had happened, they rang and spoke to someone on the investigating team. That's why they've taken this Harry bloke in for questioning. It sounds like he could be the killer.'

'We'd better not jump to conclusions,' Violet said. 'We don't know the facts, and we don't know the man.'

'True, but you have to admit, it sounds iffy . . . like he was infatuated with Angeline. Surely it's no coincidence that she's turned up dead?'

Violet shuddered. 'We'll have to wait and see if the police charge him. They'll only do that if there's hard evidence against him.'

'I bet they'll find some kind of proof,' Joyce said. 'DNA or some other type of forensics, or an eyewitness?'

'Only if he's guilty,' Violet said.

Joyce sipped her coffee. 'It sounds to me like you think he might be innocent.'

Violet shook her head and smiled. 'I'm keeping an open mind, that's all.'

'Do you have any other suspects tucked away in that open mind of yours?'

'I've not given it any serious thought. Mainly because I've been told in no uncertain terms by DS Winterton to keep out of his investigation.'

'Even so . . .' Joyce nudged her. 'You're the one who found the body. You're bound to be curious.'

Violet looked around the busy café. 'I do have a theory,' she said. 'But it's probably best if I keep it to myself.'

'Spoilsport,' Joyce said, her eyes twinkling inquisitively. 'Are you sure you don't want to share? Two heads are better than one, you know.'

Violet glanced right and left and behind her. The people on the adjacent tables were busy tucking into all-day breakfasts and were deep in conversations of their own. There was nothing to stop her airing her theory – and Joyce did have a lot of local knowledge. She'd be a good sounding board. She might even put forward a few theories of her own.

'It crossed my mind,' Violet said, keeping her voice low, 'that whoever murdered Angeline might have thought they were killing Leonie. The two of them were very much alike . . . strikingly so.'

Joyce seesawed her head as she considered the possibility. 'They were alike,' she said, 'but only from a distance. The similarities were superficial . . . the same long, blonde hair, and a similar build – but close up, Angeline was much younger, considerably more youthful.'

'What if the killer didn't get a proper look?' Violet said. 'Angeline was stabbed from behind on a dark autumn morning. Maybe it was a spur-of-the-moment thing, and the killer only realised their mistake after they'd struck the fatal blow?'

Joyce pursed her lips. 'Or they scarpered as soon as they'd done the deed and didn't realise they *had* made a mistake. Maybe they ran off and only discovered their error later . . . *much* later, when the police named the victim?'

Violet gave a nod. 'I like your thinking,' she said. 'I only wish I knew who the murderer might be, but I don't know enough about Leonie or Angeline to make an informed guess.'

Joyce squeezed Violet's hand. 'It's probably just as well,' she said. 'You have an enquiring mind, Violet, and I know you love a mystery, but you're better off leaving it to the police. The last time you got involved in a murder, you put yourself at risk. You need to take care.'

'You're absolutely right. Of course you are.' Violet smiled. 'Let's talk about something else. Tell me about your plans to become an author.'

Joyce chuckled self-effacingly. 'I doubt that'll ever happen,' she said. 'Although the masterclass has tickled my fancy. It was fascinating listening to Leonie talk about the writing process . . . before the session came to an abrupt end, that is. We were less than an hour into the lesson when the police came and took her away.'

Violet cringed. So much for changing the subject.

'Sorry,' she said. 'I should have asked about something else . . . a topic that didn't bring the conversation straight back to the murder.'

Joyce held up a hand. 'No, I'm glad you asked,' she said. 'It's a shame the class was cancelled, but it wasn't a complete write-off. As well as a full refund, we've been given copies of the handouts Leonie had prepared. I've had a quick skim through them and, I must confess, I do feel inspired to have a go at writing something . . .'

'Fiction or non-fiction?' Violet asked.

'Fiction, I think. A short story, maybe. Some of the people at the class were even talking about setting up a creative writing group in Merrywell. If that idea materialises, I'll definitely go along.'

'Were there many locals there then? At the workshop?'

'I'd say about half of the attendees were from the village. Molly Gee was there, and the guy from the garden centre . . . you know, the one with the teeth? Karen Avery was there as well, as were Rosemary and Saffy Dalloway.'

'Dalloway?' Violet said. 'Any relation to Rupert Dalloway?'

'Rosemary is his ex-wife,' Joyce said. 'And Saffy is their spoilt and very supercilious daughter. I'm not sure why *she* was there. From what I've read and heard, she's an idle little madam. I can't imagine her becoming a novelist, unless she intends employing a ghost writer.'

'You said Karen Avery was there?' Violet said. 'I met her on Friday, just before the interview. She turned up at the green room, hoping to invite Leonie for a meal. Did she get the chance to ask her about it, at the workshop, before Leonie was called away?'

'Not that I heard,' Joyce said. 'While we were waiting, Karen did make a big point of telling everyone that she and Leonie had been pals at school – but when Leonie finally arrived, she pretty much blanked Karen.'

'I bet that didn't go down well.'

'You're right,' Joyce replied. 'To be honest, it was a funny kind of atmosphere all round. Karen went very quiet. I think she must have been embarrassed or overwhelmed, or something. She was probably annoyed that Leonie hadn't embraced her like the best buddy she'd made her out to be.'

Violet smiled. 'It sounds as though she and Leonie have very different recollections of their so-called friendship.'

'Aye, so it would seem,' Joyce said, nodding sagely. 'What was it that famous artist once said . . . you know, the one with the weird, upturned moustache?'

'Salvador Dalí?'

'Yes, that's him. He said something about memories being like jewels . . . that it's the false ones that always seem more real and brilliant.'

Violet nodded, impressed with Joyce's ability to conjure up an appropriate quote.

'The question is,' she said, 'when it comes to Leonie and Karen, whose memory is true and whose is false?'

As Violet and Joyce finished their coffees and discussed the remaining festival events, two things happened simultaneously. Matthew appeared on the right, approaching from the direction of the bakery; and from the left, Paul entered the café through the main door.

If she'd been sitting at a proper table, Violet would have been tempted to duck underneath it. As it was, she had no choice but to sit and watch as the paths of the two men converged.

The pair of them came to a standstill behind her, both speaking at once, using different words to say the same thing.

'Here you are,' Paul said.

'This is where you're hiding,' said Matthew.

The two men turned to each other, their expressions puzzled.

'Matthew, this is Paul,' said Violet. 'Paul, this is my friend Matthew, and this is his mum, Joyce.'

Paul thrust out an arm and shook hands with both mother and son.

'Hello,' he said. 'I wondered if I'd get to meet any of Violet's new friends and neighbours.'

Matthew smiled politely, looking sideways at Violet, as if to say: *help me out here . . . who* is *this guy*?

Before Violet had a chance to offer an explanation, Paul opened his mouth and spoke again.

'I'm Violet's husband . . .'

'*Ex*-husband,' Violet corrected.

'I'm here for the festival,' Paul continued, staring directly at Matthew. 'Didn't I see you just now . . . at the Clive Kitchner event?'

'You did,' Matthew said, his shoulders stiffening slightly. 'It was a great session. Did you buy his latest book?'

'Already got it,' Paul said, sounding horribly smug. 'Read it last week.'

Matthew gave a perfunctory nod. When he replied, his voice sounded flat and stolid.

'Right,' he said. 'Nice one.'

Violet tried to catch Matthew's eye, but he was looking in every direction but hers. During the uncomfortable silence that followed, Joyce got to her feet.

'It's lovely to meet you, Paul, but you're going to have to excuse me,' she said. 'I need to be making tracks. My next event starts in a few minutes.'

'Maybe we'll run into each other again,' Paul replied. 'The next time I'm in Merrywell.'

Next time? Violet felt her hackles rise. If she had her way, there wouldn't be a next time.

'Hang fire, Mum. I'll come with you,' Matthew said. 'See you, Violet. Good to meet you, Paul.'

'I'll text you,' Violet said to Matthew's retreating back.

He raised a hand, but didn't turn round.

A heaviness settled in her stomach. She glared at Paul, her eyes burning into his. 'What do you think you're doing?' she said.

'What do you mean?'

'You know perfectly well.' She waggled her head and mimicked Paul's voice. '*I'm Violet's husband.* What did you say that for? We've been divorced for eighteen months.'

'Force of habit, I suppose,' Paul said. 'Chill out, Vi. No harm done. I'm going to go and grab some food. What do you fancy?'

He brought her another coffee and a toasted cheese and ham panini.

'There's a talk by a true crime author in half an hour,' Paul said. 'I thought I'd go along. Do you fancy joining me? It's your kind of thing.'

'You're OK,' Violet said, as she struggled to eat her sandwich. 'I've had enough of true crime for one week.'

'Oh, yeah. Sorry. Bit insensitive of me. I should have thought.'

'Actually, I think I'll go and do some work for a couple of hours.'

'In your office, you mean? I saw *The Memory Box* when I had a wander earlier. I'll come with you. You can show me round.'

What is wrong with him? Violet thought. *Why is he following me around like a puppy?*

'Honestly, Paul, there's nothing much to see,' she said, hoping to shake him off without reigniting hostilities. 'And I really do have work to do. You should go to the true crime session. I'll see you later.'

She drained her coffee and stood up, abandoning her half-eaten panini.

'Aren't you going to stay and finish your sandwich?' Paul said.

'I'm not hungry.'

'OK.' He seemed miffed, refusing to look her in the eyes.

'I'll see you back at the cottage, yeah?'

'All right.' He picked up the untouched half of her panini and transferred it to his own plate. 'Catch you later.'

Oh, jolly d! thought Violet. *What a memorable weekend this is turning into.*

Chapter 20

As she exited the café, a message pinged onto her phone from Eric Nash.

> Judith Talbot's just been into the bookshop to give me a dressing-down. Apparently, the police have questioned her about why she didn't want Leonie Stanwick at the book festival, and she thinks it's me who grassed her up.

Violet wondered how this weekend could get any worse.

> Oh no! Sorry, Eric. It was me who mentioned Judith's name to the police.

His reply arrived as Violet weaved her way across the courtyard.

> I guessed that, but I wasn't going to snitch on you, was I?

It was exceedingly kind of Eric not to blow her cover, but it wasn't fair that he should take the blame on her account.

I'll have a word with Judith. Set the record straight. Do you know if she's still in the shopping village?

Eric replied instantly.

You don't have to do that.

Yes, Eric. I do. It's not fair that you should get the flak for something I've done. Do you know where she went?

Violet spun around, scanning the crowds in the courtyard as she waited for his reply.

When she left the bookshop, she shot off in the direction of the deli – but really, you don't need to say anything. I'm quite happy to take one for the team.

As she read the message, Violet spotted Judith coming out of *The Epicurious*. She was carrying an old-fashioned wicker shopping basket, which was piled high with an assortment of edible goodies.

'Judith.' Violet waved her over. 'Might I have a word?'

'Of course,' Judith replied, closing the gap between them. 'What can I do for you?'

Steeling herself, Violet plunged straight in. This was going to be a difficult conversation. The sooner it was over, the better.

'I understand the police have spoken to you.'

Judith adjusted her red-framed spectacles, pushing them onto the bridge of her nose.

'A serious crime has been committed,' she said, a note of defensive haughtiness in her voice. 'I imagine they're speaking to a lot of people.'

'I'm sure you're right,' Violet said. 'But if they *have* questioned you, I just wanted to say . . . for the record . . . that it was me who mentioned your name to the police. Not Eric.'

'*You?*' Judith scrunched up her face, causing her glasses to slide down her nose again. She peered over the top of them and glared. 'Why on earth would you do such a thing?'

'When I found the body, I was under the misapprehension that the victim was Leonie Stanwick,' Violet explained. 'The police asked whether I knew of anyone who was unhappy about Leonie being in the village. I'd heard you talking with Eric in the bookshop . . . objecting to Leonie's appearance at the festival – so, feeling under pressure, I gave them your name; although I made it clear you couldn't possibly have been involved in any crime.'

Judith's face was turning the colour of pickled beetroot. 'That was big of you,' she said, her voice dripping with cynicism. 'If you were so convinced I wasn't involved, why did you give my name to the police? And why were you listening in to my private conversation with Eric anyway?'

Violet sucked air through her teeth and squirmed. So much for confession being good for the soul.

'I was up in the reading nook,' she said. 'I couldn't help overhearing.'

Judith sniffed. 'A politer person would have made their presence known,' she said.

Violet smiled apologetically. 'I'm sorry if I've caused you a problem – but I guess the police have to pursue all sorts of leads during the course of an investigation.'

'I can assure you, they won't be pursuing me,' Judith said, transferring her shopping basket from one arm to another. 'As I told the detective, my objection to Leonie Stanwick's presence at the festival was based purely on literary merit – or lack of. There was nothing more to it than that.'

'I didn't for one minute think there was,' Violet said.

'In that case, you should have kept your nose out of my

business,' Judith said, her tone icy cold. 'I have a lot of influence in this village, Violet. Trust me, you don't want to make an enemy of me.'

And with that, the councillor stuck her nose in the air and marched out of the courtyard, leaving Violet no alternative but to slink back towards *The Memory Box* feeling justifiably chastened.

Violet sat at her desk and made a concerted effort to shut Judith out of her thoughts, only to find her mind drifting back to Paul. Why was she feeling so annoyed with him? So incensed? Was it his assumption that he could turn up unannounced and expect her to spend almost every waking minute in his company? Did he not realise she had a new life now, a different circle of friends?

And why the hell had he introduced himself as her *husband*? What was that all about? Was he telling the truth when he'd said it was force of habit . . . a slip of the tongue? Or had he done it on purpose, in a peevish attempt to warn off Matthew? And, even if he had, why should that bother her? It wasn't as if she and Matthew were romantically involved. They were just friends. Close friends.

Violet recalled the look of confusion on Matthew's face as he'd stood in the café. Why was she so concerned about him getting the wrong idea about Paul's presence in Merrywell? Could it be that she wanted more from Matthew than friendship? During her break-up with Paul, Violet had sworn off relationships – but had she begun to let her guard down lately?

Her deliberations were interrupted by the piercing ring of her phone. The screen showed a number she didn't recognise. She hesitated, wondering if it was a scammer, hoping to rip her off. The too-jolly ringtone sounded for a second time, then a third. On the fourth ring, Violet picked up the phone.

'Hello?' she said, her voice cautious.

'Is that Violet?'

'Yes. Who's this?'

'It's Leonie Stanwick.'

Violet got to her feet and began to pace (not an easy feat in the limited confines of *The Memory Box*).

'Leonie . . .' she said. 'I didn't realise you had my number.'

'I got it from your business card,' Leonie replied. 'I took one from your desk when I called in yesterday. I hope you don't mind.'

'No, of course not,' Violet said. 'That's what they're there for.'

'I don't like bothering you at the weekend, but I thought you'd want to know that the police have taken someone in for questioning,' Leonie said.

'Yes, I had heard.'

'The family liaison officer called first thing this morning to update me. She says it's someone Angeline used to work with.'

'Right . . .' Violet said, not letting on that she already knew that. 'And do you know if they're planning to charge him?'

'I sincerely hope not,' Leonie said. 'You see, I have a horrible feeling they've got the wrong man.'

Violet stopped pacing and sat down again.

Leonie sighed. 'Quite honestly, my faith in DS Winterton is fading fast,' she said, sounding tired and disillusioned. 'It seems to me he's looking for an easy solution to what could well turn out to be a complex case.'

Violet felt an incomprehensible need to defend Charlie Winterton. 'I know he might not come across as particularly dynamic,' she said. 'But I've dealt with him before, and he is a good detective. Don't be put off by his scruffy appearance. Underneath that unkempt exterior lies a clever, if somewhat stubborn mind.'

'I'll have to take your word for that,' Leonie said. 'The problem is, I think he's stubbornly pursuing the wrong line of inquiry. I've been giving a lot of thought to what you said . . . about me being the killer's *real* target? I think you might be right. There were things that happened in the past . . . stuff that may be coming back to bite me. Lord knows, I've upset enough people over the years.'

'Stuff?' Violet felt her stomach lurch. Something told her this murder investigation was far from over. 'What kind of stuff? Have you talked to DS Winterton about this?'

'I've talked to him at length,' Leonie said. 'About everything. I've given him plenty of reasons to look for a culprit elsewhere, but he seems fixated on this colleague of Angeline's. He's convinced he's guilty.'

'Has he got any proof to connect this man to the murder?' Violet asked.

'I don't know. He wouldn't say. I shouldn't imagine he's allowed to.'

'I suppose it'll all come out in the wash,' Violet said. 'If this guy *is* innocent and he can prove it, the police will have to let him go. For all we know, he could have a rock-solid alibi.'

'But what if he hasn't? What if he was home alone and there's no one to vouch for him at the time the murder was committed?'

'Then a lot will depend on what other evidence the police have,' Violet said. 'What about forensics? Do you know if anything was found at the crime scene?'

'The family liaison officer told me the forensic side of things is proving difficult,' Leonie said, sounding exasperated. 'There are several footpaths around the hotel grounds and trails through the woods and fields . . . all of them open to the public. Apparently, there are hundreds of muddy footprints in the immediate area. Finding traces of the killer in the car park is going to be like looking for a needle in a haystack.'

'I take it there weren't any fingerprints on the murder weapon?' Violet said.

'No, it would seem not. The knife used was a German brand . . . expensive, but not uncommon.'

'What about the Audi?' Violet said. 'Have they found any prints or trace DNA on the door handles or bodywork?'

'Not that I'm aware of,' Leonie replied. 'The car's still being examined by the forensic team.'

'Are the police considering car theft or robbery as a motive?' Violet asked.

'I don't think they've completely ruled out car theft, but when Angeline was found, she was wearing a ring that used to belong to my mother, and her phone was in her pocket – so it definitely wasn't robbery.'

Violet let out a sigh. 'We have to trust that the police know what they're doing,' she said. 'One way or another, I'm sure they'll find out what happened.'

'You reckon?' Leonie released a groan of frustration. 'How long's that going to take?'

'I understand you want answers, Leonie, but it's only been a day. You have to be patient. Murder investigations can take months.'

'I realise that,' she replied. 'But what if my life *is* in danger? If your theory is correct, and I'm the killer's real target, what's to stop him or her from trying again?'

'If you're worried about your safety, you should speak to DS Winterton or whoever's in charge of the case. If the police think you're at risk, they'll give you protection.'

'I think the best way to protect myself is to go back to London,' Leonie said. 'If anything's going to happen to me, instinct tells me it'll be here in Merrywell.'

'What makes you say that?'

'I think someone may be rattled . . . about things that have happened in the past. And that's why I'd like to hire your services.'

'*My* services?' Violet frowned. 'I'm sorry, Leonie. I don't know what you've been told, but I'm not a private investigator.'

'I know that,' she said. 'What I'd like you to do is interview me.'

Violet gave a puzzled frown. 'Haven't I already done that? For the festival?'

Leonie laughed mirthlessly. 'It's not my books, or my writing I want to discuss this time. You told me you record family histories? It's in *that* capacity I'd like to engage your services. I want to put on record all the things I didn't allow you to ask about at our last interview. It's time I told my story . . . the whole story, about my early life in Merrywell, and my relationship with my parents and Angeline.'

'Won't all of that be included in the autobiography you're writing?' Violet asked.

'It will – but finishing that is going to take time. I need to find a speedier way to spill my guts. If Angeline's murder was triggered by my coming back to Merrywell, I need to get everything out in the open. I want to go on record – not for public consumption, at least not yet – but more as a kind of insurance policy, in case anything happens to me.'

'If you genuinely believe your life is in danger, you should alert DS Winterton.'

'I already have,' Leonie said. 'I've also filled him in on the things I intend to talk to you about – but I don't think he has the time or imagination to make sense of it all. As far as he's concerned, my past is irrelevant. What I need is someone who can sift through those irrelevancies . . . winnow the wheat from the chaff, so to speak. That's where you come in.'

'What exactly do you want me to do?'

'Eric Nash told me you have a talent for sniffing out the truth,' Leonie said. 'The answer to why Angeline was killed could well lie in the secrets I never talk about. I want you to listen to my story, and ask questions. Can you do that? Whatever the going rate is, I'll pay it.'

Violet weighed up Leonie's proposition. If she agreed to do this, it would almost certainly infuriate DS Winterton. Then again, he could hardly stop her undertaking what would, in effect, be a business transaction. And if interviewing Leonie did help to solve Angeline's murder, that had to be a good thing. Didn't it?

'OK,' Violet said. 'I'll do it. Let's fix a date for early next week. Do you have your diary handy?'

'Diary? Are you serious?' Leonie said. 'If I *am* the killer's real target, I might not be around by next week. I need to get this done *now*. Today. There's no time to waste.'

Chapter 21

They agreed to meet at the Hammond family home an hour later. Violet started to have misgivings, even as she packed her camera and recording equipment into the boot of her car.

The light in the sky was fading as she drove out of the village and turned into Stanton Lane – which was narrow and winding, with high hawthorn hedges on both sides. Almost a mile out of Merrywell, she spotted the sign she was looking for: *Birch House*. Violet braked and steered her car through the open gate and onto the driveway.

The house was large and solid. Built of stone, it was set back from the road and surrounded by fields. Violet sat and peered at it through the windscreen, wondering at the things that had happened within those grey, substantial walls. Leaving her car next to the garage at the side, she walked around to the front door.

Leonie was already waiting for her on the front step.

'Thanks for coming at such short notice,' she said. 'Especially on a Sunday. I appreciate you've probably had to change your plans.'

A trail of rose-scented perfume lingered in the air as Leonie led Violet into the house, down a central hallway into a newly refurbished kitchen.

'Are you staying here? At the house?' Violet said.

'No, I'm still at the hotel,' Leonie replied. 'I got a taxi over here this morning to sort through a few things, but I can't bring myself to stay overnight.'

'We could go back to the hotel and do the interview there, if you'd prefer,' Violet offered.

'No, I'd like to do it here. It seems fitting, somehow. I was born in this house, so it's where my story began.'

'Fine.' Violet smiled. 'I'll get set up and we'll make a start.'

'While you're doing that, I'll make a drink. Tea? Coffee?'

'Coffee, please. White, no sugar.'

As Leonie opened and closed cupboards in a search for mugs, Violet fixed her camera to a tripod and checked the ambient light with a meter.

'Do you want me to film in here?' she asked. 'Or would you like to do the interview in another room?'

'Let's do it here,' Leonie replied. 'The kitchen's the best room in the house. It was only refitted a few weeks ago.'

'I can tell,' Violet said, breathing in. 'It still has that "new" smell.'

'It breaks my heart to think Angeline won't be around to enjoy it,' Leonie said, casting her eyes over the glossy units and high-end appliances. 'She inherited the house from my mother, and made up her mind to stay, even though the place needed a lot of work. My parents hadn't made any real improvements for decades. They had a "waste not, want not" attitude to life, preferring to maintain things, rather than change them . . . including the status quo.'

She poured boiling water into a cafetière and carried it over to the central kitchen island.

'Let's get going then,' Violet said, as she switched on her camera and sound recorder. 'This is your story, so start wherever you like and tell it in your own way . . . at your own pace. If I think something needs clarifying, I'll butt in with a question or a prompt. Otherwise, I'm going to sit back, listen and record.'

Leonie smiled nervously, tucked her hair behind her ears,

and adjusted the turquoise-coloured silk scarf that was draped around her neck.

'Right then,' she said, as she poured the coffee and took a sip. 'I suppose I may as well start at the beginning.

'I was born in the upstairs bedroom of this house in 1970. At the time, my parents had been married for a little under a year. They met at work . . . a factory in Ambergate. Dad was a production supervisor there, and my mother was a typist – in the days of secretaries and manual typewriters. She left her job when she was seven months pregnant with me, and never went back. In the years that followed, money was often short, but Mum refused to go out to work. She was one of the last of the generation that thought a woman's place was in the home, taking care of the kids and the house.'

Leonie paused briefly as she gathered her thoughts.

'I can sum up the early years of my childhood in two words,' she continued. '*Unremarkable* and *uninteresting*. I never went short of much, but I was a solitary kid. I don't know if my parents *wanted* more children and it never happened, or if they chose not to bother – I didn't have the courage to ask. All I know is, growing up here as an only child was a lonely experience. It wouldn't have been so bad if we'd lived closer to the centre of the village. That way, I could have played out with the other kids . . . but I was isolated here. Very much so.

'For years my father didn't own a car – I don't think he could afford one. He used to walk half a mile across the fields to the main road, and catch the bus to work, and then half a mile back again in the evenings. It kept him fit. My mother used to say he was as *fit as a butcher's dog*. In marked contrast, she spent all her time cooking and baking, and then eating whatever it was she'd made. She didn't socialise much, but that didn't bother her. She was happy in her own company.

'I, on the other hand, was a gregarious child. I loved being at school, surrounded by friends. I suppose it compensated for the lack of playmates at home. Occasionally, I'd be invited to someone's house after school, for tea. The trouble was, I could never reciprocate. An invite to Birch House would have entailed walking back with me from the village school, trekking through the fields in all weathers. No one seemed very keen to do that. And, of course, because Dad didn't have a car, he wouldn't have been able to drive them home afterwards, which was kind of expected, even back then.

'My inability to bring friends home to Birch House put me at a distinct disadvantage at school. It meant I had to work extra hard to be popular.'

'But you did make friends?' Violet asked.

'Masses of them. I went out of my way to be sociable. I talked far too much at school, even during lessons. And if anything, my inability to get involved in out-of-school activities created a certain cachet. People were intrigued by me; they saw me as enigmatic and mysterious – although, actually, nothing could have been further from the truth.'

Violet smiled. 'My friend, Matthew Collis, remembers you from secondary school,' she said. 'He told me . . . and I quote . . . you were *popular, and clever without being swotty*.'

Leonie threw her head back and laughed. Then, as if remembering her bereavement, her smile evaporated.

'I remember Matthew,' she said. 'But only vaguely. As I recall, he was a year or two younger than me, so I don't suppose I took much notice of him.'

'Tell me about Karen Avery,' Violet said. 'Is there any truth to her claim that the two of you were best friends?'

Leonie raised her eyes heavenwards. 'We were never that,' she said. 'My best friend at secondary school was Zoe . . . Zoe Corndale. Karen was more of a hanger-on. And if our class *did* have a swot, it was definitely Karen. She was highly intelligent and exceptionally gifted, but she lacked self-confidence. She lived on a dairy farm, and her parents never encouraged her to achieve academically. From an early age, Karen was expected to help out on the farm, before and after school. Her mum and dad never liked it when she stayed on after school for the study groups. The poor kid had high hopes, but I don't think her lofty ambitions ever came to anything. As far as I know, she left school after her A levels and went to work full-time on the family farm.'

'Tell me about your own ambitions,' Violet said. 'The last time we spoke, you mentioned you wanted to become a lawyer. What changed your mind?'

Leonie pressed her palms together in a praying gesture.

'Something happened,' she said, lowering her fingers and pointing them towards Violet. 'Something that changed everything.'

Chapter 22

'It was a secret that my parents took to their graves,' Leonie continued. 'But before I tell you about it, I need to backtrack a little, to my last years at school. Like I said, I had a lot of friends, and a few boyfriends too. I was young, carefree, learning about life. It was an exhilarating time, especially when Rupert Dalloway came onto the scene.'

'He was the guy at the festival?' Violet said, pleased that Leonie was finally opening up properly. 'The one who asked about your one true love?'

'That's him.' Leonie smiled inscrutably. 'You know . . . I didn't recognise him at first, even when he put his hand up to ask a question. But when I heard him speak . . . that's when I knew. His voice transported me straight back to 1988 . . . to a time of love and excitement and heartbreak. Rupert was my first love . . . my *only* love.'

'It sounds as if you're still smitten,' Violet said. 'Tell me about him.'

Laughing, Leonie bowed her head for a moment. 'He was very good-looking when he was young,' she said. 'But other than that, he wasn't exactly love's young dream. In fact, he was only at my school because he'd been expelled from an expensive private college.

He joined the upper sixth a few weeks into the first term – and he arrived with a reputation. He was a rebel and a prankster who utterly refused to take life or his studies seriously. I suspect his parents had reached the end of their tether with him. They were furious that he'd got himself expelled – apparently it wasn't the first time he'd been chucked out of a fancy school – and they were mortified he was finishing his education at the local comp.

'At first, I kept out of his way. I was in the lower sixth and I suppose I was wary of him. I'd acted up myself plenty of times during my teens, but unlike Rupert, I always knew when to rein it in. My studies mattered to me, and I wasn't going to do anything that would jeopardise my exam results. I was *desperate* to leave home and get out of Merrywell, and going to university was my only viable escape plan.

'Life with my parents was mind-numbingly boring. They provided for me, and loved me in their own way, but they were staid and unadventurous. I was "climbing the walls", biding my time, waiting to get out of there. I'd mapped out my whole future: I was going to become a hotshot lawyer and leave Merrywell forever.'

'So, what happened?' Violet said.

Leonie gripped her scarf and pressed it against her neck.

'Rupert and I began seeing each other, in secret,' she said.

'Why did it have to be a secret?'

'Because his parents had read him the riot act. They didn't like him being at the local school, but they knew it was his last chance. They spelled everything out . . . warned him about getting distracted . . . told him he had to focus on his studies and *only* his studies. They definitely wouldn't have approved of him fraternising with a girl, especially a local girl.'

'That all sounds rather pompous and overbearing,' Violet said. 'Even if they did have their son's best interests at heart.'

'Believe me, Rupert's parents were guilty of the worst kind of snobbery. They were rich, *very* rich, and Rupert was their eldest child. Everything they owned would be his one day, and they were determined he was going to mix with the "right" kind of people.'

Violet frowned. 'It sounds like something from a Jane Austen novel,' she said. 'I didn't realise that kind of outdated thinking existed anymore.'

'It did in the late Eighties – at least as far as the Dalloways were concerned. Their airs and graces and disdain for those they considered beneath them knew no bounds. They were a ridiculous couple. Horrible, horrible people.'

'And that's why you had to keep your relationship with Rupert a secret?'

'Yes. It didn't bother me at first. What we had initially was nothing more than a flirtation . . . a reckless adventure . . . a forbidden romance.'

Violet grinned. 'Sounds like something out of one of your books.'

Leonie shook her head. 'My novels always have a happy ending. That's not how things worked out for Rupert and me.

'While we were both still at school, we'd meet in secret after lessons. If we were feeling daring, we'd go to one of the cafés in Matlock or Bakewell. We were spotted a couple of times, and eventually the kids at school put two and two together, although we neither confirmed nor denied our relationship.

'I like to think I was a good influence on Rupert, because at the end of the school year, he managed to pass his exams and get a place at university. He chose Nottingham, mainly because it wasn't a million miles from Merrywell. We continued to meet up every few weeks. I had to catch two buses to go and see him, but it was worth it.

'I won't embarrass you with the exact details of our affair. Suffice to say, the two of us went from hanging around together, having a bit of fun . . . to being madly, passionately in love. It was all very intense. And on top of being in the throes of love, I was also in my last year at school, studying like mad to get as many A grades as I could.

'It was around that time that Zoe and I cultivated a "friendship" with Karen Avery. We'd go over to her parents' farm most Saturdays, and study together. Her mum and dad weren't particularly enamoured with our little bookish study group, but they tolerated it because it kept Karen at home, and on hand to look after her little brother if required. The study group also provided me with a ready-made excuse for being absent from home on Saturdays. On the occasions I went over to Nottingham to see Rupert, my parents assumed I was at the Avery farm. They never questioned it.'

'What about Zoe and Karen? What did they think when you didn't show up? Did you tell them the truth about where you were going?'

'No, although I came close to it a few times. All I ever said was that I had to be somewhere, and if my parents ever asked, they were to say I'd been with them. I think they both had their suspicions, but neither of them had the gumption to quiz me about it. In fact, the ruse worked like a charm. My parents assumed I was at the farm, studying hard; and Zoe and Karen kept schtum, probably because they thought my absence would give them a chance to get ahead in their studies. Everyone in my year group was frantically swotting up.

'Things became massively competitive in that last year because there was a bursary up for grabs, sponsored by a local company. To be in the running, you had to be the first member of your family to go to university . . . to be honest, most of the sixth form met the criteria. The top-performing pupil in the qualifying group – the one who got the highest grades – was promised £4,000 towards a university education. That might not sound much in today's terms, but it was a hell of a lot of money back then. It was the dangling carrot that kept us focused on our studies.'

'And who won the bursary?' Violet asked.

Leonie smiled proudly. 'I did,' she said. 'I was up against some strong opposition, including Zoe and Karen, but I crammed like mad for my exams, and I won the bursary by a whisker. As you can imagine, I was over the moon. Even my parents couldn't hide their delight.

'Life stepped up a gear after that. Everything started to get serious. I was offered a place at Durham – which, as I'm sure you're aware, is a very prestigious university. It was a long way from Nottingham, but that didn't matter because Rupert and I were in love, and we'd promised each other it would stay that way. As soon as we'd both graduated, he said he'd talk to his parents . . . tell them about us.'

'It sounds like you had a bright future ahead of you,' Violet said. 'Both academically and romantically.'

Leonie leaned back and took a deep breath. 'It was good,' she said. 'While it lasted.'

'What went wrong?'

'Two things,' Leonie said. 'First up, Rupert's parents found out about us.'

'Oh.' Violet grimaced. 'How did that happen?'

'It was the end of September, and Rupert had gone back for his second year at uni. I wasn't due to start my first year until the following week, so I went over to spend the day with him in Nottingham. We knew we wouldn't see much of each other for a while, so we wanted to make the most of our time together. Rupert had moved into a shared house, and – wouldn't you know it – his sister chose that same day to roll up, unannounced. Looking back, I think she'd guessed that something was going on, but at the time she said she only wanted to see Rupert's new accommodation. Of course, when she found *me* there, it all kicked off. She wanted to know exactly what was going on, and how long it had been going on for. We were completely honest with her – we didn't really have much choice – and Rupert begged her not to say anything.'

'But she did?' said Violet.

'You betcha. She went straight home . . . couldn't wait to snitch on us. She'd always been jealous of her brother, so I imagine she took great pleasure in dropping him in it. Naturally, there was an inquisition, and the Dalloways told Rupert in no uncertain terms that he had to stop seeing me.'

'But he was an adult,' Violet said. 'Old enough to choose his own girlfriend, surely?'

'In theory, yes, but Rupert's parents put him in an impossible position. They made it clear that if he chose me, they'd cut off his allowance and withdraw the financial support they were providing to get him through uni. As their eldest child, he was also in line to inherit . . . but they said that wouldn't happen either, unless he toed the line. They held all the cards, and Rupert had no choice but to play by their rules.'

'Why did they feel the need to be so cruel and malicious?' Violet asked.

Leonie gave a cynical laugh. 'I suspect it was something in the Dalloway DNA that compelled them to act that way,' she replied. 'As far as they were concerned, they were behaving perfectly reasonably.

'Rupert rang to tell me about his parents' ultimatum just as I was finishing my first week at Durham. Their lack of humanity was hard for us to come to terms with. We were both incredulous and heartbroken – but we agreed the best thing to do was to cool things a little, in the hope they might, eventually, change their minds. Rupert said we just had to wait it out, take things slowly.

'So, that's what we decided to do . . . and, who knows . . . things might have worked out, eventually. But then I discovered I was pregnant and all hell broke loose.'

Chapter 23

Violet was dumbstruck. Of all the things Leonie could have revealed, this was one scenario she hadn't anticipated.

'Pregnant?' she said, repeating the word to check she hadn't misheard.

Leonie gave a sad smile. 'Yes,' she said. 'Not exactly the news you want to hear when you've just started your degree, is it? I was in denial at first, but it wasn't a situation I could ignore indefinitely.'

'What did Rupert say when you told him?'

'He was scared . . . and not just about what his parents would say either. He found the prospect of parenthood completely and utterly terrifying. We were both so young, and we were students. We weren't ready. The situation was a nightmare . . . a complete mess.

'It was all weighing heavily on my mind, and I desperately needed support . . . from Rupert and my parents . . . but they let me down. Every single one of them.

'When I rang to tell my mother the news, she took it upon herself to go behind my back and put the Dalloways in the picture. They asked her to go and see them at their home – Langdale Hall – and Rupert was also summoned to their little confab. I only found out about it later. Even though I had the lead role in the drama they were discussing, they didn't think to invite me along.

'I have no idea what was said. All I know is, the Dalloways and my mother conspired behind my back, and hatched a plan without consulting me. Rupert was told to stop answering my calls.

'When he stopped communicating with me, I didn't know what to do. I was anxious and frantic, and utterly lost. Then, when I was at my lowest ebb, my mother turned up at my halls of residence and took control.'

Violet sat, transfixed, as the camera continued to roll.

'Before I tell you what happened, I want you to understand that I was completely out of my depth,' Leonie said. 'My rock-solid future had turned to quicksand beneath my feet, and I was sinking fast. I was afraid . . . terrified . . . but despite everything, there was never any question in my mind about having the baby. Even so, I had to face the truth. I was eighteen and, despite my bravado, I was naïve and inexperienced. My mother and I had never been one for a lot of hugging, but when she arrived on my doorstep at uni, I fell into her arms and sobbed with relief.

'My life was shattering into pieces. Rupert had cut me off, my dream place at university was about to come to a premature end, and I was facing the prospect of going back home to Merrywell and becoming a mother. I knew that if I did that, I'd never find the strength to escape again, but I also accepted I had very little choice.

'Which is why I was so dumbfounded when my mother outlined what was going to happen. She told me she'd already sounded out the university, and they'd agreed, in principle, that I could postpone my studies for a year. She said that's what I *had* to do.

'I couldn't believe she wanted me to continue with my degree. The fact that it was even a possibility gave me a brief flicker of hope, but then, as Mother continued to spell out her carefully thought-out plan, I realised what she was actually giving me were unspeakably limited options.

'Of course, she didn't bother asking what *I* wanted. She *told* me what was going to happen, like I had no other choice. She said I'd let her down, and that she and Dad didn't want me back in Merrywell. *When you came here to university, you took great pleasure in telling us you were leaving home for good*, she said. *You can't change your mind now. There's no going back for you. Your home isn't in Merrywell, not anymore.* And then she laid it all bare for me . . . explained exactly how things were going to pan out.'

Tears were trickling down Leonie's face, and she was stumbling over her words, as if speaking them was causing intense pain.

'I'm told you have an analytical mind, Violet,' she said. 'Have you worked it out yet?'

Violet's mind was spinning, processing what Leonie had told her, shuffling everything into a logical order. Slowly, as the pieces of the puzzle settled into place, it all began to make sense.

'Of course,' she said, as she stared at Leonie's grief-stricken face. 'Angeline. She wasn't your sister, was she? She was your daughter.'

Chapter 24

'It's refreshing to be able to speak openly about it. I kept the secret for over thirty years, but there's no point in maintaining the charade now.' Leonie leaned back and released a long breath. 'When I was young, I tolerated my mother's machinations because I lacked the strength to fight back. Circumstances rendered me powerless: it was easier to stay silent and go along with her scheme – but things are different now.'

'So how did her "scheme" work?' Violet said.

Leonie pressed her hands together and leaned forward, staring straight into the camera lens. 'When the university broke up for the Christmas holidays, I was sent to stay with a cousin of my mother's, in Monmouth. That's where Angeline was born.'

'And throughout your pregnancy, your mother was pretending it was *her* who was having a baby?' Violet said. 'How did she pull that off?'

'After a few months, she told people she'd been advised to take bed rest, and that she was going to stay with her cousin until the baby was born.'

'Didn't anyone see through the ruse?' Violet asked.

'No – mainly because my parents were an antisocial pair. They didn't have friends or anyone who might have asked awkward questions.'

'And what story were the Dalloways given?'

'When Angeline was born, Rupert and his parents were told she'd been adopted. As far as they were concerned, the problem had gone away . . . swept under the carpet with the other family scandals. They cut off all communication with us; from their perspective, the situation had been satisfactorily resolved.

'When I met up with Rupert on Friday evening after the festival, he told me the Dalloways never talked about it again. Even when he got married five years later, he didn't tell his wife about me, or our baby.'

'Weren't the Dalloways suspicious when they saw your mother pushing her new "daughter" around the village?'

Leonie snorted cynically. 'The Dalloways lived on the other side of Hassop. Langdale Hall is only a few miles from here as the crow flies, but it may as well be a million miles away. Rupert and his parents rarely ventured into Merrywell. They existed in a privileged bubble, mixing only with those in the upper echelons of an elite hierarchy.

'As for Rupert, he moved to Glasgow after he graduated. He told me on Friday that . . . after what happened with me . . . things were never the same between him and his parents. He said the experience opened his eyes to what they were really like, and as the years rolled by, he grew more and more ashamed of how he'd treated me.'

'It sounds like the two of you had a lot to talk about,' said Violet.

'We did. I'd spoken to him after the festival and arranged to meet him later. He picked me up at the hotel and took me to Langdale Hall. He inherited the place a few years ago, after his parents died.'

'Did you tell him the truth about Angeline?'

Leonie pressed her lips together and nodded. 'I did. He was bewildered at first, angry and very hurt. He couldn't believe she'd been living so close all these years. He said he'd often thought about her . . . wondered where she was.'

'It was a lot for him to process,' Violet said. 'It must have come as a shock.'

'Initially, yes, but once the truth had sunk in, he was euphoric . . . thrilled about having another daughter. He wanted to arrange a get-together for us all. He was so excited about it. And then, the following morning, we found out . . . about Angeline . . . and everything came crashing down around us. Just as the wounds of the past had begun to heal, she'd been snatched away again – forever this time. Talk about lousy timing. Life can be very cruel sometimes.'

'Did Angeline know the truth?' said Violet.

Leonie nodded. 'She'd known for a while that I was her mother. My parents told her when she was fourteen. It was a difficult time for her . . . for all of us, especially as Angeline and I had never been close.

'From the minute Angeline was born, my mother insisted on taking responsibility for her, raising her as her own. When I handed her over, I felt utterly conflicted. Part of me was relieved, because I knew I wasn't in a position to raise a child myself. The easiest thing to do was let Mum take charge . . . assume control. But there was another, admittedly smaller part of me that was desperate to keep my baby. The trouble was, I was young and useless and very selfish. I'm ashamed to say, I didn't relish the idea of being tied down, or of giving up on my dreams. My mother's plan was the easy option, even if it did feel as though she'd somehow contrived to steal my child. The alternative – adoption – would have meant losing contact with Angeline altogether, possibly forever. On balance, I concluded that if my parents raised her, I'd at least have a chance of seeing her grow up . . . get to know her. But that was before I'd given birth to her, and held her in my arms.'

'Giving up your baby must have been heart-breaking,' Violet said.

Leonie nodded solemnly. 'I was devastated, and ashamed. Giving her away like that felt like the worst kind of betrayal – even though I was handing her over to my own parents. Angeline was so tiny and beautiful . . . so innocent. She hadn't asked to be born and, unwittingly, she'd become a pawn in an agonising game . . . a game I later decided I wasn't willing to play. When Mum took Angeline back to Merrywell, I couldn't bring myself to visit her.'

'Didn't you want to know how she was doing?' Violet asked.

'I got letters and photographs and the odd phone call,' Leonie replied. 'That was part of the deal. And of course, in her monthly updates, Mum went to great pains to let me know that Angeline was thriving. The implication was clear: *You see? She doesn't need you, Leonie.* But that wasn't the reason I stayed away.'

'So, what was?'

Leonie's eyes were brimming with tears. 'Seeing her would have been too painful. Giving up Angeline, losing Rupert . . . it was like my heart had been ripped open. I survived, but only just. Seeing my baby again would have opened wounds that had barely begun to heal.

'Once Mum and Angeline had gone back to Derbyshire, I stayed on in Wales for a while. I went even further west, to Pembrokeshire. I got a job in a restaurant in Tenby, and then at an estate agency. I liked being there . . . in West Wales. I was a long, long way from home, but I needed that distance. My head was telling me to bide my time until I could go back to Durham and rejoin university . . . but in the end, I couldn't face it. I didn't have the stomach for it. As soon as I realised that, I got on a train to London and threw myself into whatever work I could find to take my mind off things. Once in a while I'd ring home, but I never went back there . . . not for years. I couldn't bear to. Eventually, after six years in London, I got a job on the cruise liners. You already know the rest of the story, and what happened after that.'

'So why come back to Merrywell now?' Violet said. 'Why choose to tell the truth, after all these years?'

'Because it was time,' Leonie said. 'I've had my bellyful of duplicity and deceit. My father's been dead for over ten years, and my mother passed away six months ago. With them both gone, there was no need to maintain the secret. I wrote to Angeline to tell her how I felt, and explain that I'd be coming here for the festival. I asked if she'd meet me. I wanted us to get to know one another, try and make a connection. I was under no illusion it would be easy, but I was willing to try if she was. I also wanted to let her know that I was thinking of writing a biography. I didn't want to go ahead and sign a deal on that if she didn't approve.'

'How did she seem when you met?' Violet asked.

'Things were a little awkward at first,' Leonie replied. 'But we cleared the air, and started to make progress, especially after I gave her the car. You probably think I was trying to buy her affections . . . but that's not why I did it. She'd pumped all of her savings and the money she inherited from Mum into this house. The improvements cost a small fortune – which is why she's been driving around in an unreliable motor. I wanted to be kind to her and do the right thing – show her that I cared, you know? Now, I wish I hadn't. If I hadn't handed over the keys to the Audi, she wouldn't have been in that car park. She might still be alive.'

'You're not to blame for what happened,' Violet said. 'It wasn't your fault.'

'I'm not sure I agree,' Leonie replied. 'I only wish things had turned out differently. I messed everything up. All of it. I should never have let Angeline go. If I could have my time again, I'd make better choices.'

'I think most people would,' said Violet. 'It's easy to look back and wish you'd done things differently – regrets are part of what makes us human – but the truth is, we can only ever do our best in the circumstances we're facing at the time.'

'Did I do my best, though?' Leonie said. 'I put myself first. Shouldn't Angeline have been my priority?'

She buried her face in her hands and took a long, shuddering breath.

'You look exhausted,' Violet said. 'This must be emotionally draining. Would you like to take a break? Have another coffee?'

Leonie stood up and nodded. 'That's a good idea.'

While Leonie put the kettle on again, Violet switched off the camera and the audio recorder and reflected on the things she'd been told.

Out of the corner of her eye, she saw the screen of her phone light up. She usually switched it off during interviews, but today – to save time – she'd flicked it onto silent mode.

She peered at the screen to see who was trying to get hold of her. It was her neighbour, Toby. Whatever it was he wanted, it could wait.

But Toby obviously didn't agree. When his first call went unanswered, he rang back again immediately. Violet turned the phone over, placing it face down on the worktop. If it was important, he could leave a voice message.

Instead, he sent her a text, which pinged onto her phone as Leonie handed over another mug of coffee.

> URGENT!! Violet, if you're there and you see this, please call me. I can hear the smoke detector going off in your kitchen. I've been round and knocked, but no one's answering the door.

A knot of panic twisted in Violet's gut. Whatever the cause of this crisis, it had Paul's name written all over it.

She pushed the mug of coffee to one side, untouched. 'I'm sorry, Leonie,' she said. 'I hate to do this to you, but I'm going to have to dash back home for a while. My neighbour's just texted to say the smoke alarm's going off at my cottage. I don't know what the hell's going on, but I need to sort it out. I'm sorry to break off like this, especially at such a crucial point in your story. Hopefully, I'll get everything sorted quickly and be back in half an hour or so.'

'Don't worry,' Leonie said, her voice sounding less emotional now. 'I've already told you most of it anyway. Why don't you come back in the morning, and we can finish off then. Shall we say ten o'clock?'

'OK. That's fine with me,' Violet said, as she hurriedly gathered together her equipment. 'If you're sure.'

'Of course I am. *Now go!* Go and fix your smoke alarm.'

Violet threw on her coat, slung her camera bag onto her shoulder, and sprinted out to her car.

She called her neighbour as she drove home.

'Toby? What the hell's happening?' she said.

'You tell me,' he replied. 'I can see you've got a visitor, because there's a car parked on the driveway, but whoever it is isn't answering the door. Don't panic though. The house isn't on fire . . . nothing like that – although it might be if you don't get here soon.'

'Don't worry,' she said, pressing her foot to the accelerator. 'I'm on my way. I'll be there in two minutes.'

Chapter 25

When she got to Greengage Cottage, she swung her Toyota into the space behind Paul's car and ran to the back door. To her relief, it was already open, and the smoke detector had been silenced. The kitchen window was also open, and Paul was using a tea towel to waft frantically at the smoke that was drifting out of the back door.

'What the bloody hell are you playing at?' she shrieked.

Paul jumped at the sound of her voice.

'It's all right,' he said. 'Don't panic. Everything's under control.'

'It doesn't look like it to me,' Violet said, as she stepped into the smoke-filled kitchen. 'What's happened?'

'I thought I'd make myself some cheese on toast,' he said. 'I left it under the grill and went into the living room. I must have fallen asleep on the sofa.'

'Asleep!'

'I'm sorry. OK? Just, please, stop shouting.'

The smoke was clearing and, apart from a couple of charred pieces of cheese-topped bread lying on the draining board, there didn't appear to be any damage.

'My next-door neighbour's been knocking on the door,' Violet said. 'Why didn't you answer?'

'Like I said . . . I was asleep.'

He looked sheepish, and his hair was sticking out at an odd angle above his right ear.

'Have you been drinking?' Violet asked.

'I had a couple of pints, that's all.'

'A couple?'

'All right,' Paul admitted. 'Three . . . maybe four. In the end, I decided not to go to the true crime event. It seemed too much like a busman's holiday. I was going to go back to the café, but it was heaving, and I was thirsty . . . so I had a stroll to the White Hart. I was only going to stop for one . . . but then I got talking to a few people, and I ended up staying longer than planned. When I got back here, I was hungry, so I got the grill going . . . and then I must have dozed off. That beer they serve in the White Hart is strong stuff.'

Violet couldn't believe he was blaming his faux pas on the strength of the local beer. 'You do realise you're turning into the house guest from hell,' she said. 'What were you thinking . . . boozing in the afternoon?'

He stood with his head bowed and his hands in his pockets. 'I suppose I was looking for a bit of Dutch courage,' he said. 'The thing is . . . I want to talk to you, Vi. About us.'

Violet wrinkled her nose. 'There is no *us*, Paul. There hasn't been for a long time.'

'Oh, come on . . . don't say that.' He appealed to her with sad eyes. 'I've really enjoyed being with you again. It's been like old times. I miss you, Violet. I miss what we had.'

She felt her body stiffen. 'Please, Paul. Stop.' She held up a hand. 'This is the beer talking.'

'No,' he said. 'No, it's not. Honestly, my life's not the same without you in it.'

Cringing, Violet spun away from him. 'You're feeling nostalgic, that's all,' she said. 'You and Janis have split up, and you're hankering after the past. But we can't go back, Paul. What's done is done. We're divorced.'

She didn't like having to crush his hopes, but hardening her heart and being brutally honest was the only way to deal with this ridiculously sentimental train of thought. The truth was, Paul's feeble attempt at a reconciliation was making her acutely aware that she wanted her life to move forward, not go backwards. And as she contemplated the future, it was Matthew's face that immediately popped into her mind.

'We had some good times,' Paul said. 'Didn't we?'

'Yes, of course we did,' Violet said, pushing thoughts of Matthew aside and turning back to face Paul. 'But you need to remove your rose-tinted spectacles. You're seeing and remembering the happy times in our marriage, and conveniently overlooking the last few years. We're better off apart, Paul. And once the effects of the beer have worn off, I know you'll agree with me.'

Cold air was blasting through the open window and door. Violet picked up the remains of the incinerated cheese on toast and carried it outside to the dustbin. By the time she got back to the kitchen, Paul was filling the washing-up bowl with hot soapy water.

'I'll clean the grill,' he said, keeping his back to her. 'I'm sorry, Vi. About the smoke detector. About everything.'

She placed a comforting hand on his shoulder, feeling the warmth of his skin beneath the cotton of his shirt.

'It could have been worse. The smoke seems to have dissipated, although I think I'll be stuck with the smell of burnt cheese for a while.'

'I don't understand how I slept through the alarm,' he said, sounding relieved that she was still speaking to him. 'I must have been out for the count. It's the country air. I slept like a log last night, too. I feel relaxed here, Violet. I like your cottage, and I like the village. You did the right thing, moving to Merrywell.'

She smiled. 'I do feel at home here.'

As he picked up the tea towel to dry the grill, she took it from him.

'I'll do that,' she said. 'Why don't you go and lie down and sleep off the beer? You've got another book festival event to go to this evening . . . a nap will do you good. And if you're still hungry when you wake up, you can get yourself something to eat then.'

He nodded. 'OK. Wake me in an hour.'

Chapter 26

At six o'clock the following morning, Violet was roused by the sound of Paul's phone alarm going off in the next room. She turned over and closed her eyes, but struggled to get back to sleep. She heard the toilet flush, the sound of the shower running, and then Paul's tread on the stairs as he went down to the kitchen.

After his hour-long nap the previous evening, he'd gone off to the final event of the book festival in a subdued mood. Thinking it wise to keep out of his way, Violet had stayed at home and watched a film on Netflix. At nine-forty-five, when Paul had returned, she'd made him a hot chocolate, which he'd carried upstairs with him, declaring he needed an early night, ready for his journey back to London.

He obviously felt awkward and embarrassed – they both did. And even though Violet told herself she had nothing to feel guilty about, it didn't stop her worrying. Paul seemed lost, and a little disenchanted with life, and because she still cared about him, she wanted him to revert to his happy, chirpy self.

Turning away from the chink of pale light that was now creeping through the gap in the curtains, she plumped up her pillow and stretched out across the bed. Just as she was beginning to drift back into the transitional state of consciousness between wakefulness and sleep, a soft knock sounded on her bedroom door.

'Is it all right if I come in?' Paul said, sticking his head into the room. 'Are you decent?'

Violet pushed herself onto her elbows and sat up. 'Yeah, don't worry. I've got my jimjams on – although it's not as if you've not seen it all before.'

He came into the room and stood at the bottom of her bed. Rusty had spent the night curled up by Violet's feet – but on seeing Paul, the cat stood up, arched her back and greeted him with a meow.

'You seem to be a hit with Rusty.'

'I'm glad I'm popular with someone,' Paul said, dejectedly. 'Does she always sleep here?'

'Usually. She keeps my feet warm on cold nights.'

He smiled wistfully. 'That used to be my job.'

Violet laughed. 'But not one that you relished,' she said. 'You were always complaining my feet were like blocks of ice.'

He smirked. 'That's because they were. It's one of the few things I don't miss about you.'

Violet cleared her throat. 'Are you off?' she asked, steering the conversation towards safer ground. 'Heading back to the Big Smoke?'

'Yep . . . thought I'd better come and say goodbye, and thank you for putting up with me.' He reached out and stroked the cat. 'It's been good seeing you, Vi. I know what you said last night. You've made it clear there's no going back for us, but please think about what I said. And if you change your mind . . . you know where I am.'

'I won't change my mind,' Violet said, smiling to take the sting out of her words. 'You and I are on separate paths now, Paul. I'm happy with the way things are between us, and I want you to be happy too. I'm sorry it didn't work out with Janis, but I'm sure you'll meet someone else in the not-too-distant future.'

He pulled a face. 'I'm not sure there's anyone out there willing to put up with me.'

'Of course there is. You'll just have to keep looking and keep the faith.'

He nodded. 'Thanks, Violet. For everything.'

'You're welcome,' she replied, surprised to find that she meant it. 'Have a good journey. Text me when you get home to let me know you've arrived safely.'

His text arrived at two minutes to ten, just as Violet was pulling up at Birch House, ready for her second appointment with Leonie. Leaving her car parked in the same place as before, she went to the front door and knocked. When there was no answer, she knocked a second time and waited.

Violet glanced at her watch. Leonie had definitely said ten o'clock, so why wasn't she here? Perhaps it would have been better to meet her at the hotel.

She climbed back into the Toyota and waited. As Leonie's car was still being examined by the forensic team, she would presumably arrive by taxi.

Ten minutes later, when there was still no sign of a taxi or Leonie, Violet called her number. It went straight to voicemail. Given Leonie's poor track record on punctuality, Violet told herself she shouldn't be too worried. Even so, she couldn't shake off the creeping sense that something was wrong.

Getting out of the car, she marched to the front of the house and knocked on the door again. Then, using her fingers to shade her eyes, she peered through the downstairs front windows.

Finding no sign of life at the front of the house, she made her way along the side of the building, following a gravelled pathway onto a rear patio overlooking the garden.

Despite it being a crisp, sunny morning, an outside light was switched on. No sign of Leonie though.

Violet rapped her knuckles on the back door, and when her

knock went unanswered, a sliver of fear began to work its way under her skin. Gripping the door handle, she pressed it down and pushed, gasping when the door swung open.

Tentatively, she stepped inside.

Compared to the nippy autumn chill outside, the centrally heated kitchen felt warm and snug. There were two mugs on the island worktop: one was empty, but the other was full, and a milky skin had formed on its surface. When Violet pressed her fingers against the ceramic mug, it felt cold to the touch. There was no doubt in her mind: this was the same mug of coffee she had abandoned when she'd rushed out of Birch House the previous afternoon.

'Leonie?'

Violet listened as her voice bounced around the empty kitchen. Crossing the tiled floor, she went into the hallway and shouted up the stairs. There was no answering call. Only silence.

She double-checked the two rooms at the front of the house, and then went to stand with a foot on the bottom stair and a hand on the banister, deliberating on whether to go up to the first floor. She didn't want to intrude, but she was becoming increasingly concerned for Leonie's welfare.

She called Leonie's phone one more time, and when it went straight to the same message, she felt justified in venturing upstairs.

There were four bedrooms in all, and two bathrooms, the latter both newly fitted. Every one of the rooms was silent and empty.

Having drawn a blank, Violet returned to the ground floor and checked every room again, as well as the garden. There was no sign of Leonie anywhere and, aside from the mugs on the worktop, no indication that she had been at the house recently.

Recalling what Leonie had said about not wanting to stay overnight at Birch House, Violet wondered whether she had slept late at the Merrywell Manor Hotel. Was she worrying over nothing? Was this just another instance of Leonie's poor time-keeping?

Perhaps she was already on her way, having jumped into a taxi at the last minute – but if that *was* the case, why was the back door unlocked here at the house?

Violet pulled back the cuff of her coat and checked her watch. Quarter past ten. After leaving the house through the front door, she returned to her car and got in. She would sit and wait for ten more minutes. If Leonie hadn't turned up by then, she would call DS Winterton.

'Are you sure she's not at the hotel?' the detective said, when Violet spoke to him at twenty-five past ten.

'I called to check with the hotel a minute ago,' Violet explained. 'They put me through to Leonie's room, but there was no answer. I suppose she could be over there, having breakfast or something, but why isn't she answering her phone? And why is the back door unlocked, here at Birch House?'

'I'll send someone over to the hotel,' DS Winterton said. 'As for the back door, it's possible she forgot to lock up before she left yesterday. It's easily done. Don't you worry, I'm sure we'll be able to track Ms Stanwick down. I'll let you know as soon as she turns up. For now, I suggest you carry on with whatever it was you were planning to do today.'

'I was *planning* to interview Leonie,' Violet said. 'I talked to her yesterday. She was concerned about her safety and asked me to film an interview with her. She wanted to put a few things on record . . . she called it her insurance policy. I think she was genuinely worried, and if she *has* disappeared, it seems to me she had good reason to be.'

'Best not to jump to conclusions,' DS Winterton said. 'There's every chance she'll turn up. I'll get someone to trace her phone. That should tell us where she is.'

'Not if it's switched off,' Violet said. 'And I think it must be. I've tried calling her several times, but all I'm getting is her voicemail.'

'Ordinarily, we could check the ANPR, but Ms Stanwick's Audi is still in for forensic examination,' DS Winterton said. 'Do you happen to know if she's been using a hire car?'

'Not that I'm aware of,' Violet said. 'As far as I know, she's using taxis to get around.'

'Right . . . well, if necessary, we can check with the local cab firms. You've done your bit, Violet. You're going to have to leave it with me for now. I'll get the word out . . . we'll see if we can find her.'

'Can I ask whether the person you took in for questioning yesterday has been charged?' Violet said.

DS Winterton gave a fake cough, the sort designed to cover up embarrassment. 'No, the gentleman in question hasn't been charged. As I told you yesterday, he was never even arrested. He came into the station to answer questions on a voluntary basis.'

'And you've released him?'

'Not wishing to be pedantic, but it wasn't a case of releasing him,' DS Winterton said. 'We weren't holding him against his will. He was free to go at any point.'

'And when *did* he go?' Violet said.

DS Winterton coughed again. 'Late yesterday afternoon,' he said. 'He was able to prove where he was when Angeline Hammond was killed. We no longer believe he was involved in her death.'

'So, her killer is still out there somewhere?' Violet said.

'It would seem so,' he replied. 'Tell me . . . with regards to Ms Stanwick, can you think of anywhere she might be?'

'Not really,' Violet replied. 'All I know is, she was supposed to meet me here, at Birch House at ten o'clock.'

'Did she mention whether she's been in contact with anyone locally?'

'She knows a couple of people in the village,' Violet replied. 'And I gather she's already told you about her connection to Rupert Dalloway. She might be with him, but it's unlikely – not when she's supposed to be here, with me.'

'Maybe she's lost track of time. I'll arrange for someone to talk to Mr Dalloway. Is there anyone else you think we should check with?'

'Rupert's the only one I know of that she's definitely been in contact with, but you could talk to her old school friends: Zoe Corndale and Karen Avery. She may have been in touch with them, and there might be others that I don't know about.'

'You've done the right thing, alerting us,' DS Winterton said. 'If you do manage to get hold of Ms Stanwick, or hear from her, be sure to let us know. For now, I suggest you go home or go to work.'

After the call had ended, Violet sat for a moment, contemplating her next move. One thing was certain, she wouldn't be following the detective's advice. Going home or back to work wasn't an option. Having spent the previous afternoon listening to Leonie bare her soul, Violet felt duty-bound to do something positive to locate her. There was no way she could sit back and do nothing.

Reversing her car, she drove out onto Stanton Lane and turned left, heading towards the village and the Merrywell Manor Hotel. If she was lucky, she might get there before the police.

The haughty man wasn't on duty at the reception desk this time. Instead, a friendly, older woman offered her assistance.

'I'm trying to locate one of your guests,' Violet explained. 'Leonie Stanwick? I was supposed to meet her at ten o'clock, but I think there may have been a mix-up. I assumed we were meeting elsewhere, but maybe I should have come here instead.'

'Was it you who rang earlier?' the woman said.

'Yes, it was.'

The receptionist smiled. 'It was me who you spoke to. I can try her room again, if you like.'

Violet nodded her thanks and waited while the call was made.

'She's still not answering,' the receptionist said, as she put down the phone. 'You could try the breakfast room, or the guest lounge. We also have a guest library. She could be in there.'

Violet asked for directions to the library and lounge, and agreed to go and check. 'While I'm doing that, is it possible you could find out what time Leonie came back last night? Maybe you could check the electronic key card system. There must be a record of when her key was last used.'

The woman's affable demeanour morphed into a look of guarded suspicion. 'I'm not supposed to give out that kind of information,' she said. 'We take the privacy of our guests very seriously here at Merrywell Manor.'

'I appreciate that,' Violet replied. 'And I'm not asking for specifics. All I need to know is what time she used her key card yesterday afternoon, or last night.'

The woman gave a reluctant nod and, as she turned to check the computer, Violet zoomed over to the breakfast room. There were plenty of guests in there, but Leonie wasn't one of them. Next, she checked the lounge and the library – both of which were empty.

'Did you find her?' the receptionist asked, when Violet returned to the lobby.

'No . . . no sign of her anywhere. What about you?'

The receptionist frowned. 'I'm afraid I didn't have any luck either. Surprisingly, there's no record of Ms Stanwick having used her key card since yesterday morning.'

'Does that mean she didn't come back to the hotel at all yesterday?'

'She could have come back and spent time in the public areas, but she certainly didn't use her card to access the security door to the upper floor, or to her suite.'

'So she's definitely not in her room?'

'She can't be. Our records show that it *was* accessed this morning, but by a member of the cleaning team. Ms Stanwick's key card hasn't been used for over twenty-four hours.'

As Violet absorbed this information, she saw a movement reflected in the mirror behind the reception desk. The main door was opening and a police officer wearing a high-visibility jacket was strolling in.

Violet smiled at the receptionist. 'Thank you, anyway,' she said. 'I appreciate you checking.'

She turned and hurried back through the lobby, passing the police officer on her way out of the front door.

In the car park, she called Leonie's number – but once again, it went straight to voicemail. The situation was beginning to feel like déjà vu, and Violet didn't like it one little bit.

Common sense told her to drive to *The Memory Box* and get on with her work. She'd done her duty and voiced her concerns about Leonie to the police. She should leave it at that. Except . . . Leonie had confided in her, sharing some very personal information. Inexplicably, that had left Violet feeling a sense of responsibility for her welfare.

Before she had time to talk herself out of it, she started the car and searched for the postcode of Langdale Hall on her phone. Entering it into her sat nav, she settled back and waited for directions.

Chapter 27

When Leonie Stanwick had mentioned Langdale Hall, Violet had imagined a country manor house – something architecturally impressive, but modest in size. So, when she pulled up outside the enormous entrance pillars and looked through the wrought-iron gates to the vast, three-storey property beyond, she wondered if the sat nav had sent her to the wrong place.

The metal gates were shut, and a security camera was pointing at her from the top of one of the stone pillars. Presumably, there was someone monitoring the comings and goings at the gates, ready to open them for anyone who was expected – but to Violet and her Toyota, they remained firmly closed.

Keeping the engine running, she got out of the car and walked over to the intercom panel that was fixed to the right-hand pillar. She pressed the call button and waited.

'Hello?' said a male voice, presumably a security guard. 'Can I help you?'

'My name's Violet Brewster. I was hoping to speak to Rupert Dalloway. I don't have an appointment, but I'm a friend of a friend of his.'

'And what friend would that be?' the security guard asked.

'Leonie Stanwick,' said Violet. 'Perhaps she's here as well?'

'Nah . . . I know who you mean, but she's not here today. I'll speak to Mr Dalloway, but he doesn't usually see people he doesn't know, unless they have an appointment. What was your name again?'

'Violet Brewster. Please . . . tell Mr Dalloway I'm here because I'm worried about Leonie.'

'Stay where you are, and I'll check with him.'

There was a crackle on the intercom, followed by silence. As Violet waited, she heard the high-pitched and slightly melancholic autumn song of a robin. She looked up, scanning the high branches of a nearby tree for the elusive bird, but it seemed determined to be heard, rather than seen.

A couple of minutes later, a loud buzz signalled that the gates were opening. Violet jumped back into her car, put it into gear and entered the grounds of Langdale Hall. The driveway skirted the landscaped front gardens, and then looped back around to the front of the property, close to the house.

She parked the car, got out, and tipped her head back to gaze up at the hall's immense façade. Directly in front of her, in the centre of the house, were four stone steps leading to a porticoed and pedimented oak door, which was flanked by three sets of enormous windows on every floor.

When the door opened, it was Rupert Dalloway himself who walked out and stood on the top step. A look of recognition flitted across his face as he gazed down at his unexpected visitor.

'You're the woman from the book festival,' he said. 'The one who interviewed Leonie.'

'That's right.' Violet smiled. 'I'm sorry to drop in on you like this, but I wanted to check whether you'd heard from her. I was supposed to meet her at ten o'clock this morning, but she didn't turn up. I'm concerned.'

Rupert frowned. 'I think you'd better come in,' he said. 'I've been calling her since first thing this morning, but all I'm getting is her voicemail. I thought maybe she was avoiding me, but perhaps that's not the case.'

Violet ascended the stone steps and followed him through the door, into a palatial hallway, where a grand staircase swept majestically to the upper floors, and black and white chequered tiles covered the floor. Rupert veered right, into a high-ceilinged drawing room that was at least twice the size of the whole of Greengage Cottage.

'Please, take a seat,' he said. 'Can I get you anything to drink?'

'No, I'm fine,' Violet replied. 'I'm disappointed Leonie's not here. I was banking on her being with you. I'm assuming this is where she stayed on Friday night?'

Rupert ran a hand through his prematurely grey hair and looked at Violet warily.

'You don't have to be coy,' she told him. 'At Leonie's request, I interviewed her again yesterday. She wanted to tell me her story privately . . . the *whole* story. I know the truth about Angeline.'

He sat down, placed his elbows on his knees, and rested his head in his hands.

'I only learned the truth myself on Friday evening,' he said. 'As you can imagine, there's been a lot for me to take in over the last few days. Quite honestly, I'm struggling to come to terms with everything that's happened.'

'That's understandable,' said Violet. 'You have my sympathies.'

He rubbed his eyes, as if to keep himself awake – or maybe he was wiping away tears.

'It was a shock to learn that Angeline had been living in Merrywell all these years,' he said. 'But a pleasant kind of shock . . . if there is such a thing. Once it had sunk in, I knew I wanted to meet her and get to know her properly. I was going to invite her here, to Langdale Hall, so that we could spend some time together. I was looking forward to it.'

'I'm sorry you won't get the chance,' Violet said.

'So am I,' he replied, the words escaping on a sigh. 'On Friday night, I went to sleep happier than I'd been in years – but then, by Saturday morning, everything had turned sour. My new-found hopes and plans were snatched away overnight. Life can be vicious sometimes.'

'Was it Leonie who broke the news to you? About the murder?'

'Yes,' he said. 'As you'd already surmised, she ended up staying here on Friday night, and she went off the next morning to run some sort of writing class for the festival. The next thing I knew, she was calling to tell me that Angeline . . . the daughter I'd only just rediscovered . . . was dead. It completely poleaxed me.'

He took a deep breath and released it slowly.

'Since then, I've been riding a hideous rollercoaster of emotion. The problem is, I don't know what I'm supposed to feel or how I should behave. It's surreal. I'm in mourning for someone I didn't even know.'

'It is an unusual situation,' Violet said. 'All you can do is follow your instincts and take it one day at a time.'

'My daughter thinks I should pull myself together,' he said. 'She says it's all right to be sad, but that I shouldn't go to pieces over a stranger.'

Violet wondered whether Saffy Dalloway's advice was designed to protect her father's feelings, or nip his grief in the bud to preserve her own position in his affections.

'You've obviously told your daughter about Angeline then? Her connection to you?'

He nodded. 'Yes, I rang Saffy on Friday evening . . . invited her round. After I'd got to grips with what Leonie had told me, I wanted Saffy to join us, so that we could share the good news with her. As a child, all she ever wanted was a sister, so I knew she'd be delighted.'

'And was she?' Violet asked.

'Like me, she was taken aback initially . . . but yes, she seemed pleased. She was keen to meet Angeline, and I'm sure the girls would have got on well, had they been given the opportunity to get to know one another.'

'Does your daughter live locally?' Violet asked.

'She has an apartment here, at Langdale Hall,' he replied. 'When my wife and I divorced, we converted the rooms at the opposite end of the building into three apartments. My ex-wife lives on the ground floor, and Saffy has the apartment on the top floor.'

'And who lives in the first-floor apartment?' Violet asked.

'No one. It's empty, although we use it occasionally to accommodate visitors. It did cross my mind that Angeline could have used it. I know she had her own house in Merrywell – Leonie said she'd been doing it up – but she could have lived in the apartment and rented out her own place to bring in some extra income. It's one of the things I could have done for Angeline, to make up for lost time and atone for the way the Dalloways treated her and her family. Now, I'll never have the chance to show my daughter how much I cared. I didn't even get to meet her.'

He stared at Violet, his face pale and tired and etched with grief.

'I'm so sorry,' she said. 'It must be difficult, coming to terms with such a complex loss. I would imagine Leonie is experiencing similar emotions.'

'If she is, I wish she'd talk to me about it,' Rupert said. 'I think it would help if we could grieve together – although I'm not sure Leonie would agree. She likes to do things her own way . . . always has done. I assumed that's why she wasn't answering my calls . . . that she'd gone off somewhere, to spend some time on her own.'

'I think her phone must be switched off,' Violet said. 'As I say, I'm worried about her, which is why I'm here.'

She leaned forward, took a deep breath and – as tactfully as she could – aired the theory that Angeline could have been killed by mistake; and that Leonie might be the murderer's real target. As she spoke, the scant colour that remained in Rupert's cheeks drained away, until his skin was pale as alabaster.

'Of course, it's possible I'm letting my imagination run wild,' Violet said, as she took in his shocked expression. 'But, having had time to reflect, I believe Leonie had reached the same conclusion as me. Yesterday, she acknowledged that she could be in danger.'

'You think something terrible has happened to her?' Rupert asked.

'The longer she's out of touch, the more likely that seems,' Violet replied. 'I don't wish to seem insensitive, and I don't want to scare you, but I am concerned.'

He stood up and began to pace, striding back and forth across the antique and sun-faded rug that lay in the centre of the room.

'I couldn't bear to lose Leonie as well,' he said. 'We need to find her. I should call the police.'

'I've already done that,' Violet said. 'They're looking for her as we speak – in fact they'll probably be in touch with you at some stage soon. I'd guessed that Leonie stayed the night here on Friday, so I gave them your name. I'm sorry. I hope you don't mind.'

He waved away her apology. 'Leonie and I have nothing to hide . . . not anymore. Her visit on Friday made me realise how much she meant to me all those years ago. I was a fool to ever let her go. I should never have let my parents decide who I should be with.'

Violet gave him a sympathetic smile. 'Hindsight makes wise men of us all,' she said.

'True . . . but having lost Leonie once, I don't intend to make the same mistake a second time. Where do you think she could be? She can't have gone far. Unless . . .'

'Unless what?' Violet said.

He sat down and placed his hands on his head. 'Perhaps I put too much pressure on her,' he said. 'I told her I was keen to revive our relationship, but maybe I spoke out of turn. After the way I treated her all those years ago, I'm in no position to make demands. Leonie's the one who'll get to dictate the terms of our relationship from now on . . . assuming a relationship is still possible.'

He bent his head, stood up and began to pace again.

'She must have gone off somewhere,' he said, snapping his fingers and grasping at the safest and most bearable explanation for Leonie's disappearance. 'Perhaps she needed to get away . . . from me, and from everything that's happened over the last few days.'

'I honestly don't think she'd run away,' Violet said. 'She asked me to interview her yesterday precisely because she was ready to face up to the realities of what's happened. Even when she thought staying in Merrywell might put her in danger, she was determined to stick around long enough for the truth to come out.'

'So, what should I do?' Rupert asked, his voice a desperate wail. 'Am I supposed to just sit around and wait for the police to find her?'

Violet didn't know what to say. Her biggest fear was that the killer had already struck again; that if the police *did* find Leonie, it would be too late – but she held on to that opinion. Rupert was distraught enough already.

'Can you think of anyone who might want to harm Leonie?' she asked instead. 'Someone who might have held a grudge against her?'

Rupert released a sigh of defeat. 'The truth is,' he said, 'I don't know anything about her these days . . . who her friends are, or any potential adversaries. Leonie's been enormously successful as a writer, and she has a high-profile lifestyle, and – knowing her – she'll have rubbed numerous people up the wrong way over the years.'

'When I spoke to her yesterday, she said that if anything bad was going to happen to her, it would be here in Merrywell. She thought someone could be rattled . . . about something that had happened in the past.'

'Do you have any idea who she was referring to?' Rupert said.

'I don't think she knew herself,' Violet replied. 'As far as *I'm* aware, the only thing even remotely contentious in her past was her relationship with you.'

'I hope you're not suggesting she was afraid of *me*?' he said, sounding more hurt than angry. 'Because I'm telling you here and now, nothing could be further from the truth. Leonie was thrilled to see me again, and the feeling was mutual.'

'I believe you,' Violet replied quickly to calm him down. 'But think . . . do you know of anyone who, to quote Leonie, might be "rattled" by her presence in Merrywell?'

Rupert stuffed his hands in his pockets and shrugged. 'As far as I know, she didn't keep in touch with *anyone* from the old days. She told me on Friday that she came to Merrywell to see her parents once every five or six years, but never hung around for long. She certainly didn't mention meeting up with anyone else during those visits.'

'I gather she was a gregarious person at school,' said Violet. 'She must have had a lot of friends back then.'

Rupert stared off into the distance and smiled, as if recalling happier times. 'She was very popular, but also extremely discerning about who she confided in. Apart from Zoe Corndale, I don't remember her being especially close to anyone.'

'Do you think she could be with Zoe now?' Violet asked. 'I know they spoke at the festival. Leonie gave her a hug, so she must have been pleased to see her. Maybe they've arranged a reunion.'

Rupert didn't look convinced. 'She'd have let you know, wouldn't she . . . if she wasn't going to attend your ten o'clock meeting?'

'Maybe. Maybe not,' Violet said. 'Let's face it, Leonie isn't the most organised or punctual of people. Even so . . . there's definitely something "off" about this. Do you think I should check with Zoe?'

'I suppose it's worth a try.'

'Do you have her telephone number?'

'No, I'm sorry, I don't,' Rupert said. 'The only thing I know about Zoe is that she runs a sweet shop in Matlock Bath, and lives in the flat above it. I called into the shop a few months back, not realising it was her business – and there she was, behind the counter. A real blast from the past.'

'Is there anyone else you can think of?' Violet said. 'Any other mates Leonie might have reconnected with?'

'Not that I'm aware of, but aren't we looking for someone with a grudge against Leonie? It's unlikely to be one of her old friends, don't you think?'

'It could be anyone.'

'Or no one,' Rupert said. 'Maybe we're worrying over nothing.'

Violet thought he was being naïve, but refrained from saying so.

'What about her PR consultant, Yvette Finch?' Violet said. 'Did Leonie tell you they'd parted ways?'

'No, she didn't mention it. Does that make her a suspect? I wouldn't have thought being sacked is a motive for murder, although I suppose it depends how high the stakes are. If the survival of the Finch woman's business depends on her maintaining a working relationship with Leonie, the ending of their contract might be a huge financial blow.'

'Yvette wasn't sacked,' Violet said. 'She was the one who ended the business arrangement with Leonie.'

Rupert threw up his hands. 'There you are, then. We could sit here all morning, talking through the possibilities and going round in circles,' he said. 'To be frank, I'd prefer not to think about Leonie being in danger. It's far more likely she's feeling emotionally vulnerable and wants some time alone, to deal with her grief. It's the sort of thing the Leonie of old would have done. She always was very self-reliant . . . used to handling things on her own. She'll resurface when she's ready. I'm sure of it.'

'Let's hope you're right,' Violet said, even though she didn't think he was.

Rupert pulled a card from his wallet and handed it to her.

'That's my number,' he said. 'Please call me straight away if you hear anything.'

Chapter 28

Having told Rupert that she could find her own way out, Violet went back into the hallway, crossing the black and white tiles diagonally, like a bishop on a chessboard. As she emerged from Langdale Hall through the heavy front door, she heard the sound of female voices somewhere close by, their tone harsh and argumentative. Violet heard the words *unbelievable* and *outrageous* and *absolutely typical*.

By the time she'd reached her car, two chicly dressed women had rounded the far corner of the house and were marching towards a silver BMW parked at the far end of the driveway. When they noticed Violet, they stopped and turned their stiletto-heeled feet in her direction.

'Can I help you?' the older of the two women shouted, in a tone that suggested 'helping' was the last thing on her mind.

'No, I'm fine.' Violet raised a hand. 'I was just leaving.'

'I know you, don't I?' the woman said, as she continued to clip-clop towards Violet's car, the younger woman close on her heels.

'I don't think so,' Violet said, concluding that the two women must be Rosemary and Saffy Dalloway. 'As far as I know, we've never met.'

'You were at the book festival the other day. You interviewed that romance author.'

That romance author?

'Leonie Stanwick, you mean?' Violet said. 'Yes, I did. I take it you were in the audience?'

'We were. I'm Rosemary Dalloway, and this is my daughter, Saffy. We were at Leonie Stanwick's writing class on Saturday morning as well.'

'Ah, yes. It's a shame that session had to be curtailed,' Violet said. 'But given the circumstances, I suppose the organisers had very little choice.'

'Quite,' Rosemary Dalloway said. 'It was all most unfortunate.'

'I'm sorry for your loss,' Violet said, addressing Saffy directly.

The girl stared at her with cold grey eyes, and Rosemary tutted.

'Really!' Rosemary reeled back her head so that she could look down her nose at Violet. 'That's extremely presumptuous of you.'

'Then I apologise,' Violet said, realising she had overstepped the mark. 'I didn't mean to be impertinent . . . Saffy has lost a relative, and I simply wanted to offer my condolences.'

'Who told you that Angeline Hammond was related to my daughter?' Rosemary snapped.

'Leonie Stanwick,' Violet said. 'And I've also been discussing the matter with your ex-husband.'

'What? You've spoken to Rupert?' Rosemary said.

'Yes. Just. That's why I'm here.'

Saffy chose that moment to speak up. 'You need to butt out,' she said. 'This is none of your business.'

'Perhaps not,' Violet said. 'But in view of what's happened, Angeline's connection to your family will soon be public knowledge. Leonie Stanwick has already told the police the truth about her relationship to Angeline. That information is bound to come out in the course of the investigation. Plus, Leonie is writing an autobiography—'

'I doubt she'll bother with that now,' Rosemary interjected. 'Not now that her daughter's been murdered.'

Violet shrugged.

'On the contrary, Mummy . . .' Saffy scoffed. 'Leonie Stanwick's publishers will be rubbing their hands together. The publicity surrounding the murder is guaranteed to make the book a huge bestseller.'

Rosemary shuddered. 'Come on, darling,' she said, snaking a protective arm around her daughter's shoulder. 'Let's try and forget about this whole ghastly business. We need to get going. We'll be late for our appointment.'

'Before you go, can you tell me whether either of you saw or spoke to Leonie yesterday afternoon or evening?' Violet said.

'No, we did not,' Rosemary said, as she led Saffy away. 'Now, please, leave us alone. Unlike my ex-husband, my daughter and I aren't comfortable talking to an outsider about private matters. I suggest you get in your car and leave. Immediately.'

As the patrician pair teetered back to the BMW, Violet unlocked her own car and got into the driver's seat. She sat and watched as the Dalloway women climbed into their vehicle and sped off down the driveway, noting that the gates opened automatically as the car approached the pillared exit.

As their tail lights disappeared from view, Violet put her key in the ignition, ready to start the Toyota and follow them – but curiosity stayed her hand. Rosemary and Saffy had been contemptuously dismissive of Angeline. Did that attitude stem from an ingrained sense of arrogance, or had it been cultivated to disguise their true feelings? If so, what was it they were hiding?

Rupert had said that his ex-wife had a ground-floor flat at the far end of the building. With the Dalloway women out of the way, no one would notice if Violet had a quick scout around.

Removing the key from the ignition, she jumped out of her car and hurried to the far end of Langdale Hall, turning right at the corner. Along the side of the building were two huge ground-floor windows and, at the end, a door that presumably led to the suite of apartments. Violet scanned the area for CCTV cameras.

There were bound to be some, but for the life of her, she couldn't spot where they were.

She peered through the first window, hesitant about what she might see. What exactly was she expecting to find? Leonie Stanwick gaffer-taped to a chair, perhaps? Bound and gagged?

Violet laughed at herself. DS Winterton had hit the nail on the head when he'd said she read too many crime novels. The only thing she could see on the other side of the window was a large and extravagantly furnished drawing room, decorated with several enormous floral arrangements.

She crept along to the next window and found herself staring into Rosemary Dalloway's pristine and very swish dining kitchen.

The newly fitted units at Birch House had been impressive enough, but this was in a completely different league: gleaming marble worktops, immaculate storage cupboards and high-end appliances. Off to one side, an eight-seater dining table was laid with cutlery, napkins and sparkling crystal glasses. On the other side of the window was a double sink unit, with an inset ceramic bowl and shiny chrome taps. Further along, Violet spied a built-in wine cooler, a tall double oven and an American-style fridge. The Dalloways obviously didn't do things by halves.

Something on one of the worktops prompted Violet to press her face closer to the window. Shielding her face with her hands, she stared at the item that had captured her attention: a steel, seven-piece knife block. She narrowed her eyes and squinted. Only six of the seven slots in the block had knives in them. One was missing.

Violet pulled out her phone and held it up to the window. Tapping on the camera app, she zoomed in on the knife block and took a photo. She could see a brand name towards the bottom of the block, a little white label with a red logo and black text. Using her thumb and index finger to zoom in on the image, Violet was able to make out the word 'Wüsthof'.

She stepped back from the window and quickly googled the

name on her phone, gasping as she read the search results. The seven-knife block in Rosemary Dalloway's kitchen retailed for over a thousand pounds – but it wasn't the cost that had taken her breath away – it was the fact that Wüsthof had been manufacturing high-quality knives in Solingen for over two hundred years.

And Solingen was in Germany.

A melee of thoughts scrambled around in Violet's head as she left Langdale Hall and drove down the hill towards Bakewell. As she pulled up at a junction and waited for a break in the traffic, she mulled over a new and rather unsavoury possibility, one that completely overturned her previous theory.

What if Angeline *had* been the intended victim all along?

And what if Rosemary Dalloway was her killer?

Mindful of how easy it would be to jump to the wrong conclusion, Violet took a deep breath and carefully considered her latest discovery, thinking everything through as calmly and objectively as possible. The police family liaison officer had told Leonie that the murder weapon had been a German knife – but what were the chances it was a Wüsthof knife? How many people were wealthy enough to spend a thousand pounds on a set of kitchen knives?

If she were to check with DS Winterton, he would probably say that the knife that killed Angeline Hammond was a different brand altogether. After all, a country as big as Germany must have dozens of knife manufacturers.

Even so, Violet couldn't shake off a feeling of suspicion and unease. Rupert Dalloway had told his daughter about her half-sister on Friday evening. Had he also announced his intention to bring Angeline into the family fold and offer her the vacant apartment? He'd described Saffy as being delighted at discovering she had a sibling, but how had the news *really* gone down? Swimmingly, or like a lead balloon? The latter seemed the most likely, given Saffy Dalloway's snooty demeanour a few minutes earlier.

Had Saffy rushed straight round to her mother's ground-floor apartment to share the news? How must the Dalloway women have felt about having a cuckoo in the nest? Had they balked at the idea of a complete stranger moving into Langdale Hall?

Another factor to consider was how Angeline's sudden appearance would affect the Dalloway line of succession. If Langdale Hall was traditionally passed down to the eldest child, would Angeline have inherited instead of Saffy?

Money and status: two things the Dalloway women seemed to value highly. The desire to retain their position could be considered a strong motive for murder. But would either of the women have felt incensed enough to resort to such a drastic measure?

And if they were guilty of murder, would they still have chosen to attend Leonie's writing masterclass? They must have bought their tickets to the workshop long before discovering the author's link to Rupert – but, after learning the truth, they had chosen to go along anyway. Had that decision been driven by curiosity? Or to avoid the attention a no-show might have drawn? Had they attended the sell-out workshop in an effort to 'act normally' and evade suspicion?

Violet wondered whether she should speak to Rupert Dalloway about the empty knife slot in his ex-wife's kitchen. It would mean fessing up to snooping, but what the heck? It was even conceivable that Rupert himself was having similar suspicions about Rosemary and Saffy. Was he considering the possibility, albeit an unpalatable one, that they could have had a hand in Angeline's death?

The weather had taken a turn for the worse. A blanket of dark clouds was sliding across the hills and throwing out a steady drizzle of rain. As Violet drove through Bakewell, the lights from the houses and shops reflected on the wet road, creating a cosy, if rather damp glow. She took the turning for Merrywell, mulling over what to do next.

Perhaps she should confide in Matthew and tell him what she'd seen (or – more to the point – *not* seen) when she'd looked through Rosemary Dalloway's window. He might dismiss the empty knife slot as a coincidence and tease her about being too curious for her own good – but, whatever his view, Violet knew he would listen diligently to everything she had to say. She trusted Matthew and valued his opinion. It would be good to get his advice before deciding her next course of action.

Her first stop when she arrived back at the shopping village was to call in at the bookshop. Eric was there, leaning on the counter, looking thoroughly zonked out. Fiona was hovering close by, handing over what smelled like a strong cup of coffee.

'I'm surprised you've not taken the day off, Eric,' Violet said, as she strolled over to join them. 'After a three-day, full-on festival, you must be exhausted.'

'I'm tired, but happy,' he replied. 'It went even better than I could have hoped for. Apart from the unfortunate incident with poor Angeline, I'd say it was an unqualified success.'

'Does that mean you'll be doing it again next year?' Violet asked. 'Is the book festival going to be a permanent fixture on Merrywell's cultural calendar?'

Eric smiled. 'Ask me again in a few weeks when I've fully recovered from organising this one. Right now, I don't even want to think about going through it all again.'

'You should try and get some rest,' Fiona said.

'Easier said than done,' said Eric.

Violet smiled sympathetically. 'I know you're busy, so I won't keep you . . . I just wanted to let you know that I tracked down Judith and had a word with her. I put her straight about who it was that gave her name to the police.'

'You didn't need to do that, Violet, but thanks anyway,' Eric said. 'Did she give you an earful?'

Violet shrugged. 'It wasn't as bad as I was expecting.'

'Then why the long face?' Eric asked. 'Is everything all right?'

Violet lifted a shoulder and tried not to frown. 'Things could be better, but it's nothing you need worry about.'

Now that the stress of the book festival was finally over, Violet thought her friends deserved a hassle-free day. She didn't want to alarm them by announcing that Leonie had gone AWOL again, and she certainly wasn't going to mention that she'd been standing on her tiptoes, peering into Rosemary Dalloway's kitchen.

Eric stretched his arms and yawned. 'Well, cheers for straightening things out with Judith. And thanks again for doing the interview with Leonie Stanwick. I thought it went very well.'

'It went quickly, that's for sure,' said Violet. 'Actually, Eric, would you mind sending me a copy of the recording? I'd like to watch it again.'

'No problemo,' he said. 'I'll do it now, before I forget.'

'Thanks. I appreciate it. And congratulations . . . the pair of you . . . on a brilliant festival. You've done yourselves and Merrywell proud.'

Violet turned to leave, but when she reached the door, she realised Fiona was right behind her.

'Not so fast, madam,' Fiona said. 'Aren't you going to tell me about your visitor?'

Violet groaned inwardly. She'd guessed this was coming. Even though Fiona had been run off her feet for days, there was no way Paul's presence in the village would have passed under her radar.

'I assume you're referring to Paul?' she said.

'Yes, unless you've got another ex-husband hidden away that I don't know about.'

Violet smiled. 'One's more than enough, thank you very much.'

'He and I bumped into each other several times during the festival,' Fiona said. 'He seems like a decent-enough bloke. Is he still in Merrywell, or has he gone home?'

'He drove home this morning.'

Fiona crossed her arms, settling into interrogation mode. 'I must admit, I was surprised to see him. You didn't tell me he was coming. Or that he'd be staying with you.'

'That's because I didn't know,' Violet said, swatting away the inference that she'd behaved secretively. 'Paul turned up out of the blue on Saturday. I had no idea he'd be attending the festival, or that he planned to stay at my place.'

Fiona lifted her chin. 'Bit cheeky of him, then.'

'I'd say very cheeky – but that's Paul for you.'

'I don't think Matthew was too chuffed about him being here.'

'Why?' Violet said, feeling goose bumps forming on her arms. 'What did he say?'

Fiona wrinkled her nose. 'It's more what he didn't say. The truth is, he went very quiet when he found out your ex was in the village.'

A heavy feeling settled in Violet's stomach. She and Matthew were in the habit of exchanging regular texts and messages, but now that she thought about it, since their last encounter in the café, she hadn't heard a word from him. She hoped he hadn't got the wrong end of the stick about Paul.

'So, how was it?' Fiona asked.

Reluctantly, Violet dragged herself back to the cross-examination. 'How was what?'

'Spending time with your ex. Did it rekindle any of the old feelings?'

'No, Fiona, it didn't. At least not for me. We parted on good terms, but I doubt Paul will be visiting again any time soon.'

Her annoyance must have shown in her face, because Fiona took the hint and changed tack.

'What did he say about the murder? Did he have any theories as to who might have done it?'

'He didn't take much of an interest, to be honest.'

'Why not? He's a detective, isn't he?'

'Yes, but it's not his case. He's got plenty of investigations of his own to worry about.'

'What about you then?' Fiona persisted. 'Do you have a suspect in mind, or are your sleuthing days a thing of the past?'

Violet smiled. 'I don't know who the killer is, but . . .'

She glanced over at Eric, who was tapping the keyboard on his laptop, seemingly oblivious to their conversation.

'I didn't like to say anything in front of Eric,' Violet continued, keeping her voice low. 'But I arranged to meet Leonie Stanwick this morning, and she failed to turn up. She's not answering her phone . . . I don't know where she is.'

'Sounds like déjà vu all over again.' Fiona rolled her eyes. 'I probably shouldn't say this, seeing as she's just lost her sister, but Leonie Stanwick is a pain in the jacksie. You'd think after what happened on Saturday morning, she'd have learned her lesson and turned up on time for once.'

'It's not her time-keeping I'm concerned about,' said Violet. 'I'm worried something could have happened to her. The festival may be over, Fiona, but I'm not sure the killing is.'

En route to *The Memory Box*, Violet called in at Collis Fine Furniture. Matthew was in the workshop, shaping a block of wood on one of the lathes positioned along the back wall. When he saw her, he switched off the machine and turned to face her. Even wearing a pair of clunky, plastic safety goggles, he still managed to look good.

'What can I do for you, Violet?' His voice was friendly, but lacking its usual playfulness.

'I'm working on a new theory regarding Angeline Hammond's murder,' she said. 'I'm not at liberty to tell you everything I know, but there are a couple of points I'd like to run past you, if you can spare a few minutes. I'd really appreciate your opinion.'

'Can it wait?' He removed the goggles and rubbed a hand across his eyes. 'Only I have to finish this job by the end of play today. I need to crack on.'

His words felt like ice water in her face.

'Oh, OK,' she said, feeling crushed and crestfallen.

What was going on? This reluctance to chat was definitely out of character for Matthew. He usually enjoyed listening to her off-the-wall theories, and could always be relied upon as a trusted confidant. Why was he suddenly being so standoffish? Had she genuinely called at a bad time, or had she done something to upset him? Or was Paul behind this sudden change of attitude?

'Is everything OK?' she asked.

Matthew mustered a half-smile. 'Sure. You've caught me at the wrong time, that's all. Sorry, Violet. Let's catch up later, yeah?'

'Of course,' she said, forcing herself to maintain eye contact even though she was shrivelling up inside. 'Sorry. I'll let you get on.'

She headed for the door, swallowing her hurt feelings as she walked. Now might not be the right time, but she was determined to find out what was bugging Matthew. And whatever the problem was, she intended to fix it.

Eric was true to his word. When Violet sat at her desk and turned on her Mac, his email was waiting in her inbox. It included a link to download the recording of the interview with Leonie.

Violet opened the file and set it running, listening as she tidied her desk and completed a few essential administrative tasks. She loathed the sound of her own voice, but it was something she would have to endure in order to check on a couple of potentially significant moments during her chat with Leonie.

There were two incidents in particular that she wanted to revisit – both of which had occurred during the question-and-answer session.

Fast-forwarding to the final third of the recording, she listened to the second question in the Q&A. It had come from the woman on the balcony, who'd asked what the most important quality an aspiring writer needed in order to succeed. Leonie had replied instantly: '*That's easy. Persistence.*' And as soon as the word had left Leonie's mouth, someone in the audience had scoffed – loudly and irately.

Violet turned the volume to maximum and played the segment

several times, trying to decipher where in the audience the sound had come from – but it was impossible to tell.

Why had someone felt it necessary to react in such a way? The sound was an irritated, involuntary huff. Who had objected to Leonie offering *persistence* as a piece of advice? Had someone in the audience been persisting for years without success? An aspiring writer, maybe? Had they reacted cynically, based on their own personal experience? Or were they challenging Leonie's right to champion persistence? And if so, why? As an author, she'd achieved years of success. There was no denying she had been tenacious.

The other thing Violet was interested to view again was the moment when Rupert Dalloway had quizzed Leonie about love. The livestream cameras had been focused on the stage, so the replay didn't offer another chance to study Rupert's expression, but what Violet did see again was the warm smile his voice brought to Leonie's face. And when Rupert asked why Leonie wrote about love, she had replied in a tone that quivered with emotion. '*Because love is the most important thing there is,*' she'd said. '*Once experienced, it can never be forgotten. Not all relationships last, but love . . . true love . . . goes on forever.*'

Now that Violet knew more about their story, she understood that Leonie's reply hadn't been a sweeping generalisation. It had addressed Rupert directly. Leonie's words referred to *their* love. And when she'd insisted on answering Rupert's follow-up question, she'd also been talking about their own, personal love affair. Although she didn't go as far as to reveal who the great love of her life had been, Rupert would have known she was talking about him when she said: '*I found my one true love many years ago, but sadly it was a relationship that wasn't destined to last. But I've never forgotten that person. They will always be here . . . in my heart.*'

Violet paused the recording. From what she could remember, these two incidents had been the interview's only tricky moments. They had struck her at the time simply because they were glitches in an otherwise smooth hour-long session – glitches that, thankfully, hadn't caused an insurmountable problem, or resulted in Violet losing control of the discussion.

But had something else been said during the interview . . . something significant that could have triggered a dangerous train of thought in the mind of a killer?

She replayed the full interview, listening carefully to everything Leonie had said – but nothing jumped out, or rang an off-note. She must be overlooking something . . . she felt sure of it. What was she missing?

Chapter 29

At two o'clock, Violet had a business appointment with a local charity based in Wirksworth. Glad to get out of the office, she drove there on the B-roads, travelling via Winster and Middleton, arriving in the market town with a few minutes to spare.

The meeting was short but productive, and once it had concluded, Violet decided to drive home through Cromford, dropping down onto the main A6 road. It was a busier route, but it would take her through Matlock Bath, and provide an opportunity to check out Zoe Corndale's sweet shop.

In the warmer months, Matlock Bath was a busy tourist destination, but on a damp Monday in October, the town was almost deserted. Most of the numerous fish and chip shops were closed, as were the amusement arcades – but there was a gift shop open, as well as a couple of steamed-up cafés.

Violet steered her car into one of the parking spaces in front of the main parade of shops. At weekends, especially in the summer, this side of the road was chock-a-block with motorbikes – Matlock Bath being a bikers' paradise.

She got out of the car and crossed over to the other side of the street, which ran parallel to the river. From there, it was easier to assess the town's array of shopfronts. As she moved in the direction of the railway station, she spotted what she thought must be Zoe Corndale's shop. It was called *Sweet Dreams*, and it was tucked between an ice-cream parlour and a café. Using the pedestrian crossing to return to the other side of the road, Violet went inside.

The shop smelt heavenly: sweet and sugary. Old-fashioned confectionary jars were lined up on shelves behind the counter, containing all the treats Violet remembered from her childhood. Sherbet lemons. Pear drops. Blackcurrant liquorice. Dolly mixtures. Foam shrimps. Chocolate limes. Rhubarb and custard. It was like stepping back in time.

Behind a glass-fronted display cabinet on the counter was a selection of delicious-looking fudge pieces. Violet was peering through the glass, her mouth watering, when a woman appeared through a beaded curtain at the back of the shop.

Violet recognised the pixie haircut immediately. This was Zoe Corndale; the woman who had hugged Leonie Stanwick at the book-signing table.

'Zoe?' Violet said.

The woman narrowed her eyes for a moment, before offering up a tight smile. 'That's me,' she said. 'How can I help?'

'My name's Violet Brewster. You may remember me from the book festival? I interviewed your old friend Leonie.'

Zoe nodded slowly as recognition dawned, and her smile became warmer. 'That's right,' she said. 'I thought you looked familiar. It was a good event. I enjoyed seeing Leonie again.'

'Can I ask if you've seen her since?' Violet asked. 'Have the two of you met up at all?'

'Nooo . . .' Zoe grew wary again. 'We did talk about it, and we exchanged numbers, but when I heard what had happened to her sister, I didn't think she'd be in the mood for socialising. I sent her a text, to say how sorry I was, but she hasn't replied yet. I expect she's got a lot on her plate.'

'Can I be totally candid with you, Zoe?' Violet smiled reassuringly. 'I was supposed to meet Leonie this morning, but she didn't turn up, and I don't know where she is. I'm worried about her. I called in here on the off-chance you might know something.'

Zoe lifted an arched brow. 'And there's me, thinking you must have a sweet tooth.'

Violet smiled.

'Sorry, but I haven't the foggiest idea where Leonie is,' Zoe said. 'I do have her telephone number, but I can't give it to you without her permission. I could call her for you though . . . find out what she's up to.'

'No, that's all right. I've got her number. I've been trying it on and off all day, but I think her phone's switched off.'

'Perhaps she's been waylaid or had a better offer.' Zoe laughed. 'I shouldn't worry too much. Leonie was always notoriously unreliable. Doesn't sound like she's changed much.'

'Can you think of anyone she might be with? Someone local she was hoping to catch up with?'

Zoe looked nonplussed. 'Leonie's never been one for keeping in touch with people from round here. She doesn't even send Christmas cards. And like I said, if she's grieving, the last thing she'll want is to be socialising with friends she hasn't seen for years.'

Violet wished she could emphasise to Zoe just how concerned she was for Leonie's safety, but that wouldn't be possible without revealing Leonie's true relationship to Rupert and Angeline. Even though Leonie hadn't sworn her to silence, Violet knew it wasn't her place to share such a huge secret. Other than the Dalloways, no one seemed to know the truth. Everyone was still referring to Angeline as Leonie's sister.

'Can I ask you about Karen Avery?' Violet said, pursuing the only other contact she knew about.

'Karen? Yeah, sure, although I've not seen her for yonks. What is it you want to know?'

'Do you think Leonie could have arranged to meet her? The three of you used to hang out, didn't you? In some sort of weekend study group?'

Zoe smiled. 'That's right, we did. I'd forgotten about that. How do you know about our little club?'

'Leonie told me. I also bumped into Karen on Friday afternoon, before the festival event. She came looking for Leonie . . . said something about inviting her for dinner. Do you think Leonie might have gone to see Karen, for old times' sake?'

Zoe frowned dubiously. 'I doubt it. Karen used to irritate the hell out of Leonie. We only hung out with her because we were desperate to pass our exams with flying colours. Karen was the super-intelligent one, and I think Leonie and I hoped some of her braininess would rub off on us.'

'It obviously paid off,' Violet said. 'For Leonie anyway. She won the scholarship, didn't she?'

'Scholarship?'

'The sponsorship thing, the £4,000 bursary.'

'Oh, that.' Zoe curled her nose, as if sneering away any residual disappointment left over from not winning it herself. 'It was a bit of a travesty, actually. Karen should have romped home with it, but she totally lacked confidence, and she got horrendously nervous when it came to exams. I wouldn't say she flunked her A levels exactly, but she definitely didn't do as well as she should have done. It was a shame, because – like me and Leonie – university was her only option for escaping Merrywell. Karen's mum and dad had told her she could go to uni, but only if she won the bursary. In the end, she stayed at home and went to work full-time for her parents. It was a similar story for me . . . except, thankfully, my family didn't own a farm.'

'Why didn't the two of you go to uni anyway, without the bursary? Surely there were grants or student loans available?'

Zoe swatted Violet's words away like an errant fly. 'There were maintenance grants I think, but – realistically – that was never going to be enough. Admittedly it was before tuition fees were introduced, but even so, most parents were expected to contribute financially. Failing that, students had to get part-time jobs, often to the detriment of their studies.'

'Couldn't you have done that?'

'I suppose so, but my view was . . . if I was going to have to work my way through college, I'd be better off kicking the whole idea into touch and getting a full-time job straight away. I applied to Derbyshire County Council and was taken on as a trainee. During the three years I would have spent at university, I got loads of experience and on-the-job training.'

'But you didn't escape from Merrywell, or get to study for a degree, like you wanted. Weren't you disappointed?'

'Not especially. I didn't have high expectations, to be honest. No one in our family had been to university, and I think my parents saw studying for a degree as a bit lame. They never said as much, but I suspect they were quite relieved when I didn't go. I really wasn't bothered. Unlike Karen, I wasn't obsessed by the notion of academia.'

'Do you think Karen could have held a grudge against Leonie all these years?' Violet said, grasping at any possible motive. 'Do you think she resented missing out on the bursary, and a university education?'

'I wouldn't have thought so. I remember her being really chuffed for Leonie when she got the bursary. Karen said she'd won it fair and square. There could only ever be one winner: we all knew that. If Karen resented anyone, it would have been her parents. All they ever thought about was the farm. If they hadn't made her work so hard before and after school, she might have done better in her exams. Still, an awful lot of water's gone under the bridge since then. I shouldn't think Karen gives it a second thought these days.'

Violet nodded. 'As you say, it all happened a long time ago. I guess I'll just have to wait and hope that Leonie turns up soon.' She pulled a business card from her bag. 'This is my number. Will you let me know if Leonie gets in touch?'

'Sure. Although I don't think she will.'

'Is it worth me checking in with Karen, do you suppose? Just in case?'

'It's worth a try, I guess. It's up to you.'

'Do you have a number for her?'

'No, sorry,' Zoe replied. 'Karen and I haven't been in contact for ages. You know what it's like when you leave school. Everyone goes their own separate ways and before you know it, you've lost touch forever.'

Violet thought of her old school and uni mates, who were now scattered far and wide across the country and the world. Despite earnest promises to stay friends forever, she'd lost touch with quite a few of them.

'Can I get you anything before you go?' Zoe said. 'I noticed you were eyeing up the fudge when I came in.'

Violet smiled sheepishly. 'Go on then,' she said. 'You've twisted my arm. I'll have two hundred grams of the rum and raisin one, please.'

The purchase had been a foregone conclusion from the moment Violet had entered the shop.

Chapter 30

It was late afternoon by the time Violet got back to Merrywell and, as there was nothing urgent requiring her attention in the office, she went straight home to Greengage Cottage. Holding a mug of tea and two pieces of the fudge, she sat down at the kitchen table and checked her phone for messages. There was no word from DS Winterton and, disappointingly, nothing from Matthew either. Maybe he was steering clear because he thought Paul was still around.

As she bit into the smooth, sweet fudge, she ruminated on Leonie's whereabouts, puzzling over where she might be, and whether her disappearance was connected to Angeline's death.

Having weighed up all the likely scenarios, she concluded that there were three possibilities.

Number one: Angeline's murder and Leonie's disappearance were unconnected. On balance, Violet thought this was unlikely.

Number two: Leonie had been the intended target, and Angeline had been killed in error. In light of Leonie's disappearance, it was possible she had now become a second victim.

Number three: Whoever killed Angeline did so on purpose, and they also had Leonie in their sights. In other words, the perpetrator wanted to make sure both Angeline *and* Leonie were permanently removed from the picture.

As for who the perpetrator or perpetrators might be, Violet didn't know where to begin – although top of the list at the moment were one or both of the Dalloway women. Even Rupert Dalloway was in the frame. And what about Zoe or Karen? Or, if explanation number one was the right one, Angeline's 'stalking' colleague could still be guilty, despite having a supposedly watertight alibi.

Violet chewed over the possibilities at the same time as chewing on the second piece of fudge. When she'd finished, she fished out her phone and rang DS Winterton's number.

'It's Violet,' she said, when he answered the call. 'I'm ringing to find out if there's any news on Leonie.'

'Nothing as yet,' he replied. 'We're doing everything we can to find her, but it's proving tricky. You were right – her phone is switched off. We've requested details of the recent call activity from her service provider, but it'll be a few hours before we get that information. We've established that there's been no activity on her bank records or emails for over twenty-four hours. Other than that, there's not a lot I can tell you.'

'What about social media?' Violet asked.

'There have been some recent posts, but they're on Ms Stanwick's author accounts. Turns out they were made using one of those cross-platform scheduling tools . . . or at least, that's what the tech team tell me. Quite honestly, I haven't the first clue what a cross-platform scheduling tool is.'

Violet smiled at his self-deprecating honesty.

'We've also checked with the local hospitals,' the detective added. 'And I've been in touch with Rupert Dalloway. He said you'd been to see him.'

'Yes,' Violet said. 'I thought Leonie might have been at Langdale Hall.'

'I did tell you we'd be checking that,' DS Winterton said. 'There was no need for you to go charging over there.'

'I didn't *charge* anywhere,' Violet said. 'I certainly didn't break any speed limits, if that's what you're worried about.'

'I'm not interested in whether you've been driving too fast,' the detective replied. 'What troubles me is your habit of involving yourself in things that aren't your concern.'

Violet fought to remain calm and polite. 'Whether you like it or not, I *am* involved,' she said. 'I've been slap-bang in the middle of this since the moment I found Angeline's body. What's more, Leonie Stanwick completely opened up to me yesterday. She confided some very personal matters – which I know she's already talked to you about – and there were other things she planned to tell me this morning. It feels as though Leonie and I have unfinished business . . . I have an obligation to help her.'

'On the contrary, you fulfilled your obligations when you alerted me to the fact she hadn't turned up for your meeting. As a direct result of that, we're now treating her disappearance as a missing persons case.'

'Oh . . . well, that's something. I'm glad you're taking it seriously.'

'Of course we are,' DS Winterton replied. 'We'll be making an appeal for information later on this evening. However, as Ms Stanwick is a public figure, we're having to liaise with her publisher's PR department to make sure everything's done in a co-ordinated way.'

'Have you involved Yvette Finch?' Violet asked. 'Is she still in Merrywell? She might be able to help.'

'She's still in the village, but as she's a person of interest in the investigation, it wouldn't be appropriate to ask for her help in a professional capacity.'

'I didn't realise she was a suspect,' Violet said, mentally adding Yvette's name to the list of possible culprits.

'She's one of several people we've questioned,' DS Winterton replied. 'And please don't try to push me for any other names, because I'm not going to give them to you.'

Violet thought about the empty slot in Rosemary Dalloway's knife block. She wasn't entirely comfortable with making the woman the subject of a police investigation based on such an underhand and sneaky observation. On the other hand, DS Winterton might think it was worth checking. *No stone unturned*, and all that.

'I understand the murder weapon was a knife manufactured by a German company,' Violet said.

'How did you find that out?'

'The family liaison officer told Leonie, and Leonie told me. Do you happen to know the brand name of the knife?'

'Woost-horf . . . or Voost-hoff. Summat like that.'

'Wüsthof?' Violet said.

'Aye, that's it. Why do you want to know?'

She told him about the empty slot in Rosemary Dalloway's knife block, cringing a little as she described the way she'd all but pressed her nose against the window to get a better look.

'What did I say about involving yourself in things that aren't your concern?' DS Winterton said. 'You need to watch yourself, Violet. One of these days, you'll land yourself in trouble.'

'So everyone keeps telling me,' she replied. 'But never mind about that . . . what do you think? About the missing knife? It's worth checking, isn't it?'

DS Winterton hummed and hawed before replying.

'I'll send an officer round there,' he said. 'You're right. It's something we should look into.'

'Will you let me know what happens?' Violet said.

'Don't push your luck, lady. I'm a busy man. I haven't got time to be updating you every five minutes.'

Violet smiled secretly, feeling sure that – despite his protestations to the contrary – the detective would do his best to keep her informed.

She decided to ask one last question. 'Do you think Leonie is still alive? More than twenty-four hours have passed since I last saw her. If the killer has made contact with her, what are the chances she'll be found unharmed?'

Charlie Winterton let out a sigh. 'I'm not going to speculate with you, Violet. You're not a member of the investigation team, so there's no reason why I should. The only thing I'm willing to say is this . . . the more time that passes, the more unlikely it is we'll find Leonie Stanwick alive.'

Chapter 31

The phone call with DS Winterton had left Violet feeling helpless and inept. She was tempted to comfort herself with another piece of fudge (or three), but she knew it wouldn't do her sugar levels or her waistline any good. Instead, she got up and searched the fridge and cupboards for something savoury. Thankfully, she had the ingredients she needed to prepare a Stilton and celery risotto for dinner, which she would eat with a garlic ciabatta. It was one of her go-to recipes when she wanted to cook something tasty and quick.

Having confirmed there were adequate supplies at her disposal, she picked up her phone and called Matthew. She needed to put things right between them. She missed his funny texts, and his interesting, if somewhat random messages. She also wanted to make it clear that Paul was no longer on the scene.

'Violet,' he said, when he answered. 'How's it going?'

His tone was still a tad cool.

'Fine, thanks,' she said, feeling a flutter of panic. 'I thought I'd check in with you. You seemed out of sorts earlier. Is everything OK?'

'Yeah, everything's chipper,' he said, sounding anything but. 'You caught me on a busy day – that's all. I've been trying to catch up after taking time off for the festival.'

'Well, if you've had a hectic day, I don't suppose you'll feel like cooking tonight. I'm planning on making a risotto later. There'll be more than enough for two, if you'd like to join me.'

'Two?' he said. 'Your ex has gone back to London then, has he?'

Was it her imagination, or was there a note of irritation in the question?

'He set off first thing this morning,' she said, matter-of-factly. 'Look . . . I'm sorry I had to dip out on the quiz night, but Paul turned up completely out of the blue. I had no idea he was coming to the festival. It was all a bit awkward, actually.'

'He seemed to be enjoying his visit,' Matthew said.

'I think he was impressed with the festival,' she said, desperate to change the subject. 'Anyway . . . about dinner . . . do you want to come, or not?'

'I can't. Not tonight. I'm eating at Mum and Dad's this evening.'

'Oh . . . right.' There it was again: disappointment, poking her between the ribs. 'No problem. Some other time then. I'd better go . . . Rusty's about to make an ungainly entrance through the cat flap. She'll be pestering me for food any second.'

As Violet ended the call, her eyes filled with unfathomable tears. Throwing the phone onto the table, she delved into the bag of fudge, grabbed another comforting chunk and stuffed it into her mouth. Suddenly, the thought of making even a simple risotto seemed like too much trouble. She picked up the pack of risotto rice and plonked it back on the pantry shelf. The Hartington Stilton and sticks of celery would have to languish in the fridge for another day.

As predicted, Rusty began to weave around her ankles.

'Hello, little miss,' Violet said, bending down to gather up the cat and hold her close. 'Looks like it's just you and me this evening.'

The cat purred happily for a few seconds before scrabbling down and going to sit by her empty food bowl, looking up expectantly.

'Talk about cupboard love,' Violet said, as she ripped open a pouch of smelly cat food. 'Here you are . . . one salmon special, coming right up.'

As she tipped the wet food into the cat's bowl, her phone pinged. It was a text from Matthew.

Just spoken to Mum. She's cooking a mahoosive chicken for dinner (we're talking Foghorn Leghorn proportions) and she's adamant there's plenty to go round – so you're invited. She's serving up at six, if you're interested ☺

A wide grin spread across Violet's face. She felt a lightness in her chest, a fluttering of happiness. Was it the prospect of a home-cooked chicken dinner that was making her feel so warm inside? Or the thought of spending time with Matthew?

Smiling, she tapped out a three-word reply.

I'll be there ☺

Chapter 32

Brian and Joyce Collis lived at Well View Cottage, which was close to St Luke's Church and only a two-minute walk from Greengage Cottage. It was Matthew who opened the door when she arrived.

'Come in, Violet. You are expected.'

Smiling at her from the front step, he bowed gently and ushered her inside.

Her stomach growled as she entered the kitchen, which was filled with the mouth-watering aroma of herby roast chicken. She handed over the bottle of chilled Chardonnay she'd brought along. Joyce took it from her before folding Violet into a hug.

'How are you feeling?' Joyce asked. 'I'd say you've had quite a weekend of it.'

Violet smiled wanly as she shrugged off her coat.

'You could say that. I thought finding Angeline's body was bad enough, but then my ex-husband turned up on my doorstep, and now Leonie's gone missing again.' She clapped a hand across the lower half of her face. 'Ah . . . me and my big mouth. I wasn't going to say anything about Leonie.'

'Dunner worry, lass,' Brian Collis said, as he hung Violet's coat on the back of the door. 'You're not telling us owt we don't already know. Joyce has already heard about it.'

'How?' Violet said. 'Who told you?'

'Fiona Nash mentioned it,' Joyce said.

Violet winced. 'I hope she's not been telling everyone in the village.'

'Does it matter?' said Matthew. 'Surely, the more people who know, the better. Someone might have seen her or know where she is.'

'Matt's right, you know,' said Joyce. 'Leonie's disappearance will be public knowledge soon enough. There'll be an appeal for information before too long – you mark my words.'

'They're going to make an appeal later this evening, actually,' Violet said. 'And . . . I didn't mean to sound critical of Fiona. She's not done anything wrong. It's not like I swore her to secrecy.'

Brian tapped the side of his nose. 'There are two main forms of communication in Merrywell,' he said. 'Tele-phone and tele-Fiona. The only difference between them is that one transfers information a lot quicker than the other. I'll leave it to you to work out which is which.'

Violet laughed. 'I don't need more than one guess, but as Fiona's friend, I'm honour-bound to defend her. If you tell her something in confidence and make it clear she has to keep schtum, I can guarantee she'll keep her mouth shut.'

'Aye, and the same applies here,' Brian said. 'We have a rule in this house. What's said in Well View Cottage stays in Well View Cottage. You're among friends tonight, Violet. So, if you're worried about something and you want to talk about it, we'll be happy to listen.'

Joyce winked. 'Better let me serve up first.'

The chicken was accompanied by creamy mash, golden roast potatoes, carrots, and asparagus wrapped in Parma ham. It was a real treat for Violet to sit down and eat something that someone else had cooked.

'So come on then,' Joyce said, as she helped herself to an extra dollop of mashed potato. 'Tell us what you think's happened to Leonie.'

'I only wish I knew,' Violet replied. 'My biggest worry is that she's fallen prey to whoever killed Angeline.'

As they tucked into their meal, Violet expounded her theory that Leonie may have been the murderer's target all along – but, as she spoke, she realised she was becoming less and less sure about that. There were new possibilities emerging now, far too many for her to feel certain about anything.

'I honestly don't know what to believe,' she said. 'Angeline's death could have been a random killing for all I know. Or maybe it was pre-meditated murder and she *was* the intended victim. Her colleague has been released . . . the one the police were questioning, but there could be other people out there with a motive.'

'Such as?' said Matthew.

Violet longed to throw the 'Dalloway' name into the mix, but if she did, Matthew and his parents would want chapter and verse – and Rupert Dalloway's connection to Leonie wasn't Violet's secret to share.

'There's no clear evidence pointing to anyone in particular,' she said, evading the question. 'At least, none that I'm aware of.'

'It could be almost anyone,' Joyce said. 'I hear the police have even questioned Judith Talbot. Apparently, she was spitting feathers about it.'

Violet turned down the corners of her mouth. 'That was my fault,' she said. 'I told DS Winterton that Judith didn't want Leonie to appear at the book festival.'

Brian threw back his head and laughed. 'I'd keep that to yourself, if I were you, lass. Judith will have your guts for garters if she finds out you set the police onto her.'

Violet held up her hands and smiled. 'Too late. I've already confessed.'

Brian gave another roar of laughter. 'You're a brave woman. How did she take it?'

Violet grimaced. 'She wasn't best pleased, as you might imagine. For the record, I had no intention of setting the police onto her. I don't believe for one second that Judith was involved in Angeline Hammond's death, and I made that clear to DS Winterton.'

'Did Judith say why she didn't want Leonie at the festival?' Matthew asked.

Violet shrugged. 'She said something about lack of literary merit. You know what she's like. Judith's a book snob . . . and she likes to get her own way.'

'Mmm . . .' Matthew pronged a carrot. 'You do realise that Judith and her husband are massive cruise fans?'

'Tom Cruise?' Violet said.

Matthew chortled. 'Cruise *holidays*. It's the only time Judith misses a council meeting. She goes on a cruise at least twice a year.'

'What's that got to do with the price of fish?' Brian said.

'Probably nothing,' Matthew said. 'But if you'd been at Leonie Stanwick's event, Dad, you'd know that before she became an author, Leonie worked on a cruise ship. Maybe Leonie and Judith crossed paths at some point and the two of them had a run-in.'

Brian laughed again. 'You're not serious? What are you suggesting? Fisticuffs on the high seas?'

Matthew grinned. 'Anything's possible. And Judith does have a tendency to bear grudges, even over the most minor of spats.'

Violet's heart sank. Now that Judith knew she was responsible for tipping off DS Winterton, she'd be persona non grata in the Talbot household.

'There's no way Judith would sully herself by getting mixed up in a murder,' Joyce said. 'And anyway, I happen to know the Talbots only started cruising ten years ago, long after Leonie Stanwick worked her last cruise ship.'

'Oh,' Matthew said, looking mischievously disappointed. 'That's blown that theory then.'

'You know, Judith's not as bad as she's painted,' Joyce said. 'I don't think there's anything sinister about her aversion to

Leonie. Violet's right. It'll be a case of book snobbery, pure and simple.'

'Aye, I agree,' said Brian, smiling impishly. 'Let's face it, Judith has snootiness down to an art form.'

He reached for another slice of chicken. 'The last time there was a murder in Merrywell, I'm reliably informed you drew up a list of suspects, Violet,' Brian said. 'Rumour has it, Joyce and I were on it at one point.'

Violet shot Matthew a look. 'I wonder who you heard that from.'

'Stop teasing, Brian,' Joyce said. 'Leave the girl alone. Let her eat her dinner.'

Violet smiled gratefully. 'For what it's worth, I haven't made a list this time.'

'Then maybe you should,' Brian said. 'It might clarify a few things in your mind.'

'Violet isn't a detective, Dad,' Matthew said. 'Let her be.'

'I might not have a list,' Violet said, 'but that doesn't mean I haven't been asking questions. I spoke to Zoe Corndale this afternoon. She's an old school friend of Leonie's.'

'Aye, I know she is,' Joyce said. 'I seem to recall the pair of them were very chummy at one time. Did Zoe have anything interesting to say? Anything enlightening?'

'Unfortunately, not.'

'Are you going to put her on your suspect list?' Brian asked.

'If I *had* a list, I suppose I'd have to put Zoe's name on it,' Violet said. 'Mainly because she's one of the few people Leonie has made contact with since she came back to Merrywell.'

'This is Leonie's first proper visit in years,' Joyce said. 'But I'm struggling to comprehend why someone from the past would want to hurt her now, after all this time.'

'What about Karen Avery?' Violet said, aware that Joyce had spoken to her at the writing masterclass. 'She came looking for Leonie on Friday on the pretext of rekindling their friendship, but what if she had another reason for wanting to reconnect? Is it possible she held a grudge against Leonie?'

'A grudge about what?' said Matthew.

'Apparently, when she was in the sixth form, the school offered a bursary, sponsored by a local firm. Leonie won it, even though Karen was allegedly the more gifted pupil. It allowed Leonie to leave Merrywell . . . whereas Karen stayed behind, worked on the family farm, and never got the opportunity to fulfil her potential.'

'I don't have Karen down as the vengeful type,' Joyce said. 'She's very shy and retiring, and rather lonely. It's not easy for her to engage with people, living where she does. I see her in the village occasionally, but only ever at the shop. She never goes into the pub and she doesn't attend any of the social clubs. Mind you, she's always been a loner, although not necessarily through choice. It's a crying shame, the way her family treated her.'

'Not allowing her go to university, you mean?'

The look on Joyce's face suggested she didn't know what Violet was talking about.

'I know nothing about that,' Joyce said. 'I meant how her brother behaved, after their parents died. Her mum and dad have a lot to answer for as well. They always did favour their son.'

'Tell me what happened,' said Violet.

Balancing her knife and fork either side of her plate, Joyce took a sip of wine. 'Karen worked on the farm from a very young age. It was disgraceful really . . . verging on child labour . . . but she was a good girl and did as she was told. She was always very quiet and studious. I didn't know the Averys well, so it's probably unfair of me to say this but . . .'

'But what, Mum?' Matthew asked.

'From what I heard, they never heaped any praise on Karen, or gave her very much in the way of attention. I remember going to a sports day at the school . . . it was that year you won the high jump, Matt.'

Matthew smiled smugly. 'I reckon I still hold the school record.'

Joyce rolled her eyes. 'All right,' she said. 'No need to show off. He's only doing it because you're here, Violet.'

'Mum!' Matthew said, his cheeks flushing red. 'Stop showing me up, otherwise it'll be you who's for the high jump.'

Joyce chuckled. 'Sorry, love. I didn't mean to embarrass you. I'll admit you were a good little sportsman when you were a lad. I remember leaping up and cheering with excitement when you made that record-breaking jump . . . but Mrs Avery hardly batted an eyelid when Karen won the long-distance race. I can't remember how many metres it was the poor girl ran – but I know I couldn't have done it. She was miles ahead of the others as well.'

'Didn't Mrs Avery get on her feet and cheer?' said Violet.

'Did she heck as like. Muted applause was about all she could muster.'

'Maybe she was like Karen,' Violet said. 'Shy and quiet. Some people aren't good at showing their emotions. And at least she was *at* the sports day. She must have cared about Karen, otherwise she wouldn't have gone along to watch.'

'That's true, but Mrs Avery struck me at the time as a bottled-up sort of person. A cold fish. Maybe that's why Karen was so awkward . . . socially, I mean.'

'I wonder if the Averys were more demonstrative with their son?' Violet said.

'I'm not sure, but I do know they were more protective of him. He suffered with asthma as a child, so they tended to mollycoddle him. Someone told me he was excused duties on the farm, at least as far as the heavy work was concerned.'

'Do you know if the brother went to university?' Violet said, remembering what Zoe Corndale had said about Karen holding a grudge against her parents.

'No, I don't think he wanted to,' Joyce replied. 'He left home when he was eighteen. I seem to remember he went to work for an engineering firm or something, up in Manchester. I gather he runs his own business now. Sounds like he's done all right for himself – which makes what he did after his parents died even more unforgivable.'

'What did he do?' Violet asked.

'He insisted that the farm was sold,' Joyce said. 'Someone told me it was left to him and Karen jointly, but because he had no interest in running it, or even being a silent partner, he stipulated it had to be sold. He was hellbent on liquidating the asset, even though it meant Karen losing her home and her job.'

'Couldn't she have bought him out?' Violet asked.

'I'll bet she would have, if she'd been able to,' said Joyce. 'But the Averys' place never was very profitable. People assume that when you own a farm, you must be rich . . . but the Averys were only ever asset-rich. I shouldn't imagine they left their kids much in the way of money.'

'Couldn't Karen have raised a mortgage to buy her brother's half?' Matthew said.

'Not if the farm was barely turning a profit,' Joyce said. 'Mortgage lenders wouldn't have gone anywhere near it. Karen had no choice. The farm had to be sold. The only saving grace was that her brother agreed she could keep an old worker's cottage. It's about a mile or so from the main farmhouse. That's where she lives now. There was a derelict outbuilding at the back as well, and I hear she's converted that into a holiday apartment . . . rents it out as an Airbnb.'

'The old Avery farm . . . is that the one that's been taken over by the eco couple?' Matthew asked. 'They've got llamas now, haven't they?'

'They're alpacas, actually,' Joyce corrected him. 'Llamas are bigger, and not as soft. But you're right – the old Avery place is now a petting farm. I think the new owners make more from that side of the business than they do from traditional dairy farming.'

'It must have been a wrench for Karen,' Violet said. 'Having to leave the house she'd lived and worked in all her life . . . being banished to a cottage on the periphery . . . watching the new owners do things differently, and more successfully.'

'I'd say it's been a difficult couple of years for her,' Joyce said. 'Karen's in her early fifties now. It won't be easy for her to retrain and do a different job. Then again, she's got her half of the money from the sale of the farm, plus an income from the holiday let, so maybe she doesn't *need* to work.'

'And why would anyone work if they don't have to?' Brian said.

'People don't go to work just to earn a living, Dad,' said Matthew. 'Jobs offer a sense of purpose, and a chance to interact with colleagues and clients.'

'I agree with Matthew,' Violet said. 'Work has social as well as financial benefits. Even if I won the lottery, I'm not sure I'd give up work completely.'

'That's because you're young,' Brian said. 'Well . . . young*ish*.'

'Cheeky,' Violet said.

'Aah, I'm only pulling your leg, lass,' he said. 'Compared to me and Joyce, you're nowt but a pup. You'll have changed your tune by the time you get to my age, mind. By then, you'll have had your fill of work. Joyce and I have done our share of slogging over the years. All we want to do now is kick back and enjoy life.'

Violet smiled. 'Let's hope Karen Avery has the same philosophy.'

'She needs to make the best of her change in circumstances, that's for sure,' Joyce said. 'If she doesn't, she'll end up feeling angry and unhappy, and that's not good for anyone.'

Chapter 33

'You're quiet,' Matthew said, as he walked Violet back to Greengage Cottage. 'Penny for your thoughts.'

'They'll cost you a lot more than that,' she said, giving him a playful nudge as they walked past the village well and entered Merrywell's main street.

He smiled. 'Seriously though, I can hear your brain whirring. Are you thinking about your ex?'

'What?' Violet guffawed. 'I can assure you, he's the last person I want to think about.'

'Sure about that?' Matthew said, sounding slightly nervous as he asked the question. 'You do know I ran into him in the pub yesterday afternoon?'

'No, I didn't know,' Violet said. 'He said he'd been to the pub, but he didn't tell me he'd seen you.'

'I think he'd had quite a few pints before I got there. As soon as I arrived, he made a beeline for me. I thought he was just being friendly, but what he *really* wanted to do was let me know that the two of you are thinking of getting back together.'

Violet's face flushed with anger. 'What!' she said. 'That's utter tosh. I can't believe he said that. It's never going to happen, and he knows it.'

'So why did he tell me you were?'

'I imagine that's what he was hoping would happen – and he was telling you to warn you off. I suspect he views you as a rival for my affections.'

'I see.' Matthew smiled tentatively. 'And is he right? Am I a potential rival?'

Violet stopped in her tracks and turned to face him. Ready or not, she realised she and Matthew had reached a significant milestone. What happened next might be a turning point or it could herald the end of their friendship.

'When I first moved to Merrywell, I told you I wasn't looking for a relationship,' she said.

He nodded. 'I know you did, but that was six months ago. I guess I've been hoping you'll change your mind.'

'Well . . . maybe I have.' Violet smiled coyly. 'Weirdly, what Paul's visit *has* done is make me realise that I'm ready to move on. What is it they say? *The past is history, the future is a mystery—*'

'*And today is a gift, which is why they call it the present*,' Matthew finished.

Violet smiled, conscious of him standing next to her – close but not touching.

'Let's just say, I don't want to stay single forever,' she said. 'I like you, Matthew. You know I do.'

'Good,' he said, a smile of pleasure spreading across his face. 'Because I like you too.'

She beamed back at him. 'Let's see what happens then, shall we?'

He nodded, and they continued to walk.

'So, when I said *penny for your thoughts* a minute ago, was it me you were thinking of?'

She laughed. 'Don't get too cocky,' she said, slapping him playfully on the arm. 'As a matter of fact, I was mulling over what your mum said about Karen Avery. I wonder – if Karen *is* feeling unhappy and angry about her lot in life, how would that affect her behaviour? Do you think she might do something rash, something that would be otherwise out of character?'

Matthew shook his head and smiled. 'I might have known. There was I, hoping you were daydreaming about me, and all the time you were thinking about the murder. Violet Brewster, super sleuth, strikes again, eh?'

She frowned at his teasing and pushed her hands deeper into the pockets of her coat. 'I'm not a super sleuth, and I'm not crusading to solve this latest crime either. Right now, I'm far more concerned about where Leonie might be.'

'I have to admit, the situation is getting complicated,' Matthew said. 'I keep telling myself there has to be a logical explanation for everything that's happened, but if there is, I've no idea what it is.'

'I'm stumped as well,' Violet said. 'I've been rereading some of my favourite Agatha Christie mysteries recently, and I keep asking myself: how would Miss Marple solve this case?'

'Or Hercule Poirot.'

Violet laughed. 'That's easy,' she said. 'Poirot would use his little grey cells. I'm not sure about Jane Marple . . . she'd probably take a more laid-back approach . . . maybe mull everything over while knitting herself a new cardigan.'

'Do you have any wool?' Matthew asked.

Violet smirked. 'I'm glad you didn't ask whether I have any grey cells.'

'I didn't need to. I know you have those in abundance.'

'Why, thank you,' she said, smiling at the compliment. 'Knitting, unfortunately, is *not* my forte. Perhaps I need to find something else to pass the time . . . something that will keep me occupied while my subconscious analyses everything I've learned over the last few days. Maybe then I'll be able to make sense of it all.'

'I get the feeling you know more than you're letting on.'

Violet looked at him out of the corner of her eye. 'I do,' she said. 'I met with Leonie yesterday afternoon. She asked me to record an interview with her. She wanted to tell her story.'

‘Her *story*?’

‘Yes,’ she replied. ‘She gave me the whole nine yards, but I’m not going to share her secrets. They’re not mine to tell.’

‘But you have shared this information with the police?’

‘I didn’t need to,’ Violet replied. ‘Leonie had already told DS Winterton everything she told me.’

‘Well, that’s something at least. Hopefully, Winterton will be able to assess which parts of her story are significant, and which are irrelevant.’

‘It was a complex tale,’ Violet said. ‘I just hope he works quickly. The longer this goes on, the less likely it is that Leonie will be found alive. If only there was something I could *do*. I’m not sure why, but I feel I owe it to her to help . . . to not give up.’

Matthew placed a hand on her shoulder. ‘You’re a good person, Violet, but it’s not down to you to solve this. You don’t owe Leonie anything.’

‘But she and I have made a connection. I’ll admit, when Leonie and I were first introduced, I didn’t think I was going to like her, but over the last couple of days, she’s grown on me. The more I get to know her, the more I understand.’

‘It does sound as though the two of you have bonded. Even so, you must promise not to do anything rash.’

‘I never make promises unless I’m a hundred per cent certain I can keep them,’ Violet said. ‘But don’t fret, I’m not stupid. I won’t do anything silly. There’s no need to worry about me.’

‘That’s the thing,’ Matthew said. ‘I *do* worry. I care about you, Violet. More than you realise.’

He took her hand and squeezed it, and then let go of it almost immediately as they were forced to fall into single file past an ancient Land Rover that was parked half-on, half-off the pavement.

‘I could be wrong,’ Matthew whispered, tilting his head as they shuffled past the vehicle, ‘but I think this is Karen Avery’s Land Rover. I’ve seen her bombing around the lanes in it.’

His guesswork was confirmed when Karen emerged from the shop on the opposite side of the road. She was wearing a long trench coat, a turquoise-blue scarf, and the same purple bobble hat she'd worn at the book festival. A bottle of white wine was tucked under her left arm and, clutched to her body were two family-sized packets of crisps.

'Evening,' she said, as, head down, she brushed past them and climbed into the Land Rover.

There was something about the encounter that triggered a memory for Violet, or perhaps it was something about Karen herself that rang a bell – but whatever it was, was nebulous. It hung around the edges of her consciousness before drifting away completely.

'She was in a hurry,' Matthew said.

They heard the Land Rover's engine turn over behind them and, when it finally sputtered into life, Karen pulled onto the road and overtook them, heading north out of the village.

'Maybe her ears were burning and she's heading home to throw cold water on them.' Violet smiled. 'She was cutting it fine with her shopping though. The shop's due to close in a few minutes.'

Matthew looked pensive. 'Strange when that happens, isn't it?' he said.

'When what happens?'

'You talk about someone or something, and then . . . out of the blue, they or it turns up.'

'It's called the Baader-Meinhof phenomenon,' Violet said. 'Also known as the frequency illusion. It's when something you've just noticed, or experienced, or been told about suddenly crops up constantly.'

Matthew whistled. 'Get you! I didn't realise I was in the presence of a walking encyclopedia.'

Violet laughed. 'I'm full of useless trivia, me.'

'Not useless at all. Your explanation makes perfect sense. We talked about Karen Avery, and the next minute she's walking past us in the street. What did you call it again?'

'Baader-Meinhof phenomenon,' Violet repeated. 'Or it could simply be a kind of synchronicity . . . a meaningful coincidence.'

They had reached the front gate at Greengage Cottage.

'Want to come in for a coffee?' Violet asked.

She could tell that he was giving serious consideration to the offer, but after a few seconds, he shook his head.

'Thanks, but I'd better go home. I've got a delivery to make in Nottingham in the morning, and I want to make an early start before the traffic gets too bad.'

'OK.'

She felt a pang of disappointment, until he moved in for a brief hug.

'Goodnight, Violet. See you soon. Don't forget to let me know when you're going to make that risotto you offered me.'

She was about to say that she would text him, but something told her not to. If they *were* going to move things to the next stage, now seemed as good a time as any.

'How does Friday at six-thirty sound?' she said.

The smile he gave her made her heart skip a beat.

'It sounds perfect,' he said. 'Looking forward to it already.'

Chapter 34

When she got in, Violet abandoned the idea of coffee and instead made herself a mug of Turkish delight–flavoured hot chocolate. The prospect of cooking for Matthew on Friday was both exciting and nerve-racking, and she made a mental note to double-check she had more than enough ingredients for two people.

After carrying the mug of hot chocolate into the living room, she switched on the TV. It was still early; plenty of time left to watch a film before bedtime.

She kicked off her shoes, pulled her legs onto the sofa and began searching for something appealing on Netflix. The mug was on a lamp table close to her right elbow and it was giving off wafts of rose-flavoured Turkish delight. As the sweet scent drifted into her nostrils, Violet sat up with a jolt. The smell reminded her of the encounter with Karen Avery outside the shop.

In a flash, she remembered what had struck her at the time. When Karen had brushed past her, she had smelt of roses – the heady, rose-scented aroma of Leonie's perfume. The memory called to mind something else about Karen: she'd had a turquoise-coloured silk scarf wrapped around her neck. Had that been the source of the perfume? Was Karen Avery wearing Leonie's scarf – the same scarf she'd been wearing when Violet had last seen her?

Violet mulled over the possibilities. If the scarf *had* been Leonie's, the most innocent explanation was that she had gifted it to Karen. But if that was the case, it must have been *after* the meeting with Violet on Sunday afternoon. Had Karen visited Birch House after Violet left? Could Karen Avery have been the last person to see Leonie before she went missing? Or was she the reason Leonie had disappeared?

Leaving the hot chocolate half-finished, Violet grabbed her keys, pulled on a coat and went out to her car. She'd restricted herself to one small glass of wine with her chicken dinner, so she was OK to drive. Before she could talk herself out of it, she got into the Toyota, pulled away from Greengage Cottage, and headed north, out of the village.

She followed signs for the petting farm, which she knew was approximately one mile from Merrywell. The worker's cottage that was now Karen's home had to be somewhere close by.

As she drove, she used her hands-free device to call DS Winterton. He sounded miffed when he answered, as though she'd disturbed him from something interesting.

'What can I do for you at this late hour?' he said.

'It's twenty past eight,' Violet said, trying her best to sound chirpy. 'The night is still young – at least, it is for me.'

'So why are you ringing?'

'I saw Karen Avery coming out of Merrywell Stores a little while ago. I'm fairly certain she was wearing Leonie Stanwick's scarf – the one Leonie had on when I left her at Birch House on Sunday evening.'

'Scarf?' DS Winterton sounded incredulous. 'There must be thousands of ladies' scarves in Derbyshire. Why are you so sure it was Leonie Stanwick's scarf?'

'It was quite distinctive . . . a lovely turquoise-blue colour,' Violet said.

'That really narrows it down then.'

‘Don’t be sarky, DS Winterton. It doesn’t suit you,’ Violet said, ploughing on despite his cynicism. ‘The item I’m referring to was one of those fancy designer scarves, made of silk. The reason I’m so sure it was Leonie’s is that it smelt strongly of her perfume.’

‘Are you saying you stopped this Karen Avery woman and sniffed her scarf?’

‘Don’t be ridiculous, of course I didn’t. She brushed past me. That’s when I got a whiff of it. I’m thinking that maybe Leonie gave Karen the scarf, as a gift.’

‘I’m sorry, but this is too tenuous, even for you. You’ve already sent me off on one wild goose chase with that damned knife.’

Violet’s pulse began to pound in her ears. ‘Wild goose chase? What do you mean?’

‘I *mean* that when my officer went round to Rosemary Dalloway’s apartment, he discovered that the knife you told us was “missing” wasn’t missing at all. Turns out it was in the dish-washer. Interesting suggestion, Violet, but it appears you were mistaken. Again. Mrs Dalloway’s Wüsthof knives are all present and correct.’

Violet curled her toes. Another theory dismissed as worthless. So much for Violet Brewster super sleuth.

‘I’m sorry if your officer had a wasted journey,’ she said, determined to cling on to her dignity. ‘Even so, I still believe it was a lead worth checking. And just because I was wrong about the knife, doesn’t mean I’m wrong about the scarf.’

‘The scarf is likely to be a coincidence,’ DS Winterton said. ‘And even if it does turn out to be Ms Stanwick’s, have you considered the possibility that Ms Avery might have found it? Picked it up from somewhere? A scarf is the sort of thing that’s easily dropped.’

‘I’ll admit I hadn’t thought of that,’ Violet said, feeling deflated. ‘Shouldn’t you check with her though? Ask her where she got it? If the scarf is Leonie’s, Karen Avery might know where she is now. Or she might be the reason Leonie has gone missing.’

She heard the detective sigh.

'One of my officers has already rung Karen Avery. The last time she saw Leonie Stanwick was at the book festival event.'

'She could be lying.'

'Why would she lie?'

'Any number of reasons.'

The line went quiet. Either they'd been cut off, or DS Winterton was counting to ten.

'What is it with you?' he said, eventually. 'Why are you so determined to find work for me? Don't you think I've got enough to do?'

'Sorry.' Violet tried to sound contrite. 'I know you're a busy man. I only want to help.'

'Aye,' he said, ceding to her with a growl. 'I know you mean well, and I suppose . . . in the absence of any other leads . . . I could arrange for someone to speak to Karen Avery again. I'll get an officer to pay her a visit . . . find out about the scarf and what, if anything, she knows about Leonie Stanwick's whereabouts.'

'No need,' Violet said. 'I'm on my way to Karen's now. I'm not exactly sure where her house is, but I'll find it.'

'No, you will not.' DS Winterton's voice was instantly sharp, crackling with anger. 'You must not, I repeat *not*, go anywhere near Karen Avery's house. Do I make myself clear? If you *are* right about the scarf, there's a chance . . . albeit a slim one . . . that she's responsible for Ms Stanwick's disappearance. You'll be putting yourself at risk if you go anywhere near the house. Turn your car around, *now*. Do it.'

Violet was on a narrow, winding stretch of lane with no street lighting. It was dark out here. Pitch black. The fields on either side looked bleak and forbidding.

'I'm deadly serious,' DS Winterton continued. 'If I find out you've made contact with Karen Avery, I'll charge you with interfering with a police investigation.'

Could he even do that? Violet wondered. *Or was he making an idle threat to get her to back off?*

'All right,' she said, concluding that a criminal record wouldn't enhance her business reputation. 'I'll find somewhere to turn around and I'll go home. I promise.'

She ended the call and drove on, passing another sign that said the petting farm was two hundred yards on the left. She might be able to turn there.

But as she approached the turn-off, she saw that it was already occupied. Car headlights illuminated the area: Karen Avery's classic Land Rover was tucked into the lay-by next to the farm entrance, and parked in front of it was an RAC rescue van.

Violet slowed down, pulled up her hood, and drove past. Karen Avery was sitting behind the steering wheel of her vehicle, eating crisps from one of the bags she'd bought earlier. A roadside mechanic had his head under the bonnet, and a bright, beaming torch in his hand.

Violet whooshed past the scene, her heart pumping fast and her mind working overtime. One thing was certain: Karen Avery couldn't be in two places at once. While she was stranded in her vehicle, she couldn't possibly be at home. There was nothing to stop Violet driving to Karen's cottage and having a quick look around. No one would ever know she'd been there. OK, so she'd promised DS Winterton she wouldn't make contact with Karen Avery – but as Karen was currently at the mercy of the RAC, there was little danger of that happening, was there?

She drove on, peering into the darkness, travelling almost another mile before she saw what she assumed must be Karen's house. It was in the middle of nowhere, set back from the road, its squat limestone walls surrounded by vast open fields. Violet steered through an open wooden gate, which had a sign attached to its top bar declaring this to be Edge Cottage. The Toyota bumped along a short approach road, which had weeds growing along the middle. Violet parked in the front yard and got out.

Off to the side of the cottage was an old wooden cart; it was painted blue and filled with colourful plant pots. Only a few straggly geraniums had survived what must have been a delightful summer display.

Beyond the house, stretching out in all directions as far as the eye could see were empty, rolling fields. Somewhere in the far distance, a couple of lights twinkled, but otherwise, Edge Cottage stood like a solitary sentry, guarding the hillside.

There were four unevenly spaced windows at the front of the property, all of them in darkness.

But that doesn't necessarily mean it's empty, thought Violet, as she banged on the door.

Chapter 35

She stepped back and waited, listening carefully for any sound inside.

'Leonie?'

Her voice cut through the cloying silence of the night, but produced no answering call. Violet cocked an ear, but the only sound she could hear was an owl hooting somewhere in the distance. Across the yard was a tiny one-storey outbuilding that might once have been used to house animals or store wood. Violet tried its door, but it was locked and when she rattled the old-fashioned thumb latch, there was no response from within.

Next, she walked through a gate at the side of the house. The narrow path she followed lay in the shadows, so she used the torch on her phone to light the way. At the back of the house, two bedraggled terracotta flower pots stood either side of the toffee-coloured wooden back door. She rattled the doorknocker, but – unsurprisingly – no one appeared.

As she turned to walk away, Violet remembered the holiday let that Joyce Collis had mentioned, wondering whereabouts it was located in relation to the main house.

Holding up her phone, she swung its feeble beam around the garden, wishing she had a more powerful torch. On the right-hand side of the lawn was a path, which she decided to follow.

At the very end of the long, well-stocked garden was a two-storey stone structure. The lower portion of the building consisted of four supporting arches. The central two were open to the elements: one was being used to store wood, and a sit-on lawn mower was parked in the other. The apertures either side were closed off with arched double doors, which were painted the same shade of blue as the wooden cart at the front of Edge Cottage. Violet went over to the first set of doors. A chunky combination padlock suggested it was used for storage. She slapped her hand against the door and then moved to the far end of the building and repeated the process.

'Leonie,' she shouted. 'Are you in there?'

There was no sound from within either of the shuttered archways, but from the first floor of the building, came a frantic knock.

Violet raced around to the side, where a set of steep stone-built steps led to the first floor. There was no handrail, so she trod carefully, hugging the wall and using the torch on her phone to light the way, hoping it wasn't draining the battery too much. At the top was a blue-painted door with a sign on it that said: *Edge Cottage Holiday Apartment.*

From inside came a muted voice, and the sound of movement.

'Leonie? Is that you?' Violet shouted. 'It's Violet. Are you in there?'

'Yes, I'm here.' Leonie sounded breathless with relief, her voice increasing in volume as she moved closer to the other side of the door.

Violet tried the handle. The door was locked, but she banged on it anyway.

'What's happened?' she asked. 'Has Karen locked you in?'

'Yes. I've been stuck in here since this morning,' Leonie said, sounding exasperated and not in the least bit afraid. 'She's completely lost the plot. I think she must be having some sort of emotional meltdown.'

'Well, the good news is she's not here right now,' Violet said, telling herself not to panic. 'Her car's broken down on the lane about a mile away. Is there any chance you can climb out of a window?'

'No, and believe me, I've tried. They're all locked and Karen has taken the keys. I've been plucking up the courage to break the glass and jump out, but it's quite a drop onto the grass. Knowing my luck, I'd break my ankles and be unable to run away.'

'Not to worry,' Violet said. 'The police are on their way. They'll be able to get you out.'

She wondered whether to try and break in herself, but the door was sturdy and solid, and it would be no easy feat. Besides, she was already at risk of being arrested for interfering with a criminal investigation. Did she really want to add breaking and entering to the charge sheet? Much better to wait until the police arrived.

'How on earth did you end up here, anyway?' she asked, keeping close to the door so that she could hear Leonie's reply.

'Shortly after you left Birch House on Sunday, Karen turned up. When she knocked, I assumed it was you . . . coming back to collect something you'd left behind. I pulled open the door and there she was, staring at me with a big cheesy smile on her face. She said she was cooking a roast, and she wanted me to join her for dinner.'

'She's tenacious – I'll give her that,' said Violet.

'I tried to excuse myself . . . told her I didn't really have any appetite, but she was very insistent. *Please,* she said, *I'd love for us to catch up.* She said she wasn't living on the farm anymore, and that a lot had happened over the last few years. She wanted to tell me all about it over dinner.'

'I must admit, I'm surprised you agreed to come,' Violet said.

She heard a growl of frustration on the other side of the door. 'Trust me, I wish I hadn't,' Leonie said. 'I suppose I felt sorry for her. Karen's always been a lost soul, and I was pretty mean to her when we were at school. She considered me a friend, but I was anything but. There were times when I was horrible to her, really spiteful. I feel guilty about that now, and I suppose coming here was my way of making amends.

'I did make one last concerted effort to wriggle out of it. I told her I didn't have my car – but she batted that away by saying she'd give me a lift and drop me back at the hotel later on. Next, I told her I wasn't in the mood for company . . . and that I wouldn't be a very good dinner guest. *All the more reason to come to my place*, she said. *You shouldn't be alone at a time like this.* I ran out of excuses after that. Karen had completely worn me down, so I caved in.'

'Why did you leave your back door unlocked at Birch House?'

'I didn't know I had,' Leonie said. 'I went out to the yard to put a few things in the dustbin . . . but that was early on, ages before you arrived. I must have forgotten to lock up again. Karen whisked me away in her car, and I didn't bother checking the back door before I left.'

'It's actually a blessing that you didn't,' Violet said. 'If Birch House had been properly secured, I might not have gone looking for you. It was finding the back door unlocked that set alarm bells ringing in my head.'

'It's ironic, isn't it? Leaving my own door unlocked and then ending up locked up here. How did you know where to find me anyway?'

'It was an educated guess,' Violet said. 'I saw Karen in Merrywell. I noticed she was wearing your scarf . . . the one you had on when I last saw you.'

'I think I left it in her Land Rover,' Leonie said. 'She must have filched it.'

'Tell me what happened when you got here,' Violet said.

'Karen and I had dinner – it was lovely, actually. It felt surprisingly good, talking to her again, and I could tell she was enjoying the company. Karen always was a loner, and now that she's living out here, the daily sense of isolation must be absolutely overwhelming.

'We had a bottle of wine with dinner, and then Karen opened another. She said I could stay the night here, in the apartment. She'd had some wine herself by then, and said she wouldn't be able to drive me back. I could have rung for a taxi I suppose, but staying here seemed like the sensible thing to do.

'When Karen brought me down the garden to this place, I was impressed. She's done a great job on the conversion. There's an en-suite bedroom in here, and a living room with a kitchenette. Everything seemed to be hunky-dory, and I slept like a dream, thanks to the wine. But then, when I woke up this morning, I discovered the door and windows were locked, and Karen had taken my phone. I thought about shouting for help, but I knew I'd be wasting my time. There's nothing and no one within a mile of this place.'

'Has she explained why she's keeping you here?' Violet said.

'This morning she came and stood where you are now and told me she wanted me to stay for a few days. She said she'd like to spend more time with me. She even offered to bring me a notebook and a pen so that I could make the most of my stay . . . use it as a mini writing retreat.'

'And how did you respond to that?'

'I tried to humour her . . . told her I appreciated the offer, but that I needed to go back to the hotel.'

'What did she say?' Violet asked.

'Nothing. She walked away and left me here.'

'She's obviously not thinking straight.'

'I think she must be having a breakdown,' Leonie said. 'And I suspect it's my fault. On Sunday night over dinner, she was quizzing me about why I'd dropped out of university. You remember I let it slip during the book festival interview that I'd quit after the first term? Apparently, Karen hadn't been aware of that. She said she was disappointed in me . . . that she'd always assumed I'd graduated. At the festival, when she found out that wasn't the case, she said she was shocked and surprised. She told me I'd let the side down, that I should have persisted.'

Violet remembered the moment during the festival when Leonie had cited *persistence* as an essential quality for success. The scornful scoff somewhere in the audience must have come from Karen, mocking her old friend for what she considered hypocrisy.

'Did you tell her the truth? About why you dropped out?'

'Yes,' Leonie said. 'Like I told you before, I'm done with all the subterfuge.'

'And what did Karen say?'

'Nothing at first,' Leonie said. 'I think it took the wind out of her sails. She'd obviously been feeling extremely peeved and aggrieved, but as soon as I told her my reasons for leaving uni, her whole attitude changed. She said she was sorry . . . that if she'd known about Angeline, she would have taken the time to get to know her properly . . . looked out for her . . . been a friend.'

'I'm not sure Angeline needed anyone to look out for her,' Violet said. 'Everything I've heard about her suggests your parents did an excellent job in raising her.'

A few moments passed before Leonie replied. 'It pains me to say it, but I think you're right.'

'Did Karen say anything about Angeline's murder?' Violet said.

'No, she never mentioned it. I told myself she was avoiding the subject so as not to upset me.'

'Maybe she was keeping quiet for another reason,' said Violet. 'Has it crossed your mind that Karen might be the killer? That maybe she lashed out at Angeline in a fit of rage, thinking she was you?'

'Yes, it's crossed my mind,' Leonie said. 'Of course it has.'

'Did you ask her about it?'

'Are you kidding? I told you . . . Karen's emotionally fraught, on the verge of a complete meltdown. Accusing her of Angeline's murder might tip her over the edge. And let's not forget . . . she's keeping me here against my will. If she *did* kill Angeline, I'd be putting myself directly in the line of fire if I confronted her about it.'

'It is a volatile situation,' Violet agreed. 'We need to be careful . . . do the sensible thing. There's a police officer on the way already, but I should probably call DS Winterton as well, to let him know you're here and tell him what's happened.'

Violet pulled out her phone and waited anxiously for DS Winterton to answer her call.

'Please don't blow a gasket,' she said, when she heard his voice. 'But I'm at Karen Avery's house.'

He made a noise that sounded like a foghorn blasting in her ear. 'What did I tell you?' he said. 'I specifically instructed you to turn your car around and go home. You *promised* you'd do that. What the hell are you playing at, Violet?'

'I had every intention of turning around,' she said. 'But then I passed Karen Avery on the road . . . her Land Rover had broken down, and an RAC guy was with her. I knew she wasn't at home, and as I was close by, I thought I'd call in and have a quick look around. And it's a good job I did. Leonie Stanwick is here, locked in the holiday let behind Karen's house.'

'What?' the detective's voice snapped angrily. 'How do you know it's her? Have you seen her?'

'No, but I've spoken to her. She's fine, but Karen's keeping her here against her will.'

DS Winterton grunted. 'A patrol vehicle's already on its way, but I'll get them to switch on the blue light,' he said. 'You need to get out of there, Violet. *Now*. When my officers arrive, they'll assess the situation and, if necessary, they'll be able to break in.'

'Shall I go back to my car and wait for the patrol vehicle?'

'No, you need to get as far away from the area as you can,' he said, shouting impatiently. 'Go home, and I'll ask an officer to call in and see you later to get your statement. You've found Ms Stanwick, and that's a good thing – but this situation has the potential to turn nasty. It's time to make a hasty retreat.'

'OK,' Violet said, holding the phone several inches from her head to prevent her eardrum from being pummelled. 'I'm leaving now.'

She ended the call and leaned against the door.

'Leonie,' she said. 'The police are on their way, but DS Winterton says I've got to get out of here. Just hang in there . . . they'll soon have you out.'

Holding her phone torch in front of her, Violet descended the stone steps and hurried back up the garden path. As she dashed along the side of the house, she realised the walkway didn't seem quite so shadowy and ominous.

The reason became clear as she rounded the corner of the house. A vehicle was pulling into the yard, its headlights lighting up the darkness. Violet experienced a crushing wave of relief.

Thank goodness for that, she thought. *Well done, DS Winterton. That was quick work.*

She stepped forward, grateful for the chance to personally hand over responsibility for Leonie's wellbeing before driving away from Edge Cottage. It wouldn't have felt right somehow, leaving her alone, trapped in the holiday apartment.

As Violet held up a hand to shield her eyes from the dazzle of the headlights, her stomach clenched. The sense of relief she'd felt seconds earlier was swept away in a terrifying rush of adrenaline. The lights were round, positioned relatively high on the vehicle, and they were shining straight into her eyes.

These weren't the headlights of a police patrol car. They belonged to Karen Avery's Land Rover.

Chapter 36

'What are you doing here?' Karen said, as she jumped down from the vehicle and slammed the driver's door shut. In her left hand, she was holding the remaining bag of crisps and the bottle of wine.

Violet scrabbled around for a plausible explanation for being there, but the 'little grey cells' Matthew had praised so generously less than an hour ago, were now failing her miserably.

'I was lost.' The words were out of her mouth before she could stop them. 'I stopped for directions, but there was no one in.'

'Yeah, right. Pull the other one.' Karen was peering through Violet's car window. 'You've got sat nav. Why would you need directions?'

'It's not working,' said Violet. 'Something's wrong with it.'

'I don't believe you.'

With her right hand, Karen dug into her pocket and pulled out a set of keys.

'Do you think I don't know why you're here?' she said, using the key to point at Violet. 'You've been spying, haven't you? Found anything interesting?'

Violet put her shoulders back. 'Yes, to both questions,' she said, sounding braver than she felt. 'And I hope the key in your hand is the one to your holiday apartment. It's time you let Leonie out, don't you think?'

Karen pushed the bottle of wine into the pocket of her trench coat and threw the bag of crisps at Violet.

'You'd better come with me,' she said, gesturing towards the path at the side of the house.

Violet hesitated, weighing up her best course of action. She couldn't afford to be foolhardy. If Karen Avery was the killer, it would be unwise to make any sudden moves. For the sake of Leonie's safety and her own, she needed to keep Karen calm, and the easiest way to do that was to follow her instructions.

She walked towards the path slowly, all the while scanning the horizon, hoping desperately to spot the approach of a blue flashing light, but a visual search of the surrounding countryside proved fruitless.

Silently, Karen trailed behind her, along the garden path towards the holiday apartment. It was her muteness that scared Violet the most. It shrieked 'danger' much louder than words ever could.

'Why is Leonie locked in?' she asked, as they neared the end of the path. 'What are you planning to do?'

'Do?' Karen sounded remarkably calm and rational. 'I'm not planning to *do* anything. I just want her to stay a little longer, that's all. It gets lonely out here sometimes. It's nice to have company.'

The polite, matter-of-fact response wasn't what Violet had been expecting. Clearly, Karen didn't think she'd done anything wrong.

'The problem is, Karen, you can't force people to stay with you by locking them up,' Violet said, speaking gently so as not to further disturb Karen's state of mind.

'If I hadn't locked her in, she would have left,' Karen said, sounding petulant. 'I don't get many visitors. Nobody ever comes to see me, not willingly.'

'What about the people who come to stay in your holiday apartment?' Violet said.

They had reached the bottom of the stone steps. Above them, stars sparkled in the ink-black sky.

'Those people aren't interested in talking to me,' Karen replied. 'One couple stayed for two weeks and barely said a dozen words to me the whole time.'

'Some people are just plain rude. You shouldn't let them get to you.'

'I try to not hold it against them,' Karen said. 'Holidaymakers come here to get away from it all, not to spend time with the likes of me – but when people give me the cold shoulder like that, it confirms everything I already know about myself. I'm boring, uninteresting. Nobody wants to know me. Leonie understands that, but she came here yesterday regardless, and she was kind to me.'

'That doesn't mean you can keep her here indefinitely, against her will. Why don't we go and unlock the door and let her out?'

Karen nodded. 'Go on up,' she said, pushing Violet up the steep steps.

She climbed carefully and reluctantly, aware that Karen was right behind her, her mood unpredictable. When they reached the door, Violet stood aside and let Karen unlock it.

'Go in.' Karen thrust Violet ahead of her and, once they were both inside, she turned, locked the door and pocketed the key.

Leonie was sitting on a two-seater sofa in a compact living space. Surprisingly, rather than looking terrified, she looked annoyed and grumpy. The room had two Velux windows, and a tiny kitchen area. Behind that was a door, which presumably led to the en-suite bedroom.

Violet gave Leonie an almost imperceptible shake of her head, willing her not to reveal that the police had been called.

Leonie stood up and folded her arms. 'About time,' she said, sounding irate. 'I hope one of you is going to drive me back to the hotel. I have things to do.'

In Violet's opinion, the best way out of this situation was to appease Karen. Reason with her. Unfortunately, Leonie seemed to favour a more confrontational approach.

'What were you thinking, Karen?' she said. 'Why did you lock me in?'

Perhaps it was the anger in Leonie's voice, or the futility of what she'd done . . . whatever the reason, Karen's bottom lip began to wobble and she started to cry.

'I didn't want you to leave,' she said. 'You're the only friend I've got.'

Leonie scoffed. 'If that's true, you need to pull your socks up . . . get a grip on your life. It was nice of you to cook a meal for me, and I enjoyed spending time with you on Sunday evening, but that's as far as it goes. You and I haven't seen each other for nearly thirty-five years. Even if we were once friends, that's not the case anymore.'

Karen was blubbing now, her eyes and nose running, her whole face a wet, crumpled mess.

'There's no need to be cruel, Leonie,' Violet said, a note of warning in her tone.

'I'm not being cruel, I'm being honest. Do you have any idea how many people I've become acquainted with over the years? I've had more friends than most people have had hot dinners. It's impossible to keep in touch with each and every one of them. People move on . . . go their separate ways. It's a fact of life.'

'That's easy for you to say.' Karen snuffled. 'Miss bloody Gregarious. You were always surrounded by friends. Everybody liked you.'

'That's because I made an effort,' Leonie said. 'You could never be bothered. You always stayed on the outside, looking in. You might not realise this, Karen, but our home circumstances were quite similar. I could have chosen to be like you, an outsider, but instead I opted to make friends . . . connect with people. It was hard at first, but it got easier with time. You should try it.'

'I did make an effort,' Karen said. 'Or at least, I tried to . . . with you and Zoe. We *were* friends, whether you like to admit it or not. Perhaps not best friends, but you're one of the few proper mates I've ever had. That friendship obviously meant more to me than it did to you.'

Leonie took a deep breath. 'I'm sorry if I treated you badly,' she said, her tone conciliatory. 'I realise I could have been kinder to you, but I was a teenager, for God's sake. I was an arrogant little cow . . . selfish and self-serving. Some people might say I still am. But you, Karen . . . you were quiet and shy and self-effacing. You were also highly intelligent and extremely gifted academically. You were bloody brilliant, in fact . . . but you never had any faith in yourself. It sounds to me like you still don't.'

'What's the point in believing in myself if no one else does?' Despite the defeatist words, Karen sounded feistier now, more determined.

'It doesn't matter what other people think,' said Leonie. 'It's what *you* think that counts. That's the difference between you and me. You care what people say; I don't give two hoots.'

'Things might have been different if I'd managed to get away from here,' Karen said. 'Maybe I would have learned to like myself a little more . . . gained some self-esteem.'

'It's never too late,' Leonie said. 'There's nothing to keep you here, is there? It's a big world out there, Karen. You could sell up and go somewhere new. Or you could become a mature student and finally get your degree.'

'If I had more confidence, then maybe I would,' Karen said. 'Mind you, if I'd had any confidence, I'd have got out of here years ago.'

Unwittingly, Leonie seemed to have taken on the role of mentor. 'There's nothing you can do about the past,' she said. 'That's a fact I've had to come to terms with myself recently. All any of us can do is make the most of the here and now, and shape how we want our future lives to be.'

'Do you really think I could do that?' Karen said. 'Shape a better future?'

'Yes, I do,' Leonie replied, her voice firm. 'Now, shall we get out of here? Before the police arrive and break the door down?'

'Police?' Karen looked at Violet accusingly. 'You called the police?'

Violet nodded. 'What else was I supposed to do?' she said. 'Leonie was locked in here, and you'd taken her phone. I had no idea what you intended to do.'

'You can't possibly think I'd have hurt her?' Karen screwed up her red, tear-stained face. 'I just needed her to *stay*. I wanted to extend our time together. It was so lovely, having someone to dinner. All I wanted was more of the same . . . more friendship, more conversation, more laughter. Yesterday evening, I felt more alive than I have done for years. That's what I need. To feel *alive*.'

Violet could hear a siren in the distance, the sound growing louder with each second that ticked by. Knowing that the police were so close gave her the courage to pose the question her sleuthing-self was aching to ask.

'You say you wouldn't hurt Leonie. What about Angeline? Did you kill her, Karen?'

Karen's mouth fell open, and her eyes flashed a vehement protest.

'No!' she said. 'Of course not. Is that what you think? That I murdered Angeline?'

'Maybe you thought it was me you were killing,' Leonie said.

'No!' Karen said again, pressing her hands over her ears to block out the accusation. 'I would never kill anyone, least of all Angeline. She was a nice person, kind and caring, and a very competent nurse. She came to the farm regularly when my mother was ill. I'd never have hurt her, or you, Leonie. You have to believe me.'

Heavy footsteps sounded on the stone steps. Someone banged on the door.

'Police. Open up.'

'You need to unlock the door, Karen,' Violet said. 'Otherwise, they'll have to break in.'

Karen pulled the key from her pocket and handed it to Violet. Then she crumpled to the floor and began to weep inconsolably.

As Violet spoke to the police and unlocked the door, she could hear Leonie behind her, talking softly to Karen.

'It's all right,' she was saying. 'Everything's going to be all right.'

Chapter 37

An officer escorted Karen to the front of the main house and sat her in the back of a second police car, which appeared less than a minute after the first one. All the while, Karen continued to protest her innocence.

'Where are you taking me? I haven't done anything wrong. Ask Leonie . . . she's my friend. We've been catching up, that's all.'

Linking arms, Violet and Leonie stood and watched as she was driven away.

'I should be angry with her,' Leonie said, 'but I'm not. I feel sorry for her.'

'Me too,' said Violet.

Once the patrol vehicle carrying Karen had gone, a female police officer told Violet and Leonie that they would need to make statements.

'I hope you're not expecting us to come to the station,' Leonie said, sounding short-tempered and far more like her old self. 'I've been cooped up in that apartment all day. I need to get back to my hotel to freshen up.'

Violet thought there were worse places to be cooped up than a newly refurbished holiday apartment in the Peak District, but she sympathised with Leonie's desire to avoid a visit to the police station.

'How about if I drive Leonie back to her hotel?' Violet suggested, addressing the police officer directly. 'You can follow me, and talk to me there while Leonie has a shower and gets changed. Once she's freshened up, she can give you her statement in the comfort of her hotel room.'

'OK then, but let's not hang around,' the officer replied. 'We need to know what's taken place here. Karen Avery is likely to be charged with false imprisonment, but we also need to establish whether she was involved in the death of Angeline Hammond.'

'She told us she wasn't,' Violet said.

The officer raised an arched eyebrow. 'No disrespect, but that's for us to decide. She's hardly going to admit it, is she?'

'I really don't think she killed Angeline,' Leonie said. 'Karen's emotionally messed up, but I don't believe she's capable of murder. As for false imprisonment . . . I'd rather not press charges. She needs help . . . medical help, not punishment.'

'I'll pass that on to the interviewing sergeant,' said the officer, 'but you might not have any say in the matter. For now, the two of you can head back to the hotel and I'll follow on behind. You're staying at the Merrywell Manor, yeah?'

Leonie nodded.

'OK then,' said the officer. 'I'll be along shortly to take your statements.'

'What about my phone?' Leonie said. 'Karen took it. I'll need it back as soon as possible.'

'If it's in Karen Avery's possession, we'll need to keep it for now, as evidence.'

'Great.' Leonie rolled her eyes. 'That's all I need. Come on, Violet. Let's go.'

As they climbed into the Toyota, Violet handed her own phone to Leonie.

'I'm guessing you'd like to ring Rupert . . . let him know you're OK?' she said.

Leonie smiled. 'Yes. Problem is, I can't remember his number.'

'Don't worry. I've got it saved in my contacts.'

As Violet steered the car along the bumpy driveway and rejoined the road, Leonie made the call.

'Honestly, Rupert, I'm fine,' she said, once she'd given him a truncated explanation of where she'd been. 'I'll give you the full story later. Right now, I'm with Violet Brewster and we're heading back to the hotel. I'll call you once I've given my statement. Yes . . . don't worry. I'm OK. It's not like I've been kept overnight in a dungeon. People pay good money to stay in that apartment, although admittedly they do expect to be able to come and go as they please. Still, it had a stocked fridge, a shelf of books, and a television. No phone, of course, but worse things happen at sea, as my mother used to say.'

There was a pause while she listened. Violet could hear Rupert's deep voice on the other end of the phone, but she wasn't able to make out what he was saying.

'I don't think so,' Leonie said. 'She said she didn't, and I believe her.'

Violet guessed that Rupert was asking whether Karen had killed Angeline.

'That's all we can do,' Leonie said, in response to his next comment. 'I know, darling . . . yeah . . . no problem . . . OK, I'll ring you later. Bye.'

'Was he asking whether Karen killed Angeline?' Violet asked, as Leonie ended the call.

'Yes. He thinks it *had* to be her.'

Violet frowned, wondering whether Rupert was pointing the finger of blame at Karen to deflect suspicion away from his daughter or ex-wife.

'What do *you* think?' she said.

Leonie sighed. 'On balance, I don't think it was Karen. Her denial was very convincing.'

'It was, but given her delicate emotional state, she may not know herself what the truth is. Let's face it, she has been behaving irrationally.'

'You're right,' said Leonie. 'Her actions today were definitely not those of a rational woman. I think everything's mixed up in her head. She told me she'd had to sell the farm, said it broke her heart – but I think it broke something else as well – something in her psyche. She said she's spent ages getting the holiday let ready, but I don't think the house she's living in is good for her mental health. It's not called Edge Cottage for nothing. I thought where I grew up was isolated, but that place takes remoteness to a whole new level. It's a great location if you want to get away from it all . . . it *would* make a brilliant writing retreat, actually . . . but for someone living alone, who doesn't make friends easily? I'd say it's far from ideal. She'd be better off selling up and moving to a town, so that she can be among people.'

'For what it's worth,' Violet said, 'I don't believe she killed Angeline either, but maybe we're being gullible. The police will take a more objective approach when they question her. Only time will tell whether she's guilty.'

'I read somewhere that almost everyone is capable of murder in certain circumstances,' Leonie said. 'All it takes is for something to be triggered deep within – a feeling of anger or rage, or maybe a desire for revenge or justice. But I honestly don't think Karen is feeling any of those emotions. Instead of anger, I'd say she's possessed by an overwhelming sense of sadness. Nothing that would drive her to kill.'

In the distance, Violet could see the twinkling lights of Merrywell. It felt good to be heading back to familiar territory.

'Which leaves us with a problem,' she said, as she turned off towards the Merrywell Manor Hotel. 'If Karen didn't kill Angeline, who did?'

Chapter 38

As they pulled up at the hotel, Rupert Dalloway called back to say he was on his way over. Leonie went straight up to her room to freshen up, and Violet sat downstairs in the lobby and gave her statement to the police officer. It took less than ten minutes, and by the time she had finished, Rupert had arrived to offer his support to Leonie.

Violet drove back to Greengage Cottage feeling troubled and disappointed. When she'd discovered Leonie locked in the holiday apartment, her sleuthing brain had gone into overdrive. She'd thought she had it all worked out. The scenario she had come up with went something like this: *Karen Avery had discovered that Leonie had squandered the much-coveted bursary by dropping out of university. Convinced that Leonie had robbed her of her only chance to escape her unhappy life, Karen had decided to take revenge. She had killed Angeline in error, and intended to put that mistake right by making Leonie her next victim.*

But now, Violet's gut was telling her she had misjudged Karen. Her emphatic protestation of innocence had completely muddied the waters.

Karen's unstable behaviour and her impetuous and perfidious decision to keep Leonie under lock and key were disturbing, but

Violet didn't believe she was capable of killing anyone. She understood now that Karen's imprudent actions had been driven by a terrible sense of loneliness, with perhaps a smidgeon of anger thrown in for good measure. If she'd intended to harm Leonie, she would surely have done so quickly and decisively. Keeping her overnight in the holiday apartment had been a wild and hot-headed thing to do – but Violet was convinced the decision had been an impromptu one.

Violet slept badly, her slumber disturbed by dreams of being chased by a malicious presence, a shadowy figure pursuing her relentlessly. She woke in a sweat, feeling unsettled and cloaked in an ominous sense of dread.

She sat up in bed and thought about DS Winterton. After his actions the previous evening, Violet felt considerably more amenable towards him. He had taken her seriously and shown concern for her wellbeing, and he had acted quickly when he'd learned Leonie was being held against her will. Violet's only concern now was that the detective and his team would focus all their energies on attempting to prove that Karen was a killer.

Violet got up, showered and dressed, and went downstairs to make coffee. She drank it at the kitchen table while she texted Rupert Dalloway's number.

I hope Leonie is OK after her ordeal yesterday. Look after her, Rupert. Something tells me this isn't over yet.

As Violet sent the text, she wondered whether it was altogether wise to trust Rupert. She didn't think he was responsible for Angeline's death, but there was still a chance that his ex-wife and/or his daughter were involved. All of Rosemary Dalloway's knives were accounted for, but what about Saffy's? Was it possible she owned an identical set of expensive Wüsthof knives?

Of all the people Violet had considered as suspects, the

Dalloway women were the ones with the strongest motive. Spending time at Langdale Hall might not be a wise choice for Leonie. Maybe it would be safer for her to go back to London, away from whatever danger Merrywell might hold.

On her way to work, Violet called in at the village shop to buy a box of her favourite Derbyshire teabags. As she entered the shop, she noticed that Cathy Gee was at the counter, paying her paper bill.

Violet grabbed the teabags from the grocery shelf and placed the correct change on the counter so that she could make a swift exit.

'Just a box of teabags, please, Will,' she said to the proprietor. 'I've left the right money.'

'Cheers, lass,' he replied, scooping up the coins without counting them.

Cathy smiled. 'Wait up, Violet,' she said. 'I'll walk with you.'

They left the shop together, heading in the direction of the pub.

'I wanted to thank you for recommending us to Yvette Finch,' Cathy said.

'It's my pleasure,' Violet replied. 'I knew you had a B&B room, although when I suggested it to Yvette, I wasn't sure it would be available . . . what with the festival being on and all.'

'Oh, we had a vacancy all right,' Cathy said. 'The B&B thing is new, something to bring in a bit of extra income. We haven't really had a chance to advertise it yet – so your recommendation was much appreciated.'

'I could have filled the room twice over, actually,' Violet said, thinking about Paul's unscheduled visit. 'I'm sure you'll have plenty of takers for it, especially in the warmer months.'

'I hope so,' Cathy said. 'Billy wasn't too enamoured with the idea, but like I told him . . . needs must. Running a village pub is a hard way to make a living these days.'

'Your Billy's usually up for trying new things. Why wasn't he keen on the B&B idea?'

'He doesn't like the idea of having strangers on the premises,' Cathy said, rolling her eyes. 'I don't mean in the pub, obviously, but in our living quarters. He sees it as an invasion of privacy. It means he can't wander around in his boxer shorts first thing in the morning.'

Violet smiled.

'Thankfully, Yvette Finch has been a model guest,' Cathy said, as she began to veer off through the gate towards the pub's side entrance. 'You wouldn't know she was staying with us. Spends most of her time in her room . . . only comes out for something to eat. She can't wait to get back to London. I don't think village life is her thing at all.'

'I'm surprised she's still here,' Violet said. 'She must have given the police her statement by now.'

'She did that on Saturday, but they told her to stick around. I did wonder whether she might be a suspect, but that's obviously not the case because she was given the OK to leave late last night. She's catching a train to London later on this morning.'

'Oh well, I'm sure the room will be filled again in no time,' Violet said, as she waved Cathy goodbye.

She walked on to the shopping village, wondering about Yvette Finch's aversion to village life, and recalling her offhand manner on Saturday morning in the breakfast room. Throughout the initial search for Leonie, Yvette had maintained a detached, indifferent approach. Given that the two women had recently parted ways professionally, perhaps that was understandable – but, with hindsight, Violet found Yvette's lack of urgency odd.

An insidious thought struck Violet like lightning and lodged itself in her head. What if Yvette had struggled to muster enthusiasm for the search because she thought Leonie was already dead?

Violet remembered the visit to Leonie's room, and in particular the moment when Yvette had stood gripping one of the brocade curtains, gazing out of the window. Reflecting on that scene, she thought about the subsequent conversation they'd had about the Audi.

With her heart banging against her ribcage, she pulled out her phone and called Rupert Dalloway.

'Rupert, are you with Leonie?' she asked, when he answered the call.

'Yes, do you want a word?'

'If you don't mind.'

Violet waited as he handed over the phone.

'Good morning, Violet,' Leonie said, sounding refreshed and happy. 'I'm glad you rang. As I was falling to sleep last night, I realised I hadn't thanked you properly . . . for finding me. I might still be stuck in that holiday apartment if it wasn't for you.'

'I'm sure Karen would have seen sense eventually,' Violet said. 'Am I right in thinking we're both of a similar mind about her? Neither of us think she killed Angeline.'

'Correct.'

'Are you at the hotel?'

'Yes,' Leonie said. 'I'm in my suite.'

'Are you still in the same room? Room 22?'

'Yes. Why?'

'Do me a favour, will you?' Violet said. 'Go over to the window and stand next to the right-hand curtain, and tell me what you see.'

'OK . . . erm . . . the garden, and the car park.'

'You remember where you parked your car on Friday, after the festival event?' Violet asked.

'How could I forget?'

'Yes . . . sorry,' Violet said, aware it was also where Angeline's body had been found on Saturday morning. 'When you look out of the window, can you see the space where your Audi was parked?'

'Yes. It was over by the fir trees. I can see it clearly.'

Violet's heart was thumping. 'When Yvette Finch and I went to look for you in your room on Saturday morning, she stood for a while where you are now . . . by the window.'

‘So?’

‘Shortly afterwards, when we were back in the reception area, I asked her about your car, and whether it was still in the car park. She said she didn’t know, that she hadn’t thought to check.’

‘But if she stood here at the window, she would have seen the car,’ Leonie said, sounding puzzled.

‘Exactly. Which begs the question, why would she lie?’

‘People usually lie when they want to cover something up.’

‘Quite,’ said Violet. ‘Can I ask you something else? You told me you thought your return to Merrywell had been the trigger that led to Angeline’s death. Do you still believe that?’

‘I’m not sure what to believe anymore,’ Leonie said, sounding tired and exasperated. ‘After everything that’s happened over the last few days, I’m emotionally and physically wrung out. My brain doesn’t seem to be functioning properly at the moment. Having said that, maybe I have been focusing too much on the past, when in fact I should have been more worried about the here and now.’

‘Can you tell me why you and Yvette fell out?’ Violet asked. ‘Why didn’t she want to renew your contract? Was it something you’d done, or said?’

‘What are you talking about?’ Leonie said. ‘It wasn’t Yvette who cancelled the contract. It was me.’

Chapter 39

'When we got back to the hotel, after the festival, we had a minor altercation,' Leonie said. 'Yvette was fuming with me because I'd talked about writing my autobiography during the interview. She'd told me not to say anything. My agent is still negotiating a contract, and Yvette had warned me to keep quiet until the deal had been sealed. I told her it was my decision to make – not hers – and that I'd tell people when *I* felt the time was right.

'She got stroppy with me, said it was no use me hiring her services if I wasn't willing to take her professional advice. I told her she was right . . . and, as I like to make up my own mind about what to say and do, there didn't seem much point in carrying on with our business arrangement. The contract I had with Yvette was due to be renewed in a couple of weeks, and I told her I wasn't going to bother. It didn't go down well, but I didn't care.'

Violet was starting to question everything she'd gleaned so far. Leonie's take on how the contract was terminated was radically different to Yvette's version of events – but who was telling the truth here?

'So why did Yvette tell me that *she* was the one who'd cancelled the contract?' Violet asked, determined to ascertain the facts.

'Maybe she didn't want to lose face. Sometimes, pride makes us deny the truth. Yvette was due to head back to London on Saturday, and so was I. If we'd both left as planned, you would never have found out the truth, would you? Yvette could have told you any old rubbish and you'd have been none the wiser.'

'Or maybe she was covering her tracks,' Violet said. 'Perhaps it suited her purpose to lie, and she was under the misapprehension that you'd never be able to contradict her . . . because she thought you were already dead.'

'That's a bit of a leap, isn't it?' Leonie said. 'What are you suggesting? That she killed Angeline, thinking it was me?'

'Why not? We know the murder weapon was a high-quality German knife. DS Winterton told me it was manufactured by a company called Wüsthof.' Violet refrained from mentioning that she had suspected Rosemary Dalloway to be the owner of that knife. 'Yvette could have taken a knife from the hotel kitchen.'

'Does the hotel even use that brand?'

'I'll call DS Winterton and ask him to check,' Violet said. 'I also need to let him know that Yvette lied to me. At the very least, he should speak to her again before she goes back to London.'

'Why would Yvette want to kill me?' Leonie let out a shaky breath. 'OK, so I cancelled our contract – but that's not the end of world, is it?'

'Maybe not your world,' Violet said. 'But it might be the end of hers. You must have been her biggest client. Without the income from that contract, who knows what sort of position her business is in. Losing you would mean a massive drop in revenue, and it would also drastically reduce her professional kudos. What if she can't afford to pay her rent anymore? Or maybe there was something else she needed the money for, something more personal.'

'Why don't we ask her?' Leonie said, breathing heavily down the phone. 'She's still in the village, isn't she?'

'Yes, she's staying at the pub.'

'Let's go round there . . . confront her.'

'Is that a good idea?' Violet said. 'From what I hear, she's been lying low in the White Hart, biding her time until she can go home. If we turn up and accuse her, she might take off before the police have a chance to talk to her.'

'You'll have gathered by now that I'm not known for erring on the side of caution,' Leonie said, sounding thoroughly gung ho. 'I need to know who killed Angeline. If it *was* Yvette, we need to tackle her before she disappears back to London or goes off the radar completely. I'm going to the White Hart, Violet, with or without you.'

Violet sighed. 'When you put it like that, I suppose I'd better come with you. There's safety in numbers, after all. Give me a couple of minutes to call DS Winterton. Once I've done that, I'll meet you at the pub.'

DS Winterton's phone went straight to voicemail, leaving Violet no option but to leave a message. She kept it brief, telling him what he needed to know, and explaining that she and Leonie were heading round to the White Hart. She knew that Winterton would disapprove, but she couldn't let Leonie do this on her own.

'And you need to check with the staff at the hotel,' she added. 'Find out if they use Wüsthof knives in the kitchen. If they do, they'll need to check whether there's one missing. If there *is*, the odds are it was used to kill Angeline. Yvette could easily have snuck into the kitchens to steal it.'

Once she'd ended her message, Violet decided on a backup plan. As she hurried out of the shopping village, she rang the police station, repeating the same information to the officer on the duty desk.

'I've left DS Winterton a voicemail, but I'm worried he won't hear it until it's too late,' she said, talking as she walked. 'I'm relying on you to pass on the message.'

'I'll make sure he gets it,' the officer said. 'But I would strongly caution against going to the pub to confront this woman. No good can come of it.'

'The pub landlady told me that Yvette Finch is catching a train to London this morning. It's possible she may have left by now – but if she hasn't, someone needs to make sure she stays at the pub. That's where I come in. I'll delay her, until the police arrive.'

The officer spluttered a protest, but Violet ended the call. She had already arrived at the White Hart.

The pub wasn't yet open, so she went round to the side door, entering the bar area via the outside smoking area. It was strange, seeing the pub standing empty and silent. Tea towels were draped across the beer pumps, and chairs had been upended and placed on the tables. From somewhere in the next room came the low hum of a vacuum cleaner.

Violet walked through to the lounge area, which was the larger of the pub's two public rooms. Cathy Gee was pushing an upright Hoover back and forth over the worn Axminster carpet.

'Cathy?'

'Flipping 'eck, Violet!' she said, pressing her toe against the side of the vacuum cleaner to switch it off. 'I didn't hear you come in. You frightened the life out of me.'

Violet decided to get straight to the point. 'Is Yvette Finch still here?'

'Yes, but she's booked a taxi to the station. It'll be here any minute.'

'Is she still up in her room?'

'She is, but you'll have to be quick if you want a word with her. I promised I'd give her a shout as soon as the taxi arrives.'

'Where's the room?'

'Through the door behind the bar, up the stairs, first on the right. Try not to let Billy see you. He's down in the cellar at the moment, but he doesn't take too kindly to people trailing through the back rooms.'

'Leonie Stanwick and the police are on their way,' Violet said. 'When Leonie gets here, will you send her up to Yvette's room?'

'*Police*?' Cathy looked horrified. 'What's going on, Violet? Is it something we should be aware of?'

'I think Yvette had something to do with Angeline Hammond's murder,' Violet said.

Cathy narrowed her eyes and leaned on the silent Hoover. 'When you say *something to do with*, do you mean she killed her? Are you telling me we've been providing bed and breakfast for a felon?'

Violet held up her hands. 'I'm honestly not sure, Cathy,' she said. 'That's why I need to talk to her. There are a few things I want to clear up before she goes back to London.'

Cathy folded her arms. 'You shouldn't go up there on your own,' she said. 'Give me a minute, and I'll fetch Billy. I'll get him to bring Yvette down here. No harm will come to you if me and Billy are around when you talk to her. I'll listen out for the taxi and the police. If the taxi comes first, I'll send it away.'

Violet waited at a table near the unlit fireplace. Cathy was over by the window, keeping her eyes peeled for the arrival of the taxi, Leonie Stanwick, and the police. Violet was praying that the police would arrive first, and in double-quick time.

Cathy had been down to the cellar to brief Billy, and he was now fetching Yvette Finch from upstairs. When he emerged from the back of the pub, Yvette was right behind him. Lifting the hinged section of the bar, Billy stood aside to give her access to the lounge area.

When Yvette saw Violet, she stopped in her tracks. 'Hello,' she said. 'What are you doing here?'

'There's something I'd like to ask you,' Violet replied. 'Come and sit down.'

Yvette gave an insincere smile. 'I'm sorry, but I haven't got time. I've booked a taxi to the station. I have a train to catch.'

'Cathy's looking out for your taxi,' Violet said, nodding over to the window, where Cathy was peering out to the street.

Huffing pointedly, Yvette dragged her small suitcase over to where Violet was sitting.

'What is it?' she said. 'You'd better make it quick. I've already spent far too much time in Merrywell. The last thing I need is to miss another train.'

'I'll get right to the point then,' Violet said, bolstered by the reassuring presence of the muscular Billy Gee. 'Did you kill Angeline Hammond?'

Yvette twisted her head and gave what Violet could only describe as a cross between a sneer and a snort. A snert?

'Is this a joke?' Yvette asked.

'No, I'm deadly serious. When I saw you at the Merrywell Manor Hotel on Saturday morning, you told me you'd cancelled your contract with Leonie. That's not true, is it?'

Yvette curled her lip. 'What do you care?'

Violet chose to ignore the remark, responding instead with another question of her own.

'You also told me that you didn't know whether Leonie's Audi was in the car park. That wasn't true either. When we went up to Leonie's suite, you stood right next to the window. You must have seen her car from there. You couldn't have missed it. Why did you lie?'

Yvette squared her shoulders. 'I don't take kindly to being called a liar,' she said. 'And who appointed you chief inquisitor anyway? What business is this of yours?'

'I think you'd better answer the question,' said a voice from the far end of the bar. 'It may not be Violet's business, but it is mine.'

Leonie had arrived, sweeping into the pub lounge in a haze of rose-scented perfume.

Yvette turned. 'Leonie. What is this? Why are you here?'

'The same reason as Violet,' she replied. 'To ascertain whether you killed Angeline.'

Rupert Dalloway had also joined the gathering. He stood shoulder to shoulder with Billy Gee, the pair of them blocking the exit.

'Who the *hell* do you think you all are?' Yvette said, casting her eyes around the room. 'Are you looking for a scapegoat? Is that it? Is this a campaign designed to clear the names of everyone in Merrywell? I'm the outsider, right? So I *must* be the guilty party. Is that your theory?'

'On the contrary,' Leonie said. 'I convinced myself the killer had to be someone local . . . at least, initially. I blamed myself for Angeline's death. I thought my coming back to Merrywell was the catalyst for everything that's happened – but that's not the case, is it? *You* killed Angeline, didn't you? Did you think she was me? I knew you were furious when I cancelled our business arrangement . . . but I didn't realise you were angry enough to do something that desperate. Did you go into that car park looking for revenge? Was that it?'

'You're being ridiculous. You can't go around accusing people of murder. It's outrageous.' Yvette grabbed the handle of her suitcase and began to pull it towards the door. 'If you'll excuse me, I have a train to catch. My taxi will be waiting.'

'I think not,' Rupert said, shaking his head. 'Your taxi pulled up at the same time as we did. We sent it away. Not to worry though, because you'll be getting a ride in a police car soon enough. I suggest you sit back down until it arrives. And while we're waiting, perhaps you can tell us what happened on Saturday morning. Leonie deserves to know the truth. We all do.'

'You're not the police. I don't have to tell you anything.' Despite Yvette's words, all of her fight and bluster seemed to be seeping away. Accepting she was cornered, she sat down, looking a lot less confident and far more scared.

'Why did you tell me you'd cancelled your contract with Leonie?' Violet said, repeating her earlier question.

When Yvette pushed her lips together and folded her arms, Violet assumed she was going to give them the silent treatment.

But then, a few seconds later, Yvette leaned forward and placed her hands on the table in front of her.

'You're right. I lied. I was too proud to admit that Leonie had given me the push, but pride isn't a crime. If it was, it's one we'd all be guilty of. I'll bet every one of you has told a lie at some point in your life.' She scanned the room, looking everyone in the eyes. 'We all tell the odd fib now and again, don't we? We wouldn't be human otherwise. But telling a lie doesn't make me a killer.'

'Generally speaking, no,' said Violet. 'But I think you told that lie believing it could never be contradicted. Only you and Leonie knew the truth about how your business arrangement had ended – and you thought Leonie was dead, didn't you?'

'That's absurd. Why would I think that?' Yvette said. 'I told you at the time . . . I didn't know where she was.'

'You *thought* she was in the car park, where you'd left her with a knife in her back. When I came to the hotel looking for her, you went along with the search . . . reluctantly . . . knowing full well we wouldn't find her in her room. You were taken by surprise though . . . when you realised the bed hadn't been slept in. You said: *she must have spent the night somewhere else.* It didn't register with me at the time, but you were thrown by that, weren't you? You must have been wondering what Leonie was doing in the car park if she hadn't spent the night at the hotel.'

Yvette scowled fiercely, but said nothing.

'The police are checking with the hotel, to establish whether a knife has gone missing from the kitchen. You must have worn gloves, because there were no prints on the murder weapon, but the forensic team will be able to confirm whether it came from the hotel.'

Violet wasn't sure whether that was true, but it didn't matter – just so long as Yvette Finch believed it was.

'Why?' Violet said, determined to press hard, hoping that Yvette would crack under the pressure. 'Why did you kill Angeline?'

Yvette had gone pale. She stared at Violet, her expression hard as flint.

Leonie was over by the bar, pacing back and forth. When she spoke, her voice trembled with suppressed anger.

'I wish it had been me in that car park,' she said. 'Right now, I'd like nothing more than to swap places with Angeline. You weren't to know this, Yvette, but Angeline was my daughter.'

A collective gasp moved around the room like a Mexican wave. Yvette's mouth fell open, forming an 'O' shape. Violet took advantage of her momentary shock with another verbal onslaught.

'Angeline was a nurse,' she said. 'A kind, caring person who was well liked within the community.'

The atmosphere in the pub was crackling with tension. Everyone seemed to be holding their breath, waiting for Yvette to respond with a vehement denial.

So it came as a shock when she instead gave a strangled cry. It rose up from somewhere deep inside her chest, demanding an exit. The cry turned into a wail and once it had made its escape, Yvette began to weep uncontrollably.

'I didn't set out to kill anyone,' she said. 'You're right, I stole the knife . . . and a pair of disposable gloves from the kitchen. And yes, I went out to the car park early on . . . but all I was planning to do was slash the tyres on Leonie's car.'

She was shuddering now, all of the emotions she'd been holding on to were finally being released.

Gathering herself, Yvette turned to Leonie, her eyes flashing with anger. 'This is your fault,' she said. 'I've spent the last four years at your beck and call, running myself ragged, chasing around after you, making excuses for your tardiness. I tried my best. I did everything I could to keep you sweet – so much so that I ended up neglecting my other clients. One by one they went elsewhere, and as they drifted away, I told myself it didn't matter. The work I did for you was more than enough to make a living. Did you know that last month I finally managed to get a mortgage to buy my first place?'

'No,' Leonie said. 'I didn't know that.'

'Of course you didn't, because you're only ever interested in yourself. You weren't to know how I excited I was . . . how deliriously happy . . . and then, hey presto, you took the hump and ruined everything.' Yvette snapped her fingers. 'Just like that. You told me you weren't going to renew the contract, like I was nothing.'

'Oh, for goodness' sake! You must have seen it coming,' Leonie said. 'You and I were always clashing about something. Ours was hardly the smoothest of working relationships.'

'Everything went smoothly enough providing I did exactly as you said,' Yvette replied. 'But you were never willing to take my professional advice, were you? Why couldn't you have accepted that sometimes *I* knew best? We could have been so much more successful with our campaigns if you'd listened to me. You hired me at great cost as your PR guru, but you always assumed you knew better. You had to have the last word, didn't you? Every single time.'

Leonie took a step back, flinching from Yvette's venomous tone.

'You've sold millions of books,' Yvette said, continuing her tirade. 'You don't have to worry about money . . . how you're going to pay the rent or the next utility bill, or whether you can get a mortgage. You're Leonie Stanwick, bestselling author, with your flashy cars and your fancy house. You've forgotten what it's like for ordinary people like me. I worked my socks off for you for four years. The least you could have done was give me some notice when you cancelled our contract . . . given me some time to line up new clients – but, no. You were happy to cut me off without so much as a backward glance.'

'And that makes it all right, does it?' Leonie said. 'To lash out . . . kill someone because you thought she was me?'

'I didn't set out to kill you. I wanted to cause you some inconvenience. I'd booked myself a rail ticket back to London because I knew you wouldn't want to give me a lift. As a parting gift, I decided to delay your return by creating a little mayhem. I was feeling spiteful, vindictive . . . I wanted to get my own back but I never set out to kill anyone. You have to believe that.'

Out of the corner of her eye, Violet could see that Cathy was holding her phone. Had she called the police? Were they on the other end, listening to Yvette's confession?

'On Friday, just before midnight, I went down to the kitchen and stole the knife and gloves,' Yvette said. 'Early the next morning, when it was beginning to get light, I slipped out into the hotel gardens and went to the car park. When I approached your car, the only thought going through my mind was whether to slash all four of your tyres, or just one. I'd decided to go for all four – to cause maximum damage – and then I saw what I thought was *you* standing there, next to the car.'

She pointed at Leonie, her finger trembling.

'It was that stupid hat that got to me. I was with you when you bought it . . . remember?'

Yvette scanned the faces of everyone around her. 'Do you know how much she spent on that hat?' She waited for a beat before continuing. 'More than I earn in a week, that's how much it cost. Leonie saw it. She liked it. She bought it. Didn't even bother asking the price. What Leonie wants, Leonie gets.'

'I gave the hat to Angeline,' Leonie said.

'Well, bully for you – I wasn't to know that, was I? She had her back to me. All I saw were those stupid sequins sparkling on what looked like your head.

'For years I've been desperate to buy my first flat . . . and I was days away from achieving that dream. But when you cancelled our contract, I knew I'd have to pull out. Without a decent income, how could I possibly commit to a mortgage? I was gutted, consumed by a horrible crimson rage that took away all reason. As I stood in that car park, all I could see was *you*, standing there in your expensive hat next to your expensive car, and there was I, my business in tatters, faced with returning home on a cheap off-peak rail ticket – denied even the pleasure of slashing your tyres. Something snapped. I lashed out, and the next thing I knew you were lying face down . . . or rather, *she* was . . . lying there with the knife between her shoulder blades. I assumed it was you, and I didn't stick around long enough to discover my mistake. I turned tail and went straight back to the hotel.'

As Violet listened and observed, she realised the White Hart had become the mise en scène of an extraordinary drama. The witnesses to Yvette's confession stood frozen, stunned into silence. Billy Gee waited, his fists clenched and his complexion livid. Rupert Dalloway looked stiff, his body poised and angry. Cathy Gee watched from the window, horrified and slightly fearful. Leonie was deathly pale. She looked broken, like a wounded animal, her face etched with pain and sadness and confusion.

Into this tableau came two uniformed police officers, entering from stage right. Close on their heels was DS Winterton.

Pushing past Billy and Rupert, the police officers stepped forward to caution Yvette, indicating that she should stand up. She complied meekly. Then, with a police officer on either side, she was escorted out of the bar.

DS Winterton observed from a distance, his arms folded. Once Yvette had been taken away, he approached Leonie, checking to see that she was OK. Next, he spoke to Rupert and the Gees, reassuring them with a few muttered words. Only then did he walk over to the table where Violet was sitting.

'Are you OK?' he said, his face a fusion of exasperation and concern.

'I'm fine,' she replied, even though adrenaline was pulsing through her bloodstream, making her feel jittery. 'I'm just relieved that it's all over.'

'I suppose I have you to thank for that. Without your help, Yvette Finch would be halfway back to London by now.'

'There's no need to thank me, DS Winterton,' said Violet. 'I'm sure you'd have worked everything out for yourself soon enough.'

'You're right, I would – but maybe not quite as quickly.' The detective smiled ruefully. 'Your assistance . . . or should I say interference . . . has helped us to solve the case swiftly and satisfactorily. Having said all that, I'd prefer it if you steered well clear of future investigations. Much as I've enjoyed chatting with you, Violet, I trust we won't have any reason to meet again.'

She gave him an irreverent salute. 'I'll do my best to stay out of trouble,' she said.

She'd almost added *I promise*, but promises were something she only made if she was certain she was going to keep them.

Chapter 40

By the end of the week, life was slowly returning to normal. It was Friday, just before noon, and Violet was in *The Memory Box*, updating her website. Earlier that morning, she had paid a visit to *Books, Bakes and Cakes* and learned that the parish council had offered Eric funding to put on another book festival next year. Even Judith Talbot had given the decision her seal of approval.

Violet had also approached Molly Gee about working a few hours a week at *The Memory Box*. Molly had been overjoyed at the prospect, and Violet had agreed to employ her on a trial basis starting in the new year. Having someone to take care of the day-to-day admin would free her up to spend more time on the numerous projects she was being commissioned to complete.

At the sound of the door opening, she looked up, expecting to see Matthew, who had promised to drop in with a much-needed coffee and a Danish pastry. But instead of Matthew, it was Leonie Stanwick who strolled into *The Memory Box*.

'I've come to say goodbye,' she said. 'Or, should I say *so long*. I'm sure I'll be a regular visitor in Derbyshire from now on.'

'Does that mean you and Rupert have decided to rekindle your romance?'

Leonie smiled. 'I prefer to think of it as starting a new fire, rather than rekindling an old flame,' she said. 'What Rupert and I had all those years ago was very special, but it's impossible to turn back time. We're very different people now, so the only way to move forward is to start afresh. We're taking it slowly, waiting to see what develops. I'm not sure Saffy is too pleased about her dad seeing someone else, but I'm hoping to win her round. Maybe I can soften her up by offering some coaching in creative writing. It seems she's genuinely interested in becoming a novelist.'

'Well, I hope everything works out,' Violet said. 'I'll keep my fingers crossed for you.'

'Thanks, I need all the luck I can get.'

'Have you fixed a date for Angeline's funeral yet? Now that Yvette has been charged with her murder?'

Leonie nodded. 'The service will be held three weeks today. Eleven o'clock at St Luke's, followed by a wake at the White Hart. I hope you'll be able to make it?'

'I'll be there,' Violet said. 'And what about Karen Avery? Any news?'

'The police have let her off with a caution. I went round to see her yesterday. She's determined to stay at Edge Cottage, but I suggested she try to interact with more people . . . join some of the social clubs, here in the village. I'm hoping she'll take my advice, and I'll try to check in on her from time to time when I'm in the area.'

'That's kind of you, considering what happened,' Violet said.

'Kind? Or foolish?' Leonie smiled. 'Only time will tell.'

'I hope you'll call in to see *me* again, next time you visit Langdale Hall,' Violet said.

'Of course I will. I didn't want to leave today without thanking you. If it wasn't for you, the police might still be floundering, trying to find Angeline's killer.'

'I don't know about that. I'm sure it wouldn't have taken DS Winterton long to uncover the truth. I'm only sorry the murder happened in the first place. You're putting on a brave face, but I know it's hit you hard . . . losing Angeline.'

'It has, and it's made me all the more determined to finish my autobiography. I want the world to know the truth: that Angeline was my daughter. I've spoken to a lot of people who knew her, and they all say the same thing: she was a good, kind person – and I'm proud of that. I suppose I have my parents to thank. I'm not sure Angeline would have grown into such a lovely human being if I'd brought her up.'

'She would have turned out just fine, I'm certain of it,' Violet said. 'As for your parents, you can pay tribute to them when you write your book. I know you didn't always see eye to eye with them, but they were what they were: a product of their generation.'

'Very true. It's just a shame . . . now that they're gone . . . that I won't be able to make amends for the past. I'm not sure if I believe in an afterlife, but if there is such a thing, it comforts me to think of my parents and Angeline being together.'

Ten minutes after Leonie had left, Matthew appeared carrying coffees and a bag of pastries.

'Are we still on for tonight?' he asked, as he placed a coffee cup on Violet's desk.

'For Stilton and celery risotto, you mean?' she said. 'Of course. I'm looking forward to it.'

'Are you sure?' Matthew said. 'You've had one hell of a week.'

'I'm fine, Matthew. Honestly.'

'I was thinking, rather than you having to cook, maybe I should take you out for a meal somewhere. There's a new Thai restaurant opened in Matlock, if you fancy it.'

'Dining out?' said Violet. 'In a restaurant? Like a proper date, you mean?'

Matthew laughed. 'Yes . . . but only if you want to.'

Violet smiled at him over the top of her coffee cup. 'Do you want to make the booking?' she said. 'Or shall I?'

A Letter from Jane Bettany

Thank you for reading *Murder at the Book Festival* – the second in the Violet Brewster mystery series. It was a lot of fun to write, and I've particularly enjoyed setting a murder against the backdrop of a book festival (the idea formed during one of my stints as a volunteer at Derby Book Festival – which, I'm pleased to say, offers a varied and interesting programme of events, sans murder!).

Bibliophiles love a good book festival, and crime fiction readers *always* expect a murder – which is what prompted me to create the inaugural Merrywell Book Festival. I do hope you've enjoyed solving this latest mystery alongside Violet, as well as getting to know her and the other residents of the village a little better.

I'm currently working on the next book in the series – so if you'd like find out when it will be released, you can sign up to receive email updates and book news at my website:

janebettany.co.uk

You can also keep in touch through my social media channels:

Twitter: twitter.com/JaneBettany
Facebook: facebook.com/JaneBettanyAuthor
Instagram: Instagram.com/bettanyjane

Once again, thanks for choosing to read *Murder at the Book Festival.* Blogger and reader feedback is vitally important to writers – so if you've enjoyed the book and can spare the time, I'd appreciate you leaving a rating or a review, or letting other people know about the Violet Brewster series.

That's it for now – but, rest assured, Violet, Matthew and the gang will be back soon.

With best wishes

Jane

Murder in Merrywell

Welcome to Merrywell. Population: small. Secrets: aplenty.

Ex-journalist **Violet Brewster** is keen to make a good first impression in her new community, having just moved to the small village of Merrywell. When Violet hears about the mystery of Helen Slingsby, who disappeared from the village forty years earlier, she decides to help uncover what happened. But despite Violet's best efforts, she can find no trace of the missing woman. As Violet talks to the other residents, it becomes apparent that something sinister is lurking beneath the village's idyllic exterior. When a villager is found dead in their home, Violet becomes convinced that the murder is connected to Helen. Did Helen ever really leave Merrywell? Who in the village is hiding something? And can Violet finally solve this forty-year-old mystery before someone else gets hurt?

Acknowledgements

Firstly, a huge thank you to readers everywhere. Writing a book isn't easy – but what keeps me going as an author is the thought of people like you reading and enjoying my work. It makes the whole process worthwhile.

I'm fortunate to be published by a fantastic team at HQ. A big shout-out for my editor, Audrey Linton, whose insightful editorial comments have been (as always) spot-on, prompting revisions that have improved *Murder at the Book Festival* no end. I'm also immensely grateful to the wider HQ team who have worked hard behind the scenes to get the book published and out to readers.

Sending love and thanks to my family and friends – and remembering Alan Bettany, to whom this book is dedicated. Mondays aren't the same without you, Alan.

Finally, a huge thank you to my lovely husband, who understands and never complains when I'm on a tight deadline and have to spend hours at my desk, writing. The highlight of every working day is the forty-minute lunch break I spend with him, a cup of Ringtons tea (strongly brewed), and an episode of *Bargain Hunt* (usually a repeat). Thanks for your endless support, Howard, and for being there when I need you the most. Love you.

Dear Reader,
We hope you enjoyed reading this book. If you did, we'd be so appreciative if you left a review. It really helps us and the author to bring more books like this to you.

Here at HQ Digital we are dedicated to publishing fiction that will keep you turning the pages into the early hours. Don't want to miss a thing? To find out more about our books, promotions, discover exclusive content and enter competitions you can keep in touch in the following ways:

JOIN OUR COMMUNITY:
Sign up to our new email newsletter: http://smarturl.it/SignUpHQ
Read our new blog www.hqstories.co.uk

https://twitter.com/HQStories
www.facebook.com/HQStories

BUDDING WRITER?
We're also looking for authors to join the HQ Digital family!
Find out more here:

https://www.hqstories.co.uk/want-to-write-for-us/

Thanks for reading, from the HQ Digital team